THE EAGLE
AND THE
IRON CROSS

BY GLENDON SWARTHOUT

THE EAGLE AND THE IRON CROSS

GLENDON SWARTHOUT

THE NEW AMERICAN LIBRARY

First Printing

Published by The New American Library, Inc.
1301 Avenue of the Americas, New York, New York 10019
Published simultaneously in Canada by
General Publishing Company, Ltd.
Library of Congress Catalog Card Number: 66–26042
Printed in the United States of America

For the young men in their costumes

Therefore if thine enemy hunger, feed him; if he thirst, give him drink: for in so doing thou shalt heap coals of fire on his head. Be not overcome of evil, but overcome evil with good.

—ROMANS 12:20-21

FOREWORD

German prisoners in the United States numbered more than 300,000 by the war's end. Caged in camps from Maine to California, men waiting, men in thrall, their repatriation was not required by the Geneva Convention until the "conclusion of peace," a clause the victors might interpret according to their convenience. We did. We kept them, veterans of the Wehrmacht, the Kriegsmarine, the Luftwaffe, a huge, captive labor force, as long as they were useful. From May, 1945, to winter or spring of 1946, from the capitulation of Germany to shipment home, they existed in our midst as manpower, not as men, as spines and muscles, not as souls. They were soldiers of a cursed flag and cause. In the jest of their youth they were orphans not only of defeat but of history. Commanded, then betrayed, by their own blood, for months these beings lived beyond any logic of place, outside even the context of time. "Hostile to the past, impatient of the present, and cheated of the future," in the words of Camus, "they came to know the incorrigible sorrow of all prisoners and exiles, which is to live in company with a memory which serves no purpose." Disowned, forgotten, damned—living ghosts half a world away from that grave which had been a Fatherland—in their thousands they waited and worked and wondered. They were spoils of war, yet the war was over. They were citizens of the Third Reich, yet that state had ceased to be. To whom, to what, at that moment, did they belong?

The Eagle and the Cross is a novel about an escape from a prisoner-of-war camp in Arizona. Though based upon fact, its incidents are fiction. Its characters are representative, not real.

When prisoners escaped, they passed from a military jurisdiction. Once into the desert, they exchanged the authority of barbed wire and guns for that of sun and sand. Once into southwestern America, they belonged to what was there.

ONE

THE FOURTH REICH

1

They listened. The camp was a clock. Ticking, it told the time of war. When it stopped the war would end. Over the clock, the silence was like glass. Whistles shattered it.

"*Raus! Raus!* Move!" Corporals bellowed, running them out of the barracks. They snapped mathematically into formation.

"*Kompanie, stillgestanden!*" To ears not honed to hear it, this command, a suggestion almost, delivered in a Bavarian dialect, might have been inaudible. Master Sergeant Skubovius never shouted. His eyes were his gunnery. They counted, measured, inspected, noted, filed, went blank. As ordered, the Oberfeldwebel in delegated charge of First Stockade had it drawn up at 18.45 hours to the second. As usual, it was the *Amerikaner* who were late.

The men waited at iron attention. Sweat coursed their faces. Temperatures in southern Arizona, even in May, had soared to 40° C., and for the first time since the Führer's birthday, on the twentieth of April, the POWs had been ordered into parade dress. Some uniforms were the overseas issue, patched and cleaned out of sentiment, for such garments, together with a name, a number, a faded photograph, might be the only luggage of a man's life. Some uniforms were new, however, hand-dyed and tailor-made within the camp, exact in fit and detail. In the formation were 256 enlisted men. A few, shot out of Mediterranean skies, vaunted the collar wings and light blue of the Luftwaffe. A score, perhaps, were sailors of the Kriegsmarine, in ribboned hats and bell-bottomed trousers of dark blue, survivors of Unterseeboot, raider, and depot ship crews fished from wide and furious latitudes. Almost half, captured in Sicily, wore the familiar field gray, black belts, and jackboots of the Wehrmacht. Most dramatic of the costumes were the khaki of a full half of the complement. On the left sleeve

3

of the tunic was a band of black, silver-bordered, bearing a silver palm tree and a swastika; on the billed caps, set at defiant angle, were a silver eagle and a round cockade—black outer circle, white inner, dot of red as red as blood. The very insignia called a splendid roll of battles: Sidi Rezegh, Tobruk, Halfaya, Bir Hacheim, Mersa Matruh, El Alamein, the Faid, and the Kasserine Pass. They were the desert foxes. They were Erwin Rommel's own. Panzer men, grenadiers, infantry, engineers, and flak, they had been surrendered in Tunisia to Eisenhower and Montgomery. Leaving 40,000 of their dead behind, they were freighted away from palm trees and mountains and cruel suns and immensity, over an ocean and a continent, to a destination that only war, the idiot geographer, could decree: to palm trees and mountains and cruel suns and another immensity. They were brought to Arizona. They were the Afrika Korps.

The Afrika Korps had been, still was, even in its remnant, proud. That it had fought brilliantly, outnumbered and -vehicled, and honorably, by classic rules, had been acknowledged by its enemies. It despised the Wehrmacht, with whom it was penned. Two-thirds of the inmates of No. 80 Camp were Afrika Korps, for they were the first prisoners to reach the United States in large numbers. But in this stockade the bag was badly mixed. Here there were more Wehrmacht, which meant more SS planted like mines, and possibly SD, the Sicherheitsdienst, the thought police. That was one reason why the First Stockade was called the Fourth Reich. Another was Master Sergeant Skubovius.

He came to attention. An American officer and an enlisted man in suntans entered the stockade gate and proceeded, out of step, toward him. Neither was armed. Approaching the Oberfeldwebel, the officer returned his salute. The enlisted man hammered a notice onto a bulletin board and marched back. From his pocket the officer drew a typewritten duplicate of the notice, faced the formation, and cleared his throat once, twice. He was a young second lieutenant too conscious of his gold bars, of his language deficiency, and of the fact that his voice, a slender Massachusetts reed, must serve as history's trumpet. He cleared his throat again. He began to read in execrable German:

"The following telegram from the War Department: 'The organized resistance of the German armed forces has ceased. The Na-

4

tional Socialist Government of Germany no longer exists. The Allied occupation authorities exercise all power in Germany. Members of the German armed forces are released from any obligation entered into with a government which no longer exists. As prisoners of war you continue to be subject to American laws and regulations and must obey the orders of persons placed over you.' "

Finished, he stood uncertainly. He stepped back one pace as though the announcement might provoke a last suicidal Nazi assault upon his person. To his astonishment, there was no reaction whatever. The men had been expecting it for days. What they had hoped for, any scrap of information about their shipment home, had been withheld.

The lieutenant turned. "Sergeant, you may dismiss." Motioning to his enlisted aide, forgetting to return the master sergeant's salute, he quick-marched across the gravel and out the gate.

Oberfeldwebel Skubovius did not dismiss. He strolled to the mess hall, tore down the announcement, brought it back, crumpled it into a ball, placed it against his buttocks, made an obscene gesture, and dropped it.

"Lies," he said. "Lies and propaganda only fit for the latrine." Otto Skubovius was massive. The middle thirties were his prime. Square of face, his head was squared by tight ears and a bristle of short, brick-red hair. Each hand and wrist was a white sausage. On a finger glinted a gold ring. "Now," he said, "now the only announcement which counts today you will get from me. You heard, I am still in command of this stockade. Regulations which have been in effect will be." Among the Nuremberger's privileges was the selection of his own uniform. His GI suntan shirt and trousers had been knife-pleated by the laundry, but a black Wehrmacht belt strapped him, and on his shoulders were sewn the silver flaps of his rank. "The speaking of English. *Verboten.* The reading of *amerikanisch* books and newspapers. *Verboten.* To fraternize with guards. *Verboten.* In short, doing or saying or thinking anything disloyal to the concept of One People, One Reich, One Führer. Understand?"

The muzzles of his eyes traversed. They did not understand. They were listening, but not to him. The war was over, they had just been told, yet they were not going home. The war was over,

5

yet the clock continued to tick. The war was over, yet the time of war was not. They could not know it never is.

Mistaking their bewilderment for pigheadedness, Oberfeldwebel Skubovius hesitated. Should he challenge them with a Heil Hitler? No, the response would prove nothing. Even the Holy Ghost, administered to several of them in recent weeks, had not been enough. He must teach them all, including the Wehrmacht, a harsher lesson. *Jawohl,* he would, and this very night.

"Kompanie, abtreten!" In a gentle, almost kindly tone he let the formation go. It broke ranks and bunched up entering the barracks.

A westering sun set fire to and quenched with shadow a series of low, connecting peaks several kilometers from the camp. The Americans had no name for these mountains. To the Germans, their outline resembled that of a human figure, supine. They called them the Sleeping Indian.

2

The Post Exchange was thronged. Now they were dressed in green fatigues on which the letters POW were stenciled in white. They drank beer and played a jukebox and speculated when they would be sent home. In weeks, a month at most, in any event as soon as shipping was available, some argued, for if the *Amerikaner* had been humane in every other respect, they would prove to be in this; while others, the morose or cynical, said no, the USA was still at war with Japan, it would be a long time, at least until any work they might do was done, for if the efficient *Amerikaner* had made slaves of men before, they could again. Some were silent. They spent their work coupons for cigarettes and toilet articles, wristwatches and radios, all the sundries available in the PX of an Army installation. From Sears, Roebuck catalogues they chose and ordered such things as stockings, girdles, and brassieres. These would

6

be routed to women in Germany through the postal facilities of Sweden and Switzerland.

A soccer team practiced at one end of the *Fussball* field. At the other, two teams in American pads and helmets scrimmaged violently.

Films were being shown in several of the mess halls, usually comedies or love stories or Westerns. Occasionally a film depicting combat between Americans and Japanese was run, but never one based even remotely upon operations in the European Theater.

Prisoners whose English was equal to it read in the camp library. The most popular books, here as in the Vaterland, were the adventure novels of Zane Grey, particularly those set in Arizona.

Through the open hospital windows a handful of patients observed what they could. They were victims of recurrent malaria, contracted in Libya. They required minimal care, so that the nurses had little to do except to tend young Leutnant Heinz Buchting, once of Leipzig. He could not see through the window, could neither move nor speak. He had no sense function. All was void. For a month he had lain in an extended coma, reduced to perpetual infancy, but less than infancy for he was fed not by bottle or breast but by tube.

In one mess hall the Afrika Korps Band of thirty pieces practiced a stirring march, "From the Halls of Montezuma."

Hot night hushed the camp. Cooling slowly, degree by degree, the desert seemed to crack. A few prisoners walked the perimeter of No. 80. To the west the lights of Phoenix, a city named for the legendary bird which was reborn from its own ashes, winked on. To the north and to the east beyond the Sleeping Indian, mysterious in darkness and in myth, was vast America. To the south was Mexico.

Searchlights flared. Fixed in position atop guard towers at intervals and corners so that their beams fused, they made a wall of light around the camp's rectangle. On both sides of the wall were chain link fences twelve feet high, from the tops of which three barbed-wire strands were angled inward. Between the fences, on changing schedule, a jeep patrolled. In the wooden towers guards checked .30 caliber machine guns, sighted along the wall, their field of fire, then tuned in radios to the rebroadcast of a baseball game between the Boston Braves and the Brooklyn Dodgers played back

7

East that afternoon. Only one prisoner had ever attempted escape from within the camp, a Luftwaffe officer named Buchting who had concealed himself under a QM truck. Unfortunately for him, considering the condition in which he was returned, he had succeeded. No one had ever tried it over the fences or under, by tunneling, nor would anyone now, after the day's development. Escape would be pointless.

For the Germans, the longest, most oppressive hour was that between 21.00 and 22.00. It was then that their manhood opened like a wound which would not heal, and they were defenseless. Distance, an abstraction during the day, the soul reckoned. And it was then, locked into themselves, awaiting the pardon of sleep, that all the munitions of pride and fortitude and patience could not support their loneliness. They did what they could to make it endurable. In the heat and stifle of the barracks they stripped to GI shorts. Each barrack grew fetid with *Kommiss*, the mixture of body odors, clothing, hair oil, and boot polish peculiar to the German services everywhere. They played poker. They wrote the one letter home allotted them per month. Some made Nazi flags or carved models of U-boats or Tiger Panzers or battleships, the *Scharnhorst* or *Graf Spee*, for wholesale to the guards who retailed them in turn to civilians. For furniture each man had under his cot a footlocker and beside it a nightstand made by carpenters among them. On the latter, framed, was whatever photograph of wife or children or sweetheart or mother or father he might possess, or lacking that, a pose of Ginger Rogers or Rita Hayworth. Most of the men listened on radios to a station in Phoenix which carried every night at this time a program of Western music. The songs, sung through the nose to a twanging guitar, were laments of longing and lost love and homelessness and misspent youth and burial in strange, uncaring soil: "The Dying Cowboy," "A Wild Rattling Cowboy," "The Trail to Mexico," "The Wandering Cowboy," "Poor Lonesome Cowboy," "The Cowboy's Dream."

Lights out was at 22.00. Along the barracks in each stockade walked an accordionist. Softly he played, first Brahms's "Lullaby," then "Lili Marlene," then the *Zapfenstreich*, a refrain similar to the American "retreat." To his music the prisoners settled down. No. 80 Camp slept.

At midnight the American sergeant on duty in each stockade

8

left the office to make a cursory bed check of prisoners. As the noncom in First Stockade passed through the snores and dark of one barrack, a prisoner stirred, lay rigid as he left, timing. After a few minutes he sat up, pushed his feet into unlaced shoes, and moved cautiously outside.

He walked over the gravel to the latrine. Here the lights, naked bulbs, remained on all night. The latrines were divided into two sections, one for showers, the other lined along one wall with wash-bowls and mirrors and along the opposite wall with toilet cubicles. Blinking, he checked first to be certain he was alone.

He entered the third cubicle and closed the door. Stepping up onto the toilet seat he balanced, raised both arms, leaned forward, leaped. He caught hold of the four-by-six-inch beam which ran the length of the latrine over the cubicles, sought with his fingers, grasped a narrow packet tied with string, and dropped to the floor. Seating himself on the stool, he untied the packet.

His name was Matthe Karl Teege and he was twenty-one. He was a Reichs-German, having come from Duisburg on the Rhine. He had been surrendered as a crew driver with the 501st Tigers, attached to the Tenth Panzer Division in Tunisia. He was called "Richter," or Judge.

He first unfolded and studied a clipping from a Phoenix news-paper which ranked the various baseball teams in the major leagues by games won and lost during the current season. The Chicago Cubs led the National League, the Detroit Tigers the American. Next he unfolded several pages cut from civics textbooks. One con-tained a chart of the executive, legislative, and judicial branches of the Federal Government, together with the number of members of the House of Representatives and the Senate. On its reverse was a chronological list of Presidents and the dates of their tenure in office. This, too, he studied. The last set of pages reprinted in their entirety the Declaration of Independence and the Constitution and Bill of Rights and other Amendments of the United States, and it was these to which he devoted most effort. He seemed to be com-mitting as much as possible of them to memory or to reasonable recall. Over certain lines he lingered, frowning, trying them in the mind, judging them, his lips moving—". . . unalienable rights, that among these are life, liberty and the pursuit of happiness. . . . But when a long train of abuses and usurpations . . . evinces a design to reduce them under absolute despotism, it is their right, it is their duty, to throw off such government. . . . Neither slavery nor involuntary servitude . . . shall exist within the United States, or any place subject to their jurisdiction."

Matthe Teege glanced at his wristwatch. Refolding the clipping and pages into a packet and tying them, secreting them again atop the beam, he left the cubicle and the latrine and returned to his barrack. Inside, he removed his shoes, tiptoed to a cot not his own and awakened another prisoner.

This one's name was Albert Anton Pomtow. He was twenty-three, and his home was Taplacken, a village in East Prussia. He was always on the move. "*Rast ich, so rost' ich,*" he would say. "When I rest, I rust." Shoes on, across the open stockade yard he clomped, a walking windmill, a contraption. To his long, thin frame were jointed long, thin arms and legs and to them, big hands and feet. Albert Pomtow's nickname was "Hampelmann." The toy most coveted by German children in the nineteen-thirties was a clownish thin figure with grinning face which fitted over a hand. Pull a string behind it and Hampelmann's eyes popped and his arms and legs jerked ridiculously up and down.

So tall was Albert that he did not have to leap for the beam in the latrine. Craning an arm, he got the packet and enthroned himself on the stool for his half hour, yawning, scratching, humming "Home on the Range," and, ever practical, while broadening his knowledge of American athletic and political institutions also relieved his bladder.

When Hampelmann left the latrine on schedule he went not to his own barrack but to another, in which he roused Willi Franz Loffelbein. He was but eighteen years old. An ordinary seaman, believed to be mentally retarded by his mates and made their messboy, he had been captured only five months ago in the Caribbean when the U-305 was depth-charged to the surface by American aircraft using sonar buoys. He came from near Neukloster, in Mecklenburg.

Willi slunk across the yard, as fearful this night as on the very first sortie. He entered the latrine and looked into the showers and into every cubicle before closing the door of the third behind him. Short and stocky, the strength of his muscular legs alone propelled him from the toilet seat to the beam. He dropped with a grunt, seated himself, and set to work. To the dark-haired, dark-complexioned youth it was a half hour of torture. He did not know English as well as Matthe and Albert, and although he assured them he was making rapid progress, he was not. Words in the Declaration of Independence such as "usurpations" and "despotism" he could not even pronounce, much less comprehend. The baseball—whatever *dumm* game that might be—standings baffled him. *Ja,* he would the fly in their soup be, but help it he could not.

His second trip across the stockade yard was more dreadful than the first. Pebbles clicked under his shoes. But worse than that, four black-hooded, stocking-footed figures passed soundlessly not far away, a formation which, had he turned his head, he might have witnessed entering one of the barracks. He did not, but hurried even faster into his own barrack, his own bed. It was fortunate for him that he had neither knowledge nor premonition of the purpose of the four men.

They found what they were looking for, an infantry private named Dreschler. He had lately been reckless enough to be sarcastic about Korporal Schicklgruber and his Thousand-Year Reich. He had, moreover, expressed publicly a wish to remain in the USA rather than return to a Germany conquered and in ruins.

One man clapped hands over his mouth before he could rouse. Simultaneously another sat on his legs while each of the other two sat on his chest and extended his arms. With razor blades they slashed lengthwise the radial artery in each wrist.

Dreschler struggled but could not move. He screamed but could not be heard. The pump that was his astounded heart labored, forcing blood from the severed veins in thick gouts which splashed the floor. For eight or nine minutes they held him firmly.

He went limp then, lapsed into unconsciousness, and it was safe to release him and to slip from the barracks. As the pump failed for lack of fuel, his blood would well more slowly, but he would not revive. He would die within an hour.

To his friends in the Wehrmacht, and to the Afrika Korps, to the entire First Stockade in fact, Dreschler's exsanguinated corpse would be an object lesson in the morning. To the American military, who would take their clue from the razor blade dropped beside his cot, it would prove that to the die-hard National Socialist soldier, self-destruction was preferable to surrender.

No. 80 Camp slept. Germans dream as do all men. They dreamed of home, of beloved faces, of how a hand was formed, of how a tear had tasted. The barracks were loud with groans of protest at the horrors they had lived, the horrors they had done, on land or sea or in the air. Conscience and duty argued in the throat. In scraps of words the self begged absolution of the self. And there was no peace.

To certain prisoners, however, sleep was sweet. These were the very young, the boys in men's faces who were dressed in uniforms at seventeen or eighteen and sent on murderous errands by their elders. Now, one or two or three years later, they were boys still. In slumber they fled. In darkness they slipped from the charnel house of maturity, changed gladly from costumes of gray and blue and khaki into getups of fur and feathers and buckskin, and ran away in dreams to the very place where they now reposed—the American *Wilden Westen*. For the book of their boyhood was not *Mein Kampf*. The author of their fantasies was not Hitler or Goebbels or von Schirach. It was Karl May. What James Fenimore Cooper had been to early generations of American boys, and Mark Twain and Horatio Alger and Zane Grey to later, Karl May had been to theirs. Among the best-selling novels of all time, his seventy volumes took millions of wide-eyed German youngsters into the Near East and into Africa, but most frequently into that romantic region where tales were taller than the Rockies. There they met Winnetou, mighty chief of the Apaches, a red gentleman and natural philosopher who dressed in elk leather and perused Longfellow's *Hiawatha* in leisure moments. They met his partner in adventure, Old Shatterhand, who could fell a villain like an ox with a single blow; a combination of Natty Bumppo, Siegfried, Buffalo Bill, and Christ; a man of the Wild West who carried a magic rifle, Bear-Killer, with which he could knock out a grizzly's eye at fifteen hundred meters. With this fearless pair they rode the mountains and the prairies to survive a crisis every fifty pages. They never lost. They conquered always.

Hanging over the end of his cot, Albert Pomtow's bare toes wiggled with excitement. A tribe of howling savages surrounded him. He feared not, for he was not alone. Behind him, indomitable yet reliant on his leadership, stood a gallant band: Old Shatterhand, Buck Jones, Fred Thompson, Tim McCoy, and Hoot Gibson. *"Wie*

12

geht's, Herr Silberner Sechs-Schiesser?" they asked. "OK," he responded coolly, drawing his magic revolver. To them he was not a Hampelmann. To all the West he was The Silver Six-Shooter.

Matthe Teege lay on his back, arms solemnly at his sides. By the flickering firelight Winnetou, his bearing kingly, strode forward to address the braves. *"Heil* Teege, wearer of the Iron Cross! He will drink Winnetou's blood and Winnetou will drink his. Then Teege will be blood of our blood and flesh of our flesh. Do the warriors of the Apache agree?" In guttural shouts they gave their answer, "Howgh, howgh, howgh!"

Boys immemorial, they dreamed the Arizona night away. In those dwindling hours they were prisoners not of war but of imagination, captives not of guns and wire and light but of their youth. They dreamed of heroes and of villains, of forts and buffalo and sheriffs and cavalry. They dreamed of cowboys and the *Indianer.*

3

One of three prisoner-of-war camps in Arizona, No. 80 had been established in November of 1943. Outside its main gate were several administration buildings and the barracks of two companies of military police. The camp consisted of twelve identical fenced stockades, boxes within the larger box. Capacity was two thousand enlisted men and officers.

Six mornings of the week a line of Army trucks formed at the main gate, and from each stockade the labor details, carrying box lunches, marched through the gate and filled the trucks. Enlisted men were required by the Geneva Convention to work. NCOs were given a choice and ranks up to master sergeant did. Officers were not and of course did not. The trucks rolled.

Phoenix in 1945 was a small semitropical city supported principally by irrigation agriculture and the payrolls of two nearby Air

13

Corps bases and a naval air station. It derived income, too, from light industry and several resort hotels for winter tourists. Across the Phoenix area the trucks fanned out, moving their loads to the points at which they were needed. There was much for the Germans to do. They weeded cotton. They picked cotton. They cleaned irrigation ditches. They planted date palms. They tended the lawns and gardens of luxury hotels and painted the buildings during the off-season. They picked and packed oranges, lemons, grapefruit, melons, lettuce, and other produce. And these things they did more cheaply than migrant American or imported labor. Here the Geneva Convention, which stipulated that they be paid prevailing wages, was easily circumvented. To an Army busy with more important matters, "prevailing wages" were as low as an employer might declare them to be; there was a war on, he would justify himself to himself, and these were Germans, Nazis, the enemy. They were fortunate to be alive and in one piece.

They were, and knew it. They were well-fed and healthy, they could work and earn, they were far better off in fact than their Allied counterparts in German camps. But for one phenomenon the camp authorities could not account. It occurred irregularly, perhaps twice a month. It was a kind of contagious insomnia. Unable to sleep, a prisoner would leave his barrack in the middle of the night and appear at the fence. Soon others would join him, until the entire stockade or several stockades would muster along the fences. In the towers, guards rubbed their eyes open and trained the light machine guns. Men so long cooped up were capable of any insanity, they assumed, and two MP companies could be swiftly overwhelmed. What were the crazy krauts about to do? Goose-step through the wire in their underwear on a mass march for a port of embarkation?

They sang. They sang the songs of their services, the "Panzer Lied" of the Afrika Korps, and for the Kriegsmarine, "Wir Fahren Gegen Engeland." They sang a lilting round: "A penny and a dollar, Both of them were mine; The penny went to water, The dollar went to wine." Over the desert the chorus ebbed and tided like a restless wind, now wistful and subdued by space and rock, now a roar unruly. Listening, the guards shivered. There was something in that sound they recognized but could not understand, a counterpoint of rage.

For a soldier surrendered is a soldier betrayed. To make a soldier of a young man he must be assured that his cause is just, his flag is sacred, and that his gallantry will get him honor—but most vital, that he will triumph. This is the certitude which sustains him. But should he be handed over to his foe by general or government, he is robbed of his ultimate illusion. His youth itself is traduced. His very soul is violated. Second only to making a young man into a soldier, surrendering him is the most despicable of acts, and every nation in history has been guilty of it.

They could always sing. And they could always escape. That was another irony which attended their sojourn in Arizona. Most prisoners left the camp daily on work detail. In the fields, the two MPs guarded each truckload of twenty with something less than vigilance. Let the krauts take off like big-assed birds if they wished, the guards joked. Let them stagger around in this God-forgot desert minus food or water or maps or much English with rattlesnakes for buddies until they went loco and sang "Deutschland über Alles" to the sun. None of the Nazis had ever pulled off a real escape and none would.

It was true, if one defined a real escape as an effort which culminated in reaching neutral territory or country of origin. But from the earliest impoundment of prisoners in No. 80, many Germans had escaped in another, in an amusing, sense.

They were bored by the monotony of their routine. A little liberty was as refreshing as a cold beer in the PX after a hot day. And Germans were noted as tourists: it was their duty to see as much of America as they could while they were here. When a guard turned his back or took a nap or traded with civilians, they simply walked away from work.

One stole an Army jeep, drove to the Grand Canyon, and was recaptured standing on the rim taking photographs.

Another rode a freight train to Los Angeles and was picked up on Vine Street in Hollywood. He had been determined to meet Ginger Rogers in person.

A group of sixteen, members of the same U-boat crew, had trussed up their guards, inflated inner tubes borrowed from the camp motor pool, and set sail down an irrigation canal for the Gulf of California. To their chagrin, the canal ran dry ten miles from Phoenix.

Many turned themselves in when supplies gave out after several days of mountain-climbing, prospecting for gold, and classifying the desert flora. Some were taken wandering around in circles, hopelessly lost. They had been looking, they explained, for Indians. Trying to decipher timetables in bus terminals and railroad stations, others were apprehended by agents of the Federal Bureau of Investigation. It was the official task of the FBI to track them down, since outside the camp the Army had neither search facilities nor jurisdiction.

And then there were escape attempts which were not amusing.

4

In October of 1944 a prisoner named Heinrich Ehlert fled a labor detail. According to the map in his mind, Mexico bordered Arizona, and a guard's chance remark fixed the line, by his conversion of miles into kilometers, at roughly a hundred and thirty kilometers due south of Phoenix. His plan was to cross it, underground himself somehow to neutral Argentina, and there contact the apparatus which would have him home in time to participate in the final victory of the Reich.

Ehlert traveled by night. On the fifth morning, finding himself on a desolate plain and certain he must be close to the border, he decided to press on by daylight. Toward evening he discovered he was not alone. Like a mirage, a group of eight horsemen appeared, but they could not be a mirage for they followed rather than beckoned him. Unhurriedly they drew near. He did not run because he was hungry, thirsty, and footsore, and there was nowhere to run to.

They dismounted and surrounded him and looked him over, fascinated. "Godamighty, boys, look what we caught us," said one. "A real live kraut," marveled another. "Mostly a man has t'cross the water t'lay hands on a kraut, an' we got us one right here."

16

Ehlert was as fascinated by them. He was twenty-four. To him they were middle-aged, but in their dusty boots and faded denim clothing and broad-brimmed hats and holstered pistols they were also real, live cowboys.

They questioned him. He would give only his name, rank, and prisoner number.

"You bastard," said the youngest and tallest, who seemed to be in charge. "You dirty Nazi bastard. You're headed for the border."

"*Nein.*"

"Don't you know the war's about over and you've lost?"

"*Nein, nein.*"

The man knocked him down. Ehlert rose and in broken English demanded his right as a prisoner of war to be returned unharmed.

"Rights. You talk about rights. You're a Nazi and I'm about to beat on you till you tell us you're whipped and Hitler's whipped."

The tall man was as good as his threat. Once, twice, three times he felled the German, who did not fight back but shouted, before he blacked out, that he would never surrender, he was a soldier of the glorious Wehrmacht, which was only trying to save the world from *Kommunismus.*

When Ehlert revived he was lugged over a saddle, bound hand and foot. He listened to the men talk as they rode. The names they used, Coye, Buster, Doc, Hamp, Lloyd, Joe Mack, and Tate, he could not distinguish as names. "Makes you feel good," one said humbly, "like you done your part right t'home." The others agreed. They asked Jack, the tall, soft-spoken man who seemed to be their leader, if he intended turning the kraut in to the FBI. "Hell no. There's more where he came from, and maybe they'll try to skedaddle. So I plan to scare them off. You'll see." When they remarked it was mighty small of him to carve this one up by himself, he promised them a piece of the next, if there was a next.

Heinrich Ehlert was transferred to the trunk of a large automobile in which, bruised and exhausted, he was driven for two hours. The trunk was then opened, something was pinned to his jacket, and in the darkness he was dumped on the ground. At dawn he was found by the road near the main gate of No. 80 Camp. Pinned to his jacket was a slip of paper with a printed inscription: KRAUT KETCHERS.

He was interrogated both by the military and agents of the Bu-

17

reau. He could tell them little. He did not know where, except that it was five days south, or by whom he had been captured.

The next month, November of 1944, a prisoner in his early forties named Dieter Boehm left a detail. He had been a bosun's mate on a milch cow, or U-boat supply ship, sunk in the South Atlantic. He spoke no English. By the time he neared the border he was half crazed with thirst, and when what seemed to be a moving-picture posse of eight riders caught up with him he could respond to questions only with pleas for "*Wasser, Wasser!*"

Recalling his promise, the tall man offered the Nazi to the eldest of his posse, a man of fifty-four named Doc. Dared by the others, Doc took the seaman on. Both were small men, but the younger German began to get the better of the contest. The rest jumped in to help. They beat him badly or, as they put it, "pounded some savvy into him."

The horsemen moved the barely conscious Dieter Boehm from saddle to car trunk, unbuckled their guns, vanned the horses into Vaca, parked the vans, saw to the animals, and drove in two Cadillacs to Phoenix. After tagging his jacket with KRAUT KETCHERS and dumping him near the main gate of the POW camp, they returned to Vaca and, split up by the round trip, wanting to be together and to chin a little, they pulled in at the office of the Vaca Ginning Company at the edge of town, a small structure apart from the cotton gin itself. Joe Mack unlocked the office door, drew the window shade, opened a safe and broke out a full bottle of sourmash bourbon. They relaxed against walls or tilted chairs and big hats and lubricated their tonsils. Except for Doc they were rangy, handsome men with graying hair and tanned faces cut into like sandstone, men without fat, fine specimens, present-day descendants of Karl May's hardy Wild-West men. To Ehlert they had been cowboys, to Boehm a posse. They were neither.

"Doc, you are a ringtail cat," Coye said, winking. "You done damn well."

Doc fingered a scratch on his chin. "Had a good ten years on me, too. You don't reckon we banged 'im up too much?"

"You can't hurt a goddam Heinie, they got lead heads," Buster scoffed. "Man puts up resistance, you can chew on 'im a little, ain't that right, Jack?"

Jack Thode was thirty-six, youngest among them, but they

18

waited on his word. To themselves they called him a brush bull, the stray loner difficult to get a brand on or a rope over. He drank seldom, never ran with women, and what his personal likings were no one could rightly say. He might make you gritty in the tooth at times, uneasy, but he was a man's man, the kind who had taken this country away from the Indians in the first place and made it behave.

"Ain't that right, Jack?"

Thode nodded. "Besides, he was on reservation, remember, government land. White's accused of a crime against a white on Indian land and likely it never gets to trial. Who's going to start proceedings over some Nazi? Where'd you get a jury would convict? That's all they understand anyway, the krauts, the rough treatment."

"Kraut Ketchers, haw!" Buster exploded laughter, slapped his legs. They grinned at one another and took bottle turns. They felt good, fit as fiddles, animal.

Lloyd sobered. "You know my boy over in France, you ought t'read his letters, what them Germans do t'people. Well, we got us a lick back. Too young for the last war an' too old for this, but I damn-all wasn't tonight," he added proudly.

"You think any more will likely try it, Jack?" Hamp asked.

"Could be. They do and we better round 'em up before they cross that border. Or they might make it home and pick up where they left off." He was very long and rawboned. He still wore his gun, and as they watched, he unholstered and seemed to study the revolver. It was a show gun, a chrome-plated .38 caliber Smith & Wesson with a pearl handle and a six-inch barrel. Jack Thode palmed the chamber. His gray eyes, when not focused on an object, had a peculiar opacity, as though made of glass. He scraped the room with them. "You realize we might have saved some American kid's life stopping those two?"

Patriotism and bourbon warmed them. "Lemme have one more Nazi," said Joe Mack. "An' one more crop after this. One more crop."

What he meant was one more year of war in order to grow and market one last prime yield. It was cotton, its growing, harvesting, ginning, quality, and price, not Germans, which was their surpassing interest. Buster, Hamp, Lloyd, and Tate grew it. So did Coye and Doc, on leased land, although Coye owned a bar and Doc a

19

drugstore. In partnership, Joe Mack and Jack Thode owned the Vaca Ginning Company. And it was cotton which had made them all, in only four years, if not rich, within spitting distance of it.

It was also the war. In early 1940, Vaca had been little more than a wide place in the road ten miles north of the Mexican line. Then the world developed a craving for uniforms and high explosives. The price of cotton soared cooperatively. Speculators swarmed upon towns like Vaca, they bought desert on contract or rented it, they drove wells two hundred feet deep, they tapped that subterranean reservoir which was the precious accretion of centuries, they ditched and planted and irrigated, they weeded and sprayed and shook their fists at the heavens against the bollworm and the weevil. The fields greened, then browned, then burst with white gold. The operators, as they were known, got a short-staple crop per acre once thought impossible, and of a good grade. They imported Mexican pickers, they used whatever itinerant labor happened by. They borrowed and built gins. They ginned and baled and sold—the fiber for materials, the seed for oils and cattle fodder, the linters for cellulose. They clothed war and fed war and gave it noisy toys. Vaca prospered with them. It had a main street now and stores and gasoline stations and a population of almost two thousand. They were businessmen contributing importantly to the war effort, the operators told themselves. If it took the here-today-gone-tomorrow pumping of irreplaceable groundwater to grow cotton, if they had to hoist water till hell itself went dry, what the Christ were they supposed to do, pray for rain? If they were eating high off the hog, who by Jesus in the US wasn't? Call a spade a spade: everyone was better off for the war.

Lloyd drank deeply. "Ought t'give us a medal, an' Doc a Purple Heart. When you think what them Nazis been doin' over there to the kikes. Unhuman."

They put on appropriately sober expressions. It was Buster who released them. "Unhuman in a cat's ass—only good thing Hitler done!"

They grinned concurrence. "One thing I can't figure is," Hamp said, "how in hell, Jack, you come to know they was out there, the both of 'em."

Thode explained. Whenever prisoners escaped from No. 80, the FBI put out a bulletin. He was out on the reservation one day and mentioned the escapes to the Moencopa and asked them to keep a sharp eye out and send him word if they spotted anyone headed for the border, probably on foot. The shortest route from the POW camp was a beeline south, over the reservation, and from their mountain, the Moencopa could see a scorpion yawn ten miles away. To let him know was their patriotic duty, he told them. And it had paid off. They brought word into Vaca to him both times. So they deserved part credit for the captures.

Tate disagreed. "Hell they do. Indians an' Germans—only good one's a dead one."

"Or pickin' cotton," Buster snorted.

Two months later, in January of 1945, Jack Thode and his friends captured a brace of prisoners, Horst Mohrdieck and Bruno Fuge, who had fled a lettuce-picking detail. Again it was the Moencopa lookout which informed Thode. But this time there were two Nazis, powerful men in good condition. When surrounded after being driven half a mile, and asked how many American kids they had slaughtered, and Jews, to which they refused any reply, they put up a desperate fight before being overcome. Both prisoners were battered and kicked into insensibility. Fuge's jaw was broken. All eight of the posse were involved, themselves bruised and bloodied. It was an experience and a sensation none of them excepting Thode had ever had. They sat on the sand for a time breathing hard, each one secret unto himself, awed by the red mist which had seemed during the struggle to cloud their vision, and the lust, almost sexual, which had caressed their loins into knots. They looked at one another shyly. They were exhilarated and a little frightened. They felt like young soldiers after battle. They were renewed.

They vanned the horses onto the Moencopa reservation, saddled up and rode out together for the last time in April, 1945, less than a month before the war with Germany ended. Their quarry was Leutnant Heinz Buchting, age twenty-five, a Stuka pilot who had parachuted from his flaming plane into the sea near Bizerte. Since officer-prisoners did not work, he had escaped from the camp proper by concealing himself under a QM truck. When surrounded he identified himself readily. Lloyd stepped to the center of the circle to face him. A head taller than the German but twenty years older, he took off his hat and denim jacket. The others were silent. Lloyd said that three days ago, him and his wife had a telegram telling them their son had been wounded in action near Rosenheim.

"*Mein Herr*, I am sorry. For you and your son sorry."

"By you an' your kind. I ought t'kill you, German, but I'm too decent. All I'll do is what my boy'd do if he was here an' able."

Leutnant Buchting appealed to the ring about him. "Do not let him. I must defend myself. He should see, I am sorry and his son I did not hurt, his son I have not ever seen, we could be friends."

Lloyd hit him in the face. He did defend himself. They grappled in the dust, and when the pilot's youth began to tell, the other seven went to Lloyd's assistance. The German's use of the word "friends" seemed to trigger in them an extra fury. They pinioned his arms and legs. Long after Buchting was unconscious, they allowed Lloyd to pound his head up and down upon an outcrop of rock. It was his son and his prerogative.

Found still unconscious outside the gate of No. 80, Heinz Buchting was taken to the camp hospital. Army doctors recognized at once, by slow pulse and projectile vomiting and the condition of his head, that he had suffered massive brain damage. X rays revealed no skull fracture. The diagnosis was edema, or swelling, of brain tissue, resulting in hemorrhage and increased intracranial pressure. How long Heinz Buchting's deep coma would extend no one was medically prepared to estimate—perhaps for as long as he continued to exist. For he did not live. He took nourishment by gastric tube through the nose into the stomach. His urine was evacuated by indwelling catheter. Since he had lost control even of his rectal sphincter, he lay—man, pilot, and dullard child—in diapers.

Prisoners continued to absent themselves from labor details for sightseeing excursions, but no one risked again a flight south, toward the border with Mexico. The fate of Ehlert and Boehm and Mohrdieck and Fuge and Leutnant Buchting was general knowledge throughout the twelve *Lager*. "Kraut Ketchers" was bastardized in whispers to "the Krautfange," from the word for prisoners, *Gefangene*. There was less reason, too, after Victory-Europe Day, to attempt escape, although in several cases there was more.

5

Then Germans and Indians met at last. For those present, it was an encounter as startling and ineffable as any during the war.

American prisoners freed in Germany were already coming home, but it was rumored that the camps in Arizona would not close until every crop of every kind had been harvested, perhaps not before Christmas. Demands were made of the International Red Cross. Angry prisoner delegations inquired of the camp commandant. He had no information. He took what steps he could to placate them and to make their lot more pleasant. For one thing, two at a time the stockades would be allowed to put on their own shows, and on request, entertainment might even be provided from outside the camp, singers and dancers of USO troops, for instance.

First and Second Stockades formed a committee and produced the first show. A stage was built. One evening in June, five hundred men seated themselves on the ground before the stage. The Afrika Korps Band played a vaudeville overture.

First a magician originally from Dortmund, later a torpedoman, mystified them.

Next a quartet of parachutists from the Kleinschmid Column sang two sentimental numbers.

Next the woodwinds of the band set up a sensuous, exotic wail. To it, and to the ting of triangle and bell, a line of husky slave girls twirled onstage. But these were maidens of the Rhine, not of the Nile. Except for stocking wigs and veils they wore the scantiest of costumes. Brassieres of tin can tops glittered. Set in hairy bellies, navels from Wuppertal, Sondershausen, Bochum-Langendreer and Heiligenstadt enticed. Diaphanous skirts of cheesecloth billowed to reveal prodigious Teuton thighs and feet bejeweled with corns. Round and round they shimmied, shaking the stage, until they were joined by the harem master, playboy both of Prussia and the Sahara, Albert Pomtow and all his arms and legs, dressed and stuffed in the guise and shape of King Farouk. Gross in formal clothes, he mingled with the line of houris, clodhopping about to try their tin can tops, to pinch their panzerous behinds, to convulse the audience with lewd behavior. His harem took revenge. As they danced they unstuffed King Farouk, drawing from his person smuggled Army shirts and shorts and socks and cartons of cigarettes and sheets and pillow covers. Soon he was baggy pants and Hampelmann Pomtow once again, grinning and amiable, buffoon and black marketeer without peer in No. 80. Embracing as much of their tonnage as possible, he capered off to loud appreciation.

A pause. Ended by the beat of drums, offstage. Tom-toms. And gourd rattles. And hoof rattles. Something coursed through the five hundred men waiting in darkness, a thrill, perhaps a shiver of fore-knowledge.

Unknown to them, what their entertainment committee had asked of the camp commandant was something it did not imagine he could supply: Indians. But he had merely called the Phoenix Indian School, or government high school, and requested one of its several groups of dancers, young men below draft age, boys really, trained in ceremony.

They appeared. They were six young men, well muscled, in the elaborate and beautiful costumes which represented various gods: buckskin boots and fringed skirts; naked upper bodies striped and spotted and zigzagged with red, yellow and white paint; smooth-fitting hoods of black buckskin slitted for eyes and mouth; and on their heads crowns wider than the shoulders and not less than two feet high, woven of yellow yucca-cactus withes and painted with symbols of sun and moon and lightning, and with swastikas, one of the most ancient of Indian devices. Swastikas.

The sound the Germans made, involuntarily, was either gasp of recognition or murmur of fulfillment.

Tom-toms and rattles speeded tempo. They danced the Apache Crown Dance, performed only upon the most solemn occasions such as the setting out of a war party. They danced circularly, swinging the crowns from side to side, each dancer holding two thin swords of wood outward from flexed elbows, moving with knees bent. They made their own sounds: first the hoot of the owl,

24

a bird sacred to the Apaches, then a trilling of the tongue against the lips, exciting as a spreading fire excites. And finally, as tom-toms pounded faster and faster and rattles clacked crazily, the dancers leaped and thudded and let forth wild, unconquered yells.

They ceased. Silence again. They faced the audience. Dusky torsos glistening, they stood immobilized. For there was no applause. Instead, five hundred men had risen as one and faced them at attention.

It was an extraordinary moment, an extraordinary confrontation. Did history hold its breath? Did something ancestral in them stir, some consanguinity of bone and passion urge them on? Did civilized effect clasp hands with aboriginal cause? "He will drink Winnetou's blood and Winnetou will drink his," Karl May had written. "Then Old Shatterhand will be blood of our blood and flesh of our flesh. Do the warriors of the Apache agree?" They had, and it had come to pass half a century later, in Arizona. Through slits in black hoods, twelve eyes stared. A thousand eyes in dark formation stared. For a full hypnotic minute, blue and black eyes held. All the stories read, the films seen, the games played, the fantasies lived, surcharged the air with meaning. Germans and Indians met face-to-face at last and knew each other. They had fought a common foe, valiantly. By him both had been defeated. By him both were now imprisoned. For him both now toiled. From him both would be free. In revelation and tribute, spontaneously the audience gave the only gift within its power to the six young Indians standing in the light, that most haunting slow-march and requiem of the German services. It sang:

> *"Ich hatt' einen Kameraden,*
> *Einen bessern findst du nit.*
> I had a comrade,
> A better one you cannot find."

6

Matthe Teege, Albert Pomtow, and Willi Loffelbein went out on a cotton-chopping detail together. The prisoners detrucked, were handed hoes, and nineteen set to work while the guards leaned carbines against a fence and helped themselves to coffee from a thermos. The twentieth prisoner got down to business.

To one guard Hampelmann sold a Nazi flag for a dollar, and with the other, on Matthe's instructions, he traded a model of the battleship *Bismarck* in a bottle for a page from a book which listed the names and capital cities of the forty-eight American states. He then ambled to the far end of the field, surveyed a crew of hands chopping the adjacent acreage, and hallooed the females to him. "*Fräulein! Fräulein!* Howdy, my little dears," he jollied the plump senoritas and Negro matrons. "Observe what the good Herr Truman has sent us from Washington—*wundervoll!*" From his fatigue jacket he unpacked a half-dozen new Army shirts and displayed one like a haberdasher. "*Ist das nicht ein* damn fine shirt? *Ja, das ist ein* damn fine shirt!" He let them touch, he chucked their double chins and made them giggle, he dickered, he disposed of the shirts at two dollars each, a bargain for the ladies of the field, a happy transaction for him since the shirts had cost him fifty cents apiece.

Albert Pomtow was a born trader. "I was sad because I had no shoes," he would say, "until I met a man who had no legs." Over two years' service with the Afrika Korps, a genius at trafficking in goods and personality had literally saved his skin. He had been a cook with the Fourth Panzer-Grenadier Regiment, a clerk with the Thirty-third Reconnaissance Unit, and finally a motorcyclist with the 114th Flak, whirling back and forth across the Sahara like a dervish. As, one after another, these units were chewed up in battle, he carried his peddler's pack to the next, bartering fraternity

26

and commodity for any attachment that would keep him out of danger.

"Pomtow, you sonabitch," said one of the guards as he came up to pay the tax of fifty cents per shirt levied on all items sold under their surveillance, "you're goin' home richer'n I am."

Albert clicked his heels, raised his right arm. "Heil Amerika, land of opportunity!"

"Opportunity, shit."

"What I want to know is," said the other, "what in hell for you want them states'n capitals?"

"The slave must know his master," Albert said obsequiously. "The tourist must know where he travels."

The guard pointed at his carbine. "Fifteen rounds in that. You travelass off this detail an' I'll put more holes in you than kraut cheese. Nothin' I'd like better."

Hampelmann picked up his hoe and whistling "Whoopee Ti Yi Yo, Git Along, Little Dogies" through a gap in his buck teeth, sauntered into the cotton field. This morning's work had netted him a page from a book and six dollars in American currency, the soundest in the world, but he really disliked doing business with the guards at No. 80. They were queer ducks. If it were true, as he had long ago concluded, that war was insanity, it followed that all participants in war must be insane. Yet the guards were misfits even in an institution as huge and hodgepodge as the American Army. You could never be sure whether they were on the outside of the cuckoo clock looking in or the inside looking out. They were dressed as soldiers, but they lacked *Soldatengeist*, soldierly spirit. Albert allowed himself only one generalization: deranged enough to be taken out of the lines, yet not quite lunatic enough to be discharged into civilian life, they were here in Arizona guarding prisoners because the Army did not know what in *Hölle* else to do with them. They did not dismay him. He had seen their like in the Korps, for there had been no way to invalid them home from Africa. It was to be expected. It was war.

He joined Willi and spent the remainder of the morning hoeing up and down the green rows and catechizing him about baseball. Willi was not an apt pupil. Hampelmann sighed, leaned on his hoe, and pushed his big cowboy hat back to ventilate his brow. Flop-brimmed and battered, obtained from a guard for ten dollars, the

Stetson was his joy and trademark, a hat in his opinion worthy of *der Silberne Sechs-Schiesser*. He sighed again. Willi worshiped him, Willi tagged after him like a pup. Chastise him and he groveled for more, tail wagging. How he and Matthe were to look out for Willi when the time came, he had no idea.

"*Sehr gut*, Willi. You do your homework in the latrine every night, do you not?"

"*Jawohl.*"

"Yes. Speak only English."

"Yes."

"Then to me recite the names of teams of the League National."

"Chicago Cubs. New York Giants. Brooklyn Dodgers. Boston Braves—*Indianer*, Albert?"

"*Mein Gott*, no. Go on."

"Pittsburgh Pirates. Philadelphia Phillies. St. Louis Cardinals. Cincinnati Reds—*Kommunisten*, Albert?"

"*Herr im Himmel*, no!"

Hampelmann gave up and Willi hung his head and they chopped cotton in truce until noon.

The three friends ate their lunch under an olive tree, apart from the others yet within sight of the guards. Albert passed the new page to Matthe, who said they must begin that very night to memorize the names and capitals of all the states. Willi groaned and mopped his face with a sleeve. How could he memorize what he could not even pronounce? Richter had something else on his mind, he could tell. It was July now, and hot as an Unterseeboot submerged. In blue sky thunderheads thrust up, the white and fecund clouds which foretold summer rains and storms. In the far distance mountains wavered. Moist air streamed along their sides like milk. So much room in America, thought Willi, room to bathe in, room to swill into every pore like beer—*Lebensraum!*

Richter spoke. "I know how. At last I know."

He hesitated, not because he was uncertain but because that was his way. And it was his way, not his stature, which distinguished him. He was called "Richter," or Judge, because he seemed to carry a bench about with him, and from it, to try the world. He listened, he observed, he read, he reflected. When he spoke, it was a decision. When he acted, it was upon a weight of evidence, and others followed. His youth he rarely exposed, and then only through a smile.

"How?" they demanded.

"We will go to the Indians," Matthe said.

"The Indians?"

"Yes. I thought of it that night of the show, when the Apache dancers looked at us and we looked at them and we sang. We are friends, almost we are brothers. They live by themselves, a guard has told me, on their own lands, which are called reservations. We will find them and tell them why we have escaped. That we do not wish to return to Deutschland, but to remain here and Americans become. When they hear, they will secret us until the camp is closed and we can leave the reservation. Then we will be safe."

"But how will we find them?" Hampelmann objected.

Matthe smiled. "I do not know yet everything."

"Will they believe us?"

"If we are honest. And we will take gifts. You remember in the books, the gifts—that was how it was in the old days of the West."

"We must also get out of the camp, and carry everything also."

"There will be a method. Depend on me."

Hampelmann clapped on his cowboy hat and warbled his glee. "*Ach,* give me a home, where *die Büffel* do roam!"

To Willi, who might worship one and trust the other totally, the prospect was too miraculous to be possible, at least for him. Yet he hunkered up to pretend hope. "The *Indianer!*" he said. "With them free to be!"

Had they been overheard, what they were talking about might have convulsed the guards. But to the other men of the detail it would not have been absurd. For the incredible fact was that, given a chance, a large proportion of German prisoners in the United States in 1945 would have elected to stay and to become citizens rather than to be repatriated. While the man who had expressed this preference out loud in the First Stockade of Otto Skubovius had been executed, in most of the other stockades it was a frequent sentiment. Matthe Karl Teege, age twenty-one, from Duisburg on the Rhine; Albert Anton Pomtow, age twenty-three, from Taplacken in East Prussia; and Willi Franz Loffelbein, age eighteen, from Neukloster in Mecklenburg—these three had planned for several months to escape from No. 80 POW Camp—

29

not to cross a border or see the sights or exult in a brief liberty, but to hide out in the mountains, in a cave perhaps, to emerge when the camp was closed and the hunt for them had ended, and then, by some magic, to transform themselves into Americans, to work, to marry, to rear children, and, pioneers in a nation of pioneers, to live out their days. It was a project no more juvenile than building a house in a tree or a castle on the shore, no more lunatic than converting another by killing him. It was an ambition no more preposterous than the tricks their time had already played on them.

And if it were a scheme, indeed a game of boys, it would also be man's work, and they were both. Matthe was their leader, their brain. He made them puzzle in the middle of the night over baseball teams and standings, useful in conversation once out of camp. Since a knowledge of them might come in handy as well, he made them commit to memory and comprehension what they could of the Declaration of Independence and the Constitution. As Americans-to-be, he insisted moreover that it was their duty not only to know but to appreciate the founding documents upon which their new allegiance and citizenship would themselves be founded. Say them over and over to yourselves, Matthe urged. Hear them in the heart, the simple majesty of the words, the grandeur of the ideas, that "all men are created equal," for example, even Germans—hear them in the heart and listen later, when we are free in America, for echoes in the mind. He was moved. The somber robes parted for a moment and he was as young as they. Albert was their hands. His responsibility was supply—of study material, of American money, of civilian clothes to replace their POW fatigues, of food for any journey they might make, and of some contrivance by which to get these things out of camp with a labor detail. Head and hands, they were friends in treason. Sent to the same camp, assigned to the same stockade, they played together in the Afrika Korps Band, by coincidence the same instrument, the tuba, and they plotted escape together. They also shared an impediment of the flesh, a blister, a headache in the pathetic person of Willi, who tangled himself in their compassion by a kind of umbilical cord of helplessness. The miserable messboy had as little reason as they to return to Germany. And if Matthe sought truth in the USA and Albert opportunity, Willi would be content with a mere crust of that which the country promised in greatest abundance: freedom. How could they

30

deny him? To join their search, to have their friendship, he would pay an absolute devotion.

"OK, partner, name and capital of every state," Hampelmann agreed. "What also?"

More of the same, replied Matthe. Be patient, continue to study and to earn and hoard dollars for purchase or bribery. Albert said he had turned $7 that morning for a flag and some shirts, so that they were up to $171. Matthe directed him to give the $7 to Willi. They kept the currency in three fairly equal parts, and on their persons at all times. "And yes," Matthe remembered, "to decide what we will take to the Indians."

"If we find them. Maybe we should up on a mountain go and make a, a—how do you say—a signal, with fire and smoke. Hello, *Indianer!* We are here, where are you? Howgh, howgh!"

Matthe smiled. "Leave that to me."

He was as good as his word, although in this instance he came by the information through sheer good fortune. Trucked out one day with a detail to plant young date palms, he noticed the other men take from their jackets and hand over to the guards two cartons of cigarettes each before commencing work. Matthe Teege knew at once that by mistake he had been put on what the prisoners with sardonic humor called a Whore-*Kommando*. Pandering to the appetites of the thousands of servicemen training in Arizona was an industry almost as lucrative to the state as mining and agriculture. Much of downtown Phoenix had been declared off limits to military personnel by the authorities, to small effect. Attracted to the market by the hundreds, in all shapes, ages, colors, and nationalities, the whores moved elsewhere, to other sections of the city. When No. 80 Camp opened, it was not long before someone realized that the desires of German soldiers, sailors, and airmen might be similar, although of a more bestial order, to those of the American, and not long before a system of gratification was devised by a captain at the camp named Cohen. At punctual, four-week intervals, every one of the two thousand prisoners who wished to be was serviced. The medium of exchange was cartons of cigarettes. Out of his 80¢ a day wage he purchased for $2 in the PX two cartons of brand cigarettes worth, under the counter to civilians, $6. When his name came up on the schedule maintained by Skubovius and the other stockade overseers, he took them on detail and gave them to

31

the guards, who passed them on to ultimate resale. Grateful for day work, a whore was brought to the designated location and, between the cotton rows or in a packing shed, on the ground or on a bed of mouldy lettuce leaves, in a bower of onion sacks or orange crates, she made herself available. The twenty prisoners took turns. She was finished by noon and $40 better off. The difference in price between the $40 each truckload of men had paid for the cigarettes and the remaining $80 they eventually brought was divided in various percentages between the guards, the master sergeants, and Captain Cohen, who was scrupulous in his insistence that the whores be inspected and free of disease. It was an admirable arrangement, in its precision almost German, in its scope and remuneration truly American. There were of course occasional errors. The guards grumbled when Matthe Teege explained his misassignment, but nothing could be done about it.

After he and a companion, a Wehrmacht man in his middle forties, had dug several holes for the palm shoots, one guard pointed into the grove of mature trees nearby. The whore was there, evidently, and the older man was to begin. Somewhat sheepishly he left Matthe, only to return within five minutes, pick up his shovel, and work quietly. Presently he said he wished he were ten years older, or twenty, and lust would let him be, because he could not do it, not with this one. Two dollars, more than two days' work wasted. But she was only a girl. It would be like coupling with a daughter. Two daughters he had back home in Stuttgart, and a son, and a wife. Besides, he thought she was Indian.

Matthe stopped. He asked the older man how much time he had not taken with her. Five, ten minutes. Matthe looked for the guards. At a far corner of the grove one was asleep, the other reading a newspaper. He ducked into the trees.

He entered *Paradies*. Pillars of old palms were spaced in architectural order. Among their tops, among the male and female blossoms of the dates, bees dallied. The green and lacy fronds formed arches. Shafts of sun were driven downward through the arches. Light and shadow alternated. One walked in light and then in shadow, in dawn and then in dusk, in idol gold and then in templed purple. Except for birdsong, the oasis was purified of sound.

Matthe Teege found the girl and could not speak. What he had expected he did not know himself. Someone with feathers in her

32

hair? Dryad from a silver screen, copper child of nature and imagination?

"You got a cigarette?" she asked.

"I do not smoke."

"Gum?"

"My name is Matthe. What is yours?"

"Miss America."

She lit her own cigarette and blew sullen smoke. Chipped pink, her fingernails were bitten to the quick.

He did not smile at her sarcasm. "The other night, in the camp, your young warriors danced. We Germans have read of the Apaches of Arizona in many books, how they were brave. We salute them."

"Thanks. Say, let's get goin'."

She stunned and repelled Matthe. She did not enhance the spell of the grove; she desecrated it. A small, thin girl with the figure of a boy, her urchin hair, with the blue-black glint of a new weapon, was tangled and dirty. In blouse and skirt and bobby sox and scuffed flat shoes she sat against the trunk of a palm and hummed a tune he recalled hearing on the jukebox in the PX—"Pistol Packin' Mama." Disillusion angered him.

"This you should not do," he said, "lie with soldiers. It is not acceptable for one of your tribe. I would not myself lie with you."

"Blow it out your barracks bag."

Her skin was not even copper, but brown, like that of adobe brick long dried in the sun. Matthe grew anxious. The guards must soon notice his absence, and he had learned nothing from this slut-child. "Listen to me," he said. "I know how much you will gain from this, this unproper thing. I have more. I will give you to tell me certain information and go away now from this place and not to lie with soldiers."

"How much?"

"Sixty dollars."

She opened great black eyes. She rubbed a snub nose. "Crap," she said. Matthe unpinned the bills from the inside of his jacket. She held out a hand. She counted and wadded them tightly in her fist. "Now be quick," he said, and tumbled questions at her. Where was the reservation of the Apaches? South, she said, on a line south from Phoenix. How many kilometers? She did not know, or miles

33

either. To walk then, how many days? Four, maybe five. How would one tell it? There was no way, but it could not be missed if you traveled south, it was very big, all along the border. What towns was it near? Taft and Vaca. What was the terrain? Flat, and with mountains, the Lagartos, or Lizards. Very well, would she go now, and promise not to conduct herself without morals and to return to her reservation and family? She nodded. "And what is your name?"

"Me to know an' you to find out, soldier."

Matthe frowned. "You will tell me. In order that if you have not told the truth, I may search you and punish you."

She sprang up and would have run. He reached for her, taking hold of one wrist, and his hand covered something metallic. He forced her about and, as she struggled, raised her wrist. She wore a cheap identification bracelet of aluminum, of the sort affected by soldiers, a chain with a strip on which was stamped a name: TANSIE SCOUT. He let her go and watched her out of sight among the palms.

Retracing his path out of the grove, Matthe met a guard tracking him. "Hey, Heinrich, where you been? Where's Pocahontas?"

"Who?"

"The Indian babe."

"A man came. He took her away."

"After you got your ashes hauled, huh?"

"I would not lie with her."

"Why not?"

"She was Indian."

"So what?" The guard looked at Matthe, then split into sudden, unnatural laughter. "Indian, I get it! Buddies! Like laying your sister—priceless!" He stopped laughing, lowered his carbine, and with mock ferocity aimed it at Matthe's crotch. "I ought to deball you. They'll have my tail in a sling for this foul-up." He laughed again. "Indian!"

He waved his weapon. "Move on out." Still chuckling, he followed his prisoner. "Indian. You crazy goddam krautheads. One more thing, Heinrich. Anthropologically speaking, how come you had to start this motherscrewing war?"

"When it started," Matthe said, "I was age fifteen."

7

They knew now where to go and how to get there. The money Matthe Teege had given the young whore could not have been better spent. They were going to the Apache reservation four or five days south of the camp, a journey which would require only minimum funds and for which, now that they had a destination and a route, they might plan specifically.

They would travel in the guise of field laborers. Hampelmann began to trade new Army issue for three ragtag outfits. Piece by piece, together with provisions, he hid them under the flooring of an unused room in the recreation hall.

Richter had a double responsibility. He must devise a way to get food, clothing, and gifts for their Indian allies out of the camp via a work detail from which the three of them could disappear. A related matter was timing, when to go, and this must be his decision alone.

That they must go soon, that every week's delay added to the peril of discovery, was clear to them. It was American policy to allow the Germans, subject to the Articles of War and the Geneva Convention, to govern themselves, to maintain their own notorious discipline. On the whole, the policy had worked well. After the failure of von Rundstedt's Ardennes offensive in January of 1945, most prisoners had accepted the inevitable defeat with reasonably good grace. True, there were occasional thrashings, but men always quarreled. True, there was a death, but men now and then slashed their wrists. To the authorities, a German was a German and a Nazi as well, so that an administration which would never have housed American paratroops and infantry in the same barracks had no qualms about mingling Wehrmacht and Afrika Korps in fairly equal strength in the same stockade. It was a mistake. And if the ranking NCO happened to be Wehrmacht, a fanatic Nazi, and suspected of being SS or SD to boot, organizations which Erwin Rommel had never permitted to foul the ranks of his Afrika Korps, it was a tragic mistake. It put innocent men at the mercy of guilty. It put soldiers at the mercy of killers. It delivered Germans who had already lost everything except their lives into the hands of Nazis who had much yet to lose, including their lives.

Otto Skubovius founded his Fourth Reich soon after certain of his charges began to admit openly that the Third was doomed. To several the Holy Ghost, a severe beating, was meted out by night. Others he put into his own disciplinary cage to broil on bread and water. When there were mutterings, he salted the barracks with spies.

He drew up his own regulations. He demanded undiminished loyalty to Volk, Reich, and Führer, unequivocal faith in ultimate victory, unconditional belief in the flatness of the earth.

While the rule of terror disintegrated in the Third Reich, he imposed one in the Fourth. When it was announced that the war was over, he ordained that the inmates of First Stockade fight on. To add bite to his bark, that very night he had one of his own Wehrmacht, the man named Dreschler who had dared to utter a preference for life in the USA over repatriation, bled to death.

One morning there was brought to him a scrawled notice put up during the night on the bulletin board. It warned that another execution would result in his own. It was signed with a palm tree, an insignia of the Afrika Korps.

The master sergeant deliberated. The men might guess but they could not prove. They might threaten but would not be rash enough to go to the Americans. Besides, he had no choice but to crack down harder. He tightened barracks inspections. To test for dust he donned white gloves. He instructed his spies to report as much as one mutinous hair out of place.

June burned into July and July into August. The fields in which the prisoners toiled were fiery furnaces. The air was parched. Rain slaked it. But even rain was given grudgingly here. Dust storms, reminding the Germans of the ghibli, the sandstorm of the Sahara, advanced across the desert like an artillery barrage, passed in thunder, and preceded rain. A few hours of comfort and the temperature marched again to 110°F., exacerbating men whose captivity had been prolonged beyond justice and whose release no one in authority would date or discuss.

The law of averages overtook Matthe Teege, Albert Pomtow, and Willi Loffelbein one night during a dust storm. Last of the three, Willi labored an extra fifteen minutes in the latrine. He memorized the names of the states from North Dakota to Utah, the capitals from Bismarck to Salt Lake City, leaped twice, replaced the packet on the beam above his cubicle, and left the building.

The corporal who, by simple abdominal coincidence, had come to use the latrine, noted his acrobatics through a window, went inside, felt along the beam to the packet, opened it, glanced, and scurried immediately to the office. Whispering, he handed it through the Oberfeldwebel's open window and was ordered to wait. The master sergeant closed the window, drew the shade, turned on a light, and examined the documents. He sat down. Outside, a wind wailed and the corporal stood by. For whatever he chose to do, it was a good night. It had not been a good day. That morning he had found pushed under his door another love letter from the Afrika Korps. It repeated the earlier warning: any more of the Holy Ghost or another execution and his would be next. And if it were inconvenient to beat him or bleed him dry here in No. 80, or on the train East, or on the ship, he might rest assured the matter would be arranged within an hour after he set foot again on the soil of the Vaterland.

He lit a cigar. Except to tap ash, he sat without moving for five minutes. Loffelbein, Willi. Seaman. Eighteen years approximately. Stupid. Planning escape to stay in United States or these papers unnecessary. Too stupid to get them himself or understand them. Therefore with others, one or more. Who read or speak English well and intelligent enough to see the need for acquaintance with baseball and government if questioned. Who? How to find out who? Must. And go with them.

That was the irony. The situation of Otto Skubovius was as desperate as that of any of the two thousand inmates of No. 80, his need to escape more crucial than that of the youth, asleep on his cot, whose dice he must now cast. For the Bavarian had reached the end of the road, or the rope, or almost. Beginning in an orphanage in Nuremberg, the ham-fisted master of his dormitory. Brawling with *Kommunist* gangs in the streets. Then, after years alone, a home, security, a father and mother: the Reichsparty. And a uniform, that of the Brownshirts. Beating Jews, painting swastikas on their synagogues, looting and burning their shops. A perfect recruit for Heinrich Himmler's thought police, the SD, the Sicherheitsdienst. War. Assignment to the 331st Division in Sicily, a division made up in the main of Poles, Czechs, and Bulgars, who would require much surveillance and education by the SD. Invasion in 1943. Conscripts in flight or surrendering like sheep. To buck them up before Agrigento, a lesson. Select a batch caught advancing to the rear, forty-one in all. March them before the regiment and shoot them. Salutary improvement in the regiment's will to fight. Capture by Americans. Shipment to the USA, to No. 80. Command as ranking NCO of First Stockade. And now, no Reichsparty, no SD, no war except that which he could wage himself, no authority except that which the *Schweinehund* Americans granted him, no comrades except the personal Gestapo of ex-SS men he could bully into obedience, no home, no security, no mother or father, the rope looped, the road ending exactly where it had begun thirty-five years ago. An orphan again.

Otto Skubovius tapped ash. He had four alternatives. *Eins,* he could stay. Yet if he stayed, he could not keep power without continued resort to violence, and the men were already near the breaking point. *Zwei,* he could stay, relax discipline, play the jolly fellow, and sail home with the lot. But an officer had mentioned reading a magazine article to the effect that the occupying powers intended to track down and try all Germans responsible for battlefield atrocities, and there had been hundreds of witnesses to his education-by-bullet of the conscripts in Sicily. *Drei,* he could somehow exit the camp himself and make for Argentina by way of Mexico and there join the other Reichs-refugees. But he spoke no English, in two years he had never been outside No. 80, beyond the wire he had no data whatever on the region. *Vier,* he could hitch a ride on someone else's plot. He could bribe or coerce his way into an escape attempt already well planned and provided for, with men who spoke English, who knew the country, and once they had outlived their usefulness, once they got him close enough to Mexico to cross the border on his own momentum, he could dispense with them.

He tapped ash. Loffelbein, Willi. A sailor, a fish out of water. His accomplices would have to be men trained to the desert, to heat and thirst and mirage. *Jawohl,* Loffelbein, Willi, must go with Afrika Korps. But who, when, where?

Problem: how to get information out of an idiot.

Solution: poke fear down his throat till he pukes.

Oberfeldwebel Skubovius butted his cigar neatly, checked his wristwatch, gave instructions through the window to the corporal, and began to make ready.

Half an hour later four men in fatigue trousers and black hoods rushed Willi Loffelbein across the stockade yard through a raving wind—a Willi Loffelbein too stupefied by fear to note the resemblance of their hoods to those worn by the Apache dancers.

They took him into an unused room in the rec hall, forced him into a chair, stood at his back. The windows of the room were covered against flickering light by blankets. Quaking in his GI undershorts, he huddled before a ping-pong table draped in black. Above him, on the wall, was a large replica of the Nazi swastika flag. On the table were the packet of book pages and newspaper clips, a Bible, a portrait of Adolf Hitler cut from a magazine and framed and flanked by a candle on each side, and a large dagger made from a butcher knife, that dagger which was part of the NSDAP uniform, into the handle of which was carved the inscription BLUT UND EHRE, Blood and Honor. Facing him sat a white whale of a man, naked from the belly up except for a black hood. His hands and wrists and forearms were flukes. On a finger a gold ring glinted. Through slits in the hood were eyes so expressionless, so opaque, that they might have been glass.

Willi recognized them as the eyes of Otto Skubovius. He recognized the room as the very one in which, under the flooring, probably under the black-draped table itself, were the garments Albert had procured and hidden.

He sprayed tears.

Over his wails, over the wailing of the wind, the dispassionate voice of the judge presiding announced that this was a court-martial and ordered him to swear on the dagger to tell the truth. He bawled that he would not.

Using a wide Wehrmacht belt as a whip, one of the men behind him snapped him beside the head. His ear burst blood.

He was informed that he was on trial for failure to observe the

39

regulations of First Stockade. The evidence lay before him, documents in English the possession or reading of which, as he knew, were *verboten*. He was charged further with high treason to the Third Reich, to People, Führer, and Fatherland, a crime punishable by death after trial by military proceeding. The documents testified to an intent not only to renounce his oath to the Reich but to take up permanent residence in the United States, an enemy power. How would he plead? Guilty or not guilty?"

Willi babbled that the Führer was dead, the Reich did not exist, the war was over, the German armed forces were *kaputt*, but fright and pain and sobbing made him incoherent.

The candles were snuffed. In darkness a voice pronounced judgment. "Guilty, then, this court declares you, Loffelbein, Willi. You are sentenced to be hung by the neck until dead. Unless now, before this court, you name those also guilty. Speak."

Willi could not have had he tried.

Arms raised him from the chair. He went rigid. He was lifted off his feet and taken outside, into the screaming wind, and borne upright like a figure of wood, a dummy, across the yard, up steps, and into the latrine. A man was posted at the door to bar entry to anyone, but no one would come, for just then the entire camp was cut off by a mighty eminence of dust, the gathering from fifty miles of desert which, like doom's door, slammed shut upon it. The latrine trembled. Against its thin board walls, dust flailed.

Still in their hoods, Skubovius and the other three worked hastily. A rope was flung over the beam from which the packet had been retrieved, the noose on its other end placed round Willi's neck. Hands under his shoulders lifted him, two men pulled the rope taut, and his weight was released against the noose. Inches above the floor, hands clawing at the rope, legs kicking, face purpling, he died a little.

They let him fall onto his hands and knees. His ear dripped blood. In extremity, he had urinated.

"The names, Willi," Skubovius said into his ear. "Give me the names of the others!"

Willi gagged.

"Too bad, see, he has befouled himself like a child. He is bleeding also. Wash the *Schwein*."

They dragged him to a toilet, pushed his head into the stool, underwater, and flushed it.

On the Oberfeldwebel's nod they dragged him back, hauled him upright, noosed him a second time, hoisted, let him dangle writhing and clawing a moment, and a second time let him fall. He fell flat, his eyes closed.

Otto Skubovius nudged him with a foot. "Out with you," he said to his assistants. When they were gone, from a trouser pocket he took the cigar he had butted earlier, relit it, puffed, and sat down beside his victim. "*Ach,* Willi, how interesting it is," he said in sad, gentle Bavarian, to himself actually, below the wind. "You think I will kill you, but if I do, I kill myself. You are my only chance. To get out of this camp with your friends, to *Südamerika.* So you must tell Otto, your *Kamerad.*" He sighed. "You do not listen, Willi." He applied the hot cigar butt to Willi's injured ear, swabbed it out in blood. The youth's eyes flew open. He moaned. Skubovius clucked greeting. "Good evening, Willi. You are a good, brave, stupid boy. Tomorrow night we will hang you permanently. Do not go to the *Amerikaner* with your whimperings. They will give you a card for the chaplain, a TS card they call it, tough *Scheisse,* and give you back to me to put in my cage. Tomorrow night. But if you tell me the names before then, I will let you go. You will be free. Until tomorrow night, Willi. *Auf Wiedersehen.*"

He left the latrine. Willi lay for a long while trying to breathe. Eventually, on hands and knees he crawled into the storm. His instinct was to reach the barrack where Matthe and Albert slept, but he could not see it through the dust, he could not even locate his own. Gravel cut into his palms and kneecaps, dust smothered him, and finally, somewhere in the yard of First Stockade, he collapsed, trapped in dust.

8

He had never been free, really. For all his eighteen years, four months, two weeks, and five days of existence he had been a prisoner.

Rain revived him. Rain cleansed the air and swept his head. Rags of rain slapped him to his feet. But he took no more than a step toward the barrack of Matthe and Albert before he stopped. What if the hooded ones were watching? And he led them straight to his friends? He whirled toward his own barrack and ran for it, dived into bed, and drenched and shivering with cold and the error he had almost made, doubled himself into the fetal position.

Willi Loffelbein had been born into bondage. The stableboy son of peasants, serfs actually, on a junker estate in Mecklenburg, stolid folk who cared for him no more assiduously or tenderly than they did their pigs or ducks, not until fourteen was he delivered, and then into the Jungvolk. And if, besides his life, he offered what was more important, his heart, to Adolf Hitler, it was because no one else would have it.

In the two hours of drizzle before the bugle he did not sleep. He rose with the others, dressed in POW fatigues, lined up for the count, washed laggardly, but did not go to the mess hall. He might see Matthe and Albert, they might speak to him. His best chance was to be sent out on the same labor detail. Working together in a field, he could safely tell them what had happened in the night, the trial and sentence and torture and proposition. But when he went to the gate, a noncom informed him he was confined to First Stockade, orders of the Oberfeldwebel. Only then did Willi grasp the dimensions of his predicament. He lay on his bed, picking at the dried blood on his ear, alone with his panic. He was helpless, he was hopeless. To persuade the Americans to believe and to protect him he would have to reveal the escape plan. Passing so much as a single glance or word of warning to Richter and Hampelmann would give them away to the SS or SD.

In the late afternoon he looked out the window. His eyes met others, those of Skubovius, watching him from the office. Shuddering, Willi jumped out of sight.

To cast off the shackles of class and origin, to explore the thrilling vistas which had opened up to him in the novels of Karl May, he had enlisted in the Kriegsmarine on his seventeenth birthday. Rather than liberation, however, it was a new enslavement—first within the cramped galley of the U-305, then behind ·the barbed wire of No. 80 POW Camp. His worlds had been a set of Chinese boxes, smaller and smaller, with the final one, in which he was now enclosed, that of his own despairing flesh.

After the count formation he dodged into the room in the rec hall in which he had been court-martialed, burrowing for almost five hours under the ping-pong table draped the night before in black. He dared not go to dinner. Not until lights out at 22.00 hours did he slink back to his barrack to lie on his bed and pray that his friends would not seek him out and to count the time he had left before midnight.

You are a good, brave, stupid boy, Skubovius had murmured into the very ear he had just used as an ashtray. Good he might not be, brave he certainly was not, but was he so stupid he could think of no way to strike back at the master sergeant? Or defend his friends so that they might make their vision durable? Or live himself, *grüss Gott*, to be an American? Tomorrow night, boy, we will hang you permanently.

It was 21.00 hours. In another hour and ten, perhaps fifteen, minutes, as soon as the American sergeant had walked through on bed check, they would come for him, the hooded men.

Around him others snored and gibbered, unaware that they slept with one condemned.

His ear throbbed. Remembering the rope, his neck hurt.

He had not slept the night before. His stomach begged. He had missed three meals.

Terror took him. He wet the sheets with sweat.

He had read how, by gnawing, wild beasts sometimes amputated their own legs to free themselves from traps.

43

Steps. The sergeant walking through.

The instant he had gone, Willi was out of bed and rummaging through his footlocker. The things he took from it he bundled into a sheet and hurried outdoors, across the yard and into the latrine. After eighteen years, four months, two weeks, and six days, he might have five minutes more at most while the noncom completed his rounds.

On the beam in the place where they had kept the packet he put $59 in currency, his share of the escape fund. Coming to do his research on schedule, Matthe might find it.

Before the mirrors he dressed himself in his Kriegsmarine uniform—bell-bottomed trousers creased fore and aft rather than at the sides, blue blouse with red torpedo on the left sleeve and broad white collar and black scarf. Thankful that he did not yet need to shave, he combed his dark, curly hair carefully and put on his sailor hat, the blue ribbons of which hung to his shoulders. It was a beautiful uniform, and except for his deformed ear, Willi thought he looked very well indeed.

Going then to a cubicle, he tossed one end of the sheet over the beam, tied a slipknot, and cinched it up. The sheet was too long. Chewing a start, he tore it in half, made a noose, tested it, and placing the noose around his neck, stood upon the toilet seat and balanced and faced himself in the mirrors on the opposite wall.

To admire the sight of himself, to participate fully in his own sacrifice, he intended to stand at attention for a moment. It could not be *ein Heldentod,* the hero's death glorified in the German services, but it must be more than an act of mere terrier loyalty, more than a frightful, meaningless puppetry in which brutal hands not his own actually pulled the strings. There must be in it elements of resolution and gallantry and even, *ja,* even the mysticism of Tom Mix. It must signify the proud acceptance by one who had been a prisoner all his life of a final, everlasting imprisonment. But in coming to attention on the toilet seat, his foot slipped. Death surprised Willi Franz Loffelbein. Quite by accident he fell into the first freedom he had ever known.

9

His discovery, by another seaman too horrified even to cut him down, brought men piling out of the barracks and rushing toward the latrine. In a minute or two it rocked on its foundations as prisoners attempted to get out while others fought to get in. Roused, the inmates of adjacent stockades streamed to their fences to inquire. It was as though No. 80 Camp had been waiting storm by storm, rain by rain, month by smoldering month for the entire fierce and humid summer to explode.

Beyond the wall of light sirens screamed, noncoms yelled that the krauts had finally blown their tops, and a company of MPs was turned out to double-time through the main gate, carbines at the ready. Extra jeeps sped out to patrol. In the towers, guards trained machine guns on First Stockade.

Senseless fights erupted at once between sailors of the Kriegsmarine, whose uniform the dead boy wore, and soldiers of the Wehrmacht. But to most of the men, particularly the Afrika Korps, men already in a mood made ugly by restriction and by an almost manic tyranny which turned fact upside down, the meaning of the hanging was immediate: it was another execution, disguised like that of Dreschler to appear a suicide, which could only have been carried out on orders of the Führer of the Fourth Reich.

Drawn to one another, the Afrika Korps assembled in the latrine. Someone began a chant. Others joined. In seconds a hundred throats swelled with it. To the MPs the chant sounded like the hee-haw of a hundred donkeys braying in lower-register unison. It reminded the Germans in other stockades of the high-low horns which substituted for sirens on police cars throughout Europe. To the Oberfeldwebel leaning out the window of his quarters in the office, the vengeful chanting was his name: "Ot-to! Ot-to! Ot-to!"

45

He did not know what had happened, but for the implications of the chant he had long been prepared. He plunged himself into a white shirt and a gray worsted civilian suit. From a desk drawer he swept up a wallet containing over a thousand dollars in American money, his commissions from Captain Cohen, and a pair of heavy wire cutters and a .45 caliber Army automatic, loaded.

Wire cutters in his left hand, pistol in his right, he strode from his room head on into the American duty sergeant, also quartered in the office, whom he clubbed to the floor with a single sideswipe of the gun.

Once out the door he did not run. He walked as though inspecting a formation, slipping the weapon into a pocket and transferring the tool to his right hand. Around First Stockade was a simple three-strand fence. He snipped the strands. As the last parted, he sprinted for the wall of light and its double barrier, only thirty meters away. For one of his bulk, he ran with amazing speed.

The men of the Afrika Korps had by this time become a mob. Moving from the latrine, chanting "Ot-to! Ot-to!" in cadence, it swirled about the office, its intent lethal. Windows were broken. Several men rushed inside. He was gone.

It was this mob which concerned the guards in the towers. In one, the soldier at the machine gun was a private named Billy Cahoon, age eighteen. A tight-strung, imaginative youth, his adolescence of war movies and war books had caused him to break out with a type of patriotic acne and had induced him at seventeen to leave high school and enlist, with his parents' permission, in the Army. He was trained as a rifleman, an infantry replacement, at a camp in Georgia. During Billy Cahoon's sixteen weeks of basic, one problem came up again and again. What would happen overseas, in combat, a trainee would ask his officer-instructor, when it encountered the real thing, if a platoon were pinned down by fire, pinned down so completely that it could not move a muscle toward its objective? The officer's response was stock. There was no need to worry, he would say with officer-candidate-school confidence; in such an emergency, some one man in the platoon, and which one no one could predict, would for some mysterious reason take the initiative, risk his life, and by his heroism lead his buddies safely to their objective. He might die in the doing, but rest easy, men, shit no bricks, there would always be someone. It might be the man sitting next to you even now. It might be you. Me.

At the first chain link fence Otto Skubovius flung himself prone, lying just at the edge of the wall of light, and with the tool made two vertical incisions a foot high and several feet apart. He pushed, he bent the rectangle inward and up, and twisting, squeezed through the opening and into the fused beams of the searchlights.

Billy Cahoon knew, knew positively, the someone would be Billy Cahoon. He became obsessed by his own eventual heroism, his own sacrifice, his own casualty. He dreamed in theatrical sound and color of the Distinguished Service Cross, the Silver Star, the Bronze Star, all awarded him posthumously and presented, together with the ten thousand dollars from his service life insurance, to his exalted parents. When he woke, his blankets were damp with sweat. When he was shipped to France in December, 1944, the Army had machined this likely lad, except for a single loose screw, into a strong and battle-ready item of equipment.

The riot in First Stockade seemed to be under control. MPs were surrounding it. Something lodged in the corner of Billy Cahoon's eye. He looked below. He blinked.

In the glare a man wearing a gray civilian suit was halfway through an opening at the base of the outer fence, his shoes kicking dust as he wedged himself butt and belly down. Billy Cahoon howled at his fellow guard and swung the machine gun on its tripod. He began firing before he had the barrel depressed. Instead of firing in bursts, as he had been trained, he clenched the trigger. Like a boy with a string of firecrackers, he let go the whole belt of two hundred fifty rounds. He ripped holes in the fence. He skipped ricochets off rocks. Hanging on, he sprayed even the darkness into which Otto Skubovius had fled in one childish, inaccurate, delighted ejaculation.

10

They went together the next night to the latrine. On the beam they found the money. It was like a message from the grave. It did not reveal whether he had been executed or had died by his own hand or to what extent Skubovius had been responsible. But it told them that the packet had been discovered by the SS or SD and that its possession had incriminated him. It explained why he had avoided them all of one day and hidden from them that evening. But you are safe, you are safe, for I did not give you away, it seemed to say most clearly. That is why I put the money here, where you might find it. Please find it, please use it, please, for my sake, and be American and free. And do not, dear Albert, dear Matthe, for me grieve. By my death I gain *Kameraden* better and more lasting than by my life I could have gained.

Hampelmann was inconsolable. "In a latrine," he said. "He could not have even a decent place to die." GI undershorts sagging about his gaunt hips, he stood against the wall and turned his face to it. "*Ach*, poor Willi," he said. "To him *alles* we were, *alles*."

"I know," said Matthe. "It is my blame. I made him study."

Over his shoulder Albert stole a glance. The Judge's face was expressionless, but Albert knew his sorrow was as deep, perhaps deeper, than his own. Sometimes it seemed to him that Matthe Teege resembled one of the ruined buildings he had seen in Tobruk, of which there must have been hundreds more in London and Berlin and Leipzig and Rotterdam, one of those freaks of bombing in which the walls were left standing while the interior was gutted. He had some knowledge of how the last three years had rubbled the youth that Matthe Teege once had been.

"To lay hands on the bastard Skubovius I would a year of my life give." With his lank, bare arms Albert pushed against the wall.

"Matthe, I must get out of this *verdammt* place. I have been here too long."

The latrine stank of death and futility and disinfectant. A faucet drip, drip, dripped its tears.

"Soon," said Richter.

It was sooner than that. It was so unexpected, in fact, that even Hampelmann, ever prowling the main chance, did not recognize it.

Immediately after they left band practice the next evening Matthe gripped his arm and walked him rapidly to the perimeter of No. 80. The time had come, he said, and the opportunity—something told him the instant the bandmaster had announced. For once, Albert did not understand. What the bandmaster had said was that the Afrika Korps Band would play in a stadium the following night, in Phoenix. So? So they would be out of the camp, and at night, Richter said, and sometime during the performance they could give the guards the slip, and best of all, they would finally have something in which to transport everything needed—change of clothing, personal effects, provisions, gifts for the Indians—and pass it out right under the guards' noses! What? Well, what instrument did they both play? The tuba. Was it a large instrument? *Gross!*

"Albert, do you not see?" demanded Matthe.

"No. *Ich komm'* from Missouri."

Matthe gripped his arm again. What did you transport a tuba in? A big case—so? So suppose you hung the horns over your shoulders and simply carried the cases at your sides as though empty. Hampelmann jumped straight up.

Matthe Teege and Albert Pomtow lived the next twenty-four hours as though a sulfa of excitement had been administered them. During the night they unearthed from beneath the flooring of the rec hall the supplies and gear Trader Pomtow had procured—Baby Ruth and Butterfinger candy bars, cans of beans and cheese, nondescript civilian shirts and trousers and jackets—and brought them to their barrack to store in footlockers. Willi's outfit they left under the floor as a kind of memorial.

After the next day's labor detail they did not go to supper. Instead, alone in their barrack they uncased the tubas, packed the cases, then showered, shaved again, and dressed.

At 19.30 hours, big silver bass horns over their shoulders, black cases held nonchalantly in one hand, they strolled out of First Stockade, the Fourth Reich, and down the street to the main gate of No. 80 POW Camp. The Afrika Korps Band consisted of thirty pieces—twelve woodwinds, fourteen brass including two tubas, and three drums and a cymbal. Two QM trucks pulled up for them. Four guards, wearing only sidearms and too disgruntled by extra duty to note anything untoward in the separation of bass horns and cases, counted them off into two groups of fifteen. They mounted, flutes and clarinets and saxophones and cornets and French horns and trombones and drums and instrument cases and jabber. Into the red August evening the trucks rolled.

On the way into Phoenix they sang "A Penny and a Dollar." In the city, with the exception of the two tuba players, who were strangely silent, they did what all young men do. They whistled at pretty girls.

11

The Afrika Korps Band was to participate in the climax of the Seventh War Loan Drive, the last of the war. Civilian bond sales had lagged in Arizona, and the local War Finance Committee, whose inspiration it had been to add to other attractions a musical unit of prisoners, had synchronized its effort to put the sales drive over the top with the arrival in Phoenix of a touring Army exhibition called "Here's Your Infantry!" According to the newspapers it was to be the most spine-tingling, hair-raising, bloodcurdling, thrill-packed show ever staged in the city. Tickets were given to adults with the purchase of war bonds, but since the show by its nature was educational, children were admitted free.

Baited by the publicity, bored with rodeos and movies and circuses, a crowd of several thousand was already inside the high school stadium while hundreds more milled about the parking lot as the two trucks from No. 80 Camp arrived. The prisoner-musicians unloaded and formed. To reach the tunnel entrance to the stands, they had to march across the parking lot. What they saw caused them to fall out of step, to bump into one another, to halt. They gaped.

They halted amid their own weapons. They were surrounded by a comprehensive display of German war materiel captured in Europe. They stood among Americans as fascinated by it as they themselves were stunned. The sides of vans were opened to racks of .09 Mausers and Lugers, of .98 carbines, of rifles and Schmeisser machine pistols and grenades. Mounted on the beds of Army trucks were .34 and .42 Spandau machine guns, 21 cm. *Granatwerfer,* or mortars, and *Nebelwerfer,* the six-barreled rocket launchers. Behind two Mannesmann and two Henschel diesel trucks were attached a howitzer, a 17 cm. field gun, a 5 cm. antitank gun of the *Panzerjäger,* and that most dreaded of all antitank, anti-aircraft and anti-personnel weapons, an 88 mm. gun. But even more startling to the desert foxes than these was the huge gray prehistoric beast chained upon a long, olive-drab, thirty-wheeled Army tank transporter. It had been the old reliable, the iron mascot almost, of the Afrika Korps. It was a forty-ton Mark IV Special Cruiser tank. Last model before the Tiger, it had been repainted even to the black-and-white cross gleaming on its turret, and restored to operating condition, its tracks and rear and forward driving sprockets and eight bogie wheels intact. American boys and girls, like Bedouin youngsters, peered curiously into its open hatches. Its nine-foot-long gun barrel and muzzle brake pointed ludicrously across the parking lot at a grocery store.

Guards shouted at them to move on out. They resumed step and marched across the lot and into the tunnel. A block of seats had been saved for them at ground level. They uncased instruments, stacked the cases along the railing, and sat down.

"Anyway, my motorcycle they do not have," Albert Pomtow whispered. "Did you ever drive the Mark IV?"

Matthe shook his head. "The Tiger only."

Hampelmann shook his. "I do not see how to do it. *Ach,* so many people."

About them vendors hawked refreshments. Babies cried. It was almost dark. Batteries of floodlights on poles above the stadium burst suddenly bright, greening the field. The crowd buzzed. A loudspeaker system scratched. "Testing, one, two, three. Ladies and gentlemen, our national anthem."

To the roll of drums, a guard of fat American Legionnaires, professional veterans of the First World War, marched the colors across the field. The crowd stood. The Afrika Korps Band stood. As a high school band played "The Star-Spangled Banner," the colors were run up. Some in the crowd saluted. Some yawned. The Afrika Korps Band did not salute. People ate hot dogs. There were cheers. The crowd seated itself. The show began.

The chairman of the War Finance Committee introduced the master of ceremonies for the evening, a local radio announcer noted for his programs of recorded Western music and his ability to sell war bonds. He said howdy, folks, and congratulated the crowd on its patriotism, reminding it that although the Germans had thrown in the towel and the Nips were on their last legs and expected to belly-up any day now, for the sake of the brave boys still fighting and dying in the Pacific it behooved everyone on the home front to support them one hundred and ten percent, if not with bullets, then with wallets.

The crowd grumbled. The night was very hot and the lights made it hotter. People drank soft drinks.

While the Army was setting up its big bang, the announcer said, the committee had arranged for a couple of jim-dandy extra features. He couldn't exactly say he was proud to, but he would now present one guaranteed to curl their hair. By right kind permission of the commandant of No. 80 prisoner-of-war-camp right here in Phoenix, folks, the Afrika Korps Band, former enemies and Hitler's best on the hoof! There was no applause.

They formed at the field edge, hesitated, and on the bandmaster's "*Vorwärts, marsch!*" paraded onto the field playing Sousa's "Under the Double Eagle." They could not hear the crowd, but they could sense its incredulity. They marched down the field, right-flanked, right-flanked, finished Sousa, marked time ten beats, and marched up the field to the "Horst Wessel Song." It was their little joke. They had bet with one another that no one in the audience would recognize it. Whether anyone did or not, the joke did not now seem amusing. Billed caps at a devil-may-care tilt, silver and

52

brass instruments flashing, the young Germans strained for perfect order, they tootled and blew and banged the drums with might and main and tried to produce the volume of a hundred pieces rather than thirty. Towering over the rear rank, the bell of the tuba still higher over his head, Hampelmann winked at Richter and compelled from it an almost Wagnerian oom-pah, oom-pah. It was bravado. The more they tootled and blew and banged, the less audible they seemed to themselves; the more they struggled to impress, the less self-confident they became. It was a relief to halt in the center of the field and offer, lento and with much feeling, their last selection, Irving Berlin's "God Bless America."

After the last note the Afrika Korps Band waited. There was neither applause nor hostility. The crowd simply did not know what to do. Babies cried. People ate peanuts.

As they marched off the field Matthe twiddled his valves and spoke to Albert out of the corner of his mouth: "When we pass the cases, pick them up and bring them and stand them by our seats." This they did, and seated on the aisle, stood the tubas upright between their knees.

While the Army was getting ready for the big shoot-'em-up, the announcer said, it was his pleasure and privilege to introduce an attraction well known to all of Arizona, a colorful, hard-riding group which had come up here from Vaca at its own expense, and folks, here they were, the Vaca Valientes!

Out they rode, eight horsemen on eight gray steeds. They wore identical broad-brimmed Stetson hats and outfits of silver-gray whipcord, shirts with silver buttons and breeches tucked into leather boots hand-tooled and stitched with silver. In the costly holsters of their cartridge belts were pearl-handled revolvers. Their saddles and stirrups were inlaid with silver Indian conchos, their bridles rich with Indian turquoise. Brilliant floodlight struck them and reflected spangles of more brilliant light into the stands. They made the Afrika Korps Band chatter German. They took Albert's breath away. To him they were the glorious embodiment of all the Western heroes of the silver screen—Buck Jones and Fred Thompson and Tim McCoy and Hoot Gibson. *"Die Silberne Sechs-Schiesser!"* he gulped. *"Ach,* to have Willi here, for him to see!" To a quick-step played by the high school band they cantered in and out of intricate and beautiful patterns, they trotted through lines and circles and figure-eights, they gathered and dispersed, sitting their mounts erectly and directing them not by rein but by thought, eight haughty, virile figures, imperturbable and pure. Gauging the attention of the guards, estimating how long it would take from his seat to the tunnel mouth, even Richter Teege was stirred by the Valientes. Take care, he warned himself. It is perhaps only their costumes, even more splendid than ours. If you ask the Americans to judge us not by ours, do you not judge them by theirs. Do not too soon judge. Mistakes you have already made, remember. But the crowd appreciated the Vaca Valientes unreservedly, with spatters of applause. In recent years similar groups had sprung up everywhere in the Southwest, clubs or fraternities of men of means dedicated to preserving hardihood and valor and dash and horsemanship and drama—in short, the best traditions of the Old West, that singular hell-for-leather era now so obviously on the wane. For a climax the Valientes lined up, spurred forward, and waving hats, with a loud "Yahoo!" charged the length of the field to rein in and rear their mounts in the classic pose. The crowd cheered.

One of the horsemen trotted to the announcer, spoke to him, and returned to the line. Over the loudspeakers the announcer relayed the conversation to the stands.

"Folks, that was Deputy Sheriff Jack Thode, head honcho for these boys, an' I just want to pass on what he told me. Now you know I've asked you to dig down deep an' buy bonds till it puckers. Now these eight boys from Vaca, solid businessmen in their community, Jack tells me they want each of them to pledge another bond in the amount of one thousand dollars! Folks, that's what you call patriotism with a capital P an' these boys here, they're what made America what it is, an' while they ride off what say we stand up on our hind legs an' give them the hand they deserve! Folks, our own Vaca Valientes!"

The crowd rose and cheered as the horsemen cantered from the field. In German, Matthe whispered to Albert, "Your horn turn and fix against the seat before you in order that it will by itself stay." Eyebrows raised, Hampelmann did as directed.

"An' now folks, you been waiting long enough an' here's where you get your money's worth. Here's Your Infantry!"

Mortar shells boomed air-bursts over the stadium. The crowd jumped and shrieked. Babies cried.

54

For once the newspapers had not exaggerated. To civilians the show was indeed spectacular. The traveling company which had staged it perhaps thirty times in as many cities across the country was well rehearsed and prodigally supplied with equipment and blank ammunition.

There was mass firing with M1 rifles, carbines, Browning automatic rifles, light and heavy .30 caliber machine guns.

Grenades were thrown and exploded.

Using the thrust-and-parry with ballet grace, a team of riflemen cut and smashed into pieces a row of dummy enemies dressed in Japanese uniforms.

People ate popcorn.

A papier-maché medium German tank lumbered onto the field. A squad of infantry assaulted it on foot, piercing its turret with a bazooka shell, blowing it off its tracks with grenades, and lobbing another into its turret until it blazed luridly and recorded screams of agony issued from its hatches.

The floodlit air in the coliseum became hellish with smoke and smell. The stands vibrated with detonation. The Afrika Korps Band sat motionless. People ate ice cream.

Over the loudspeaker an Army officer in shouts announced the final demonstration of the evening: a night attack by two squads of riflemen upon a German pillbox under battle conditions as realistic as it was possible to make them.

Crews of Army stagehands sped onto the field, rolling into place the lifelike replica of a concrete pillbox, its apertures bristling with machine guns. Soldiers in Wehrmacht uniforms and jackboots and helmets ran to man the pillbox. The floodlights over the stadium were dimmed to half-power.

Richter put his mouth to Hampelmann's ear. "Make ready. When I rise, rise and follow. Slowly. Exactly as I do. Comprehend?" Hampelmann nodded and swallowed.

As soon as the two rifle squads in full combat dress appeared like gladiators at one end of the field, the Spandau machine guns in the pillbox began their familiar blurt, firing at the rate of twenty-five rounds per second, much faster than the Americans'. The squads deployed to flank the strongpoint, one from the left, one from the right—rush, fall and fire, rush, fall and fire. Several GIs leaped as though struck, fell writhing. Closer they came. Grenades were hurled and exploded harmlessly against the concrete slopes of the pillbox. The body of a German sprawled halfway out of an aperture. A bulky apparatus strapped on his back, a GI got to his feet. Suddenly the lights in the stadium went out entirely, as though for a display of fireworks. Instead, through the black the dragon stream of a flamethrower spewed at the pillbox, licking through the gunports with a roar, turning its interior into an inferno. There were death yells as Germans were incinerated.

Matthe rose, edged past his tuba, picked up its case, and in the darkness stepped down into the aisle one, two, three rows, turned left, turned left again into the tunnel, waited. Albert joined him.

Together they walked unhurriedly through the tunnel. The parking lot was deserted. If there were Americans guarding the exhibit, they had idled inside the stadium to watch the Fourth-of-July finale. Without breaking stride, Matthe slightly in the lead, they walked between the Henschel diesels. From the arena came the waves of an ovation. The show was over. They had only seconds.

Matthe headed for the Army tank transporter, a specialized vehicle consisting of a long iron chassis mounted on thirty pneumatic-tired wheels, onto and from which a tank could be driven and hauled over highways by the truck tractor in front. As they reached it, and Matthe's audacity came clear, Albert's eyes popped.

Perhaps it frightened them both. The lights were on above the stadium, it would disgorge its crowd any instant, they would be seen. They panicked. They cursed and scrambled about in a clumsy, slapstick comedy.

There were three hatches into the Mark IV Special Cruiser, all closed. Jumping onto the lower track, they opened the side turret hatch and tried wildly and absurdly to cram both unwieldy tuba cases into it at once. "*Gott verdammt!*" they swore at each other, closed the hatch, clambered around to the driver's hatch, Hampelmann butting his head on the gun barrel, and found that one too small, even, for one case at a time. "*Herr im Himmel!*" They could hear people's voices echoing ahead of them in the stadium tunnels. Babies cried.

Matthe slammed shut the driver's hatch, vaulted to the upper track of the tank and, standing on it, exposing himself as a last resort, threw up the hatch atop the turret, dropped his case in, grabbed Albert's case, dropped it in, and pleading "*Los, los,* let's go, let's go!" half pushed, half untangled Albert himself in, leaped down on top of him, and buttoned the turret.

Armored in pitch darkness, they could hear nothing, see nothing. Cramped, panting, sweating, they scarcely moved for at least an hour. "Here's Your Infantry!" had to pack and load its props. And the search for them must have been on. A hatch might be flung open at any moment.

Then a tremble! A rumble! And they were on their way!

It was safe now to make themselves comfortable. Passing the tuba cases to the loader's and radio operator's seats behind them, Matthe took the driver's seat and Albert the gunner's. Cautiously Richter opened the driver's slit. Fresh air flowed into the turret, and the massed hiss of thirty rubber tires on pavement. He peered through the slit. The infantry show had become a military convoy traveling down a well-lighted avenue. The tank transporter must have been the tail of the convoy, for ahead of them, over the cab of the tractor and the muzzle brake of the nine-foot gun barrel, were jeeps, personnel carriers for the actors, loaded trucks, and the vans and German trucks and hitched field guns.

It was only then that the sublime farce of their situation struck them. They chuckled. All they lacked was the Afrika Korps Band playing out in front! They laughed. They choked with laughter. They pounded each other. Here were two German prisoners of war escaping from prison in a German Panzer! With an American Army convoy for an escort! In Phoenix, Arizona, USA! And escaping not to escape but to stay!

"*Wunderding, Wunderding!*" Albert gasped. "When did you think of it?"

"When I saw it," Matthe grinned.

"A fox you are—a Rommel!"

On the convoy rolled, through the downtown area of the city, between buildings, the turret of the Mark IV barely clearing the traffic lights above intersections, in a direction and toward a destination neither of the tank crew could know. By touch, Matthe acquainted himself with the interior of the turret. He gripped the steering sticks, he pushed a foot down on the throttle, he bent to squint through the telescopic sight and press the electric firing button and the traverse controls, he ran his hands over the racks for heavy explosive and armor-piercing shells, empty now. Everything was familiar to him, except that it was on a smaller scale. This was a Mark IV. The Mark VI, or Tiger, he had driven in Tunisia had weighed half as much again, sixty tons, and carried an 88 mm. gun which fired shells three feet long. Tank and transporter gave his driver's seat a gentle, rocking motion. Matthe closed his eyes. Yet machine gun tracers crisscrossed red before him. His mouth filled with the sharp taste of cordite, his ears with the awful swish of AP shells and the crackle of the radio through his earphones. Behind him the loader pulled down the ejection lever, slammed in the new shell and closed the breech, and tapped the gunner "ready" on the shoulder. It was afternoon of February 15, 1943, near the village of Sidi bou Zid, southwest of the Faid Pass, and the 501st Tigers, attached to the Tenth Panzer Division, had spent the cold wet day picking off the General Grants and Shermans of Battle Group A, First Armored Division. Raw to armored reality, the Americans had allowed themselves to become encircled. From flanks and rear, where they were most vulnerable, the Tigers waded into them. Neither had the Americans ever seen Tigers before, low-silhouette behemoths built to counter Russian T-34s and mounting .88s with full traverse which would penetrate a turret at 3000 yards while the 75 mm. guns of the American tin cans could not pierce theirs point-blank. It was like shooting cows with a cannon, cows with names painted insouciantly on their sides: "Antsy Pants," "Rita Baby," "Don't Fence Me In," and "Jumpin'-Jehosaphat." Out-gunned and -armored and -maneuvered, dive-bombed by Stukas and strafed by ME-109s, the Americans would that day suffer their worst mechanized defeat of the war, would surrender 2000 prisoners and leave 165 tanks and other vehicles burnt out on the field by nightfall. The Tiger which Matthe Teege drove had already killed three Grants and two Shermans when its commander, reckless with success, unbuttoned and ordered it down into a wadi to look for more. Facing forward, he could not have seen the enemy 105 mm. howitzer propel itself to the rim of the wadi behind him and leer down its barrel at the backside of the ponderous Panzer.

Concussion, anticipated and recalled, made Matthe Teege cry out in fear and loathing. His eyes flew open. He sat at the steering sticks of a Mark IV, not a Mark VI, and a friend's hand was on his shoulder. "Easy, easy," said Hampelmann. "Tunisia this is not, you squarehead. It is Arizona."

"We must swear an oath," Richter said, his tone urgent, hoarse. "Not to injure an American, not if we are captured even, by force not to resist force. To you I swear it, Albert. So must you to me."

"*Jawohl*, I swear it." Hampelmann removed his hand.

"So help you God."

"*Gott* help me." He changed the subject. "Where in *Hölle* are they taking us? To Hollywood maybe? And we can get parts in movies, to play the dirty Nazi *Soldaten?* Even uniforms we have!"

Matthe peered through the slit again. The convoy was out of the city now. Lights were scattered. To a bivouac area somewhere, he thought. The infantry show company would doubtless camp somewhere for the night.

He was right as always, for within minutes the convoy slowed, the transporter turned, slowed and stopped, airbrakes blowing. Now they must wait, Matthe whispered, closing the driver's slit to a crack, wait until the Army was bedded down and snoring. He checked his wristwatch. It was 00.05 hours. He corrected himself. It was five after midnight. He was no longer a soldier, and he would no longer keep military time.

In steel they sweltered. They heard voices, sleepy voices, a snatch of song, shoes on gravel and pavement, the clank of gear. Men passed, going somewhere. Then silence.

A demon of impatience was in Hampelmann. He fidgeted and mopped and heaved long martyred sighs. But Matthe made them wait a full half hour after the last sound. Then slowly, slowly, he eased himself upward and slowly, slowly raised the turret hatch an inch to stand and reconnoiter.

The convoy was parked in an open area beside a brick building with a rounded roof, a military armory of some sort. "Here's Your Infantry!" must be barracked in the building. He could see no guards. It should be easy.

He raised the hatch full up, bent to whisper instructions, then hoisted himself out of the tank and let himself down on the upper track. Albert passed the tuba cases to him, levered himself out, stepped to the lower track, to the ground, and took the cases handed down.

Each lifted his case. Matthe slightly in the lead, they tiptoed away from the Mark IV, the convoy, the armory. It was easy. Now a hundred meters away, down a road they walked.

Grüss Gott! Someone walking toward them, a soldier! They must pass. He would be accustomed to fellow-actors in Wehrmacht uniform, but not Afrika Korps! Perhaps in darkness, though. But why, why had they neglected to change!

They passed. Behind them, he stopped.

"Hey, Joe."

Matthe made Albert stop. "Yes?"

"How'd the Phils do today?"

"Phils?"

"Phillies."

"Oh. The Cardinals defeated," Matthe said.

"Yeah? Thanks."

The soldier turned, walked on. They walked on, another hundred meters down the road, now two.

Now they ran.

12

They ran from the Fourth Reich. They ran from No. 80 POW Camp. They ran from war. They ran from Europe, that old, diseased, exhausted continent over which men had fought for hundreds of years as over a bitch in heat. But being boys, it was what they ran to, not from, that mattered most.

Lungs balloons, horn cases heavy, leaping ditches and throwing themselves at fences, they ran until they let themselves fall flat on earth new-plowed.

When they had reclaimed their breath, they stood. Overhead, the great guttering stars of summer waxed. They were in the center of a field. Soldiers' training made them carry the cases to a line of trees for cover. They did not know or care where they were. Matthe Karl Teege of Duisburg on the Rhine and Albert Anton Pomtow of Taplacken in East Prussia were free.

Hampelmann clapped on his head the belov[e]
danced out into the field, flapping his wings and [
kicking his heels in antic, barnyard elation. *"Ist a[
dreams?"* he crowed. *"Ja, das ist* a land of dreams!"*

Disabled by the dance, its artlessness and ecstas[
turned away. Tightly, as though to brace the struc[
he put his arms about the trunk of a tree. He was a[give
way to emotion, but he could not help himself. He was twenty-one
and weary to his soul. Of pomp and cannon and cheers and death
and costumes. Of the betrayal of the few by the many. Of waiting
and weighing and reserving judgment, of being Richter. Of saying
no. In his life, however, he had already blundered twice, and
grossly. As consequence of the first, faith in another's love had
proved false. As consequence of the second, faith in Führer and
Fatherland had won him the Iron Cross that carnal day in Tunisia
and made of him, at the same time, a murderer. Had he not in fact
erred a third time, even murdered again? Had his kindness in sharing their aspiration with Willi Loffelbein not been, in the end, as
sordid and fatal as its result? It was true—whatever truth was. But
he was weary even of the search for that. Truth, it might be, was a
sky, and not a star to steer by; a vision, not a printed declaration.
Truth, it might be, was in the reassurance of a tree, in the poetry of
a feather, in a jig of joy danced in a new world. Let this be my
Albert's land of dreams, prayed Matthe Teege. And let myself be
young as my years, not before my time old. Let me say yes, not no.
Friend or foe, innocent or guilty, let me kill no more. Let me instead love. Let me again have faith. Let me go out now into *Amerika,* and to *Amerika* myself give, and with the giving, these things
get.

It was time to start. He summoned Albert. They changed into
gray, ill-fitting shirts, faded blue denim trousers and jackets and
packed the khaki uniforms into their cases.

They set out south at a steady pace, marching, swinging the cases
in rhythm. They crossed one cultivated field after another, fields
prepared for cotton planting. They wondered what was being said
about them in First Stockade. They wondered if there were two
other tuba players among the Afrika Korps in No. 80. "Here's Your
Infantry!," barracked in the armory by the Mark IV Panzer, they
wished a sound repose. The girl had told Matthe that her reserva-

lay along the Mexican border, near the towns of Taft and Vaca, by mountains called the Lagartos. They would travel by night and hide to sleep during the day. Passing through a citrus grove they picked oranges from the trees, peeled and ate the fruit, and let juice run lavishly down their chins. They were not at all tired. They were full of vitamins and adventure. Rather than slowing as the night declined, they almost skipped.

For they were beginning a new life. They were on their way to Winnetou, his incarnation, and Old Shatterhand, his. They were on their way to greet friends, to be welcomed as brothers, to take refuge among the Apaches. But they were not fugitives, they were explorers. The long miles as cargo, the long months as captives, and then as stateless persons, were over.

Hampelmann swung his case to his shoulder like a banner and sang as he marched, and Matthe let him:

> "Whoopee ti yi yo, *vorwärts*, little dogies,
> It's your *sauerbraten und* none of *mein* own,
> Whoopee ti yi yo, *vorwärts*, little dogies,
> For you know Arizona will be your *neu* home."

The land to which men vow their true allegiance has no hemisphere. It is bordered by their flesh. Its drum their pulse, its anthem is composed within their blood, and dreams are all its institutions. Love lets them belong to it, not birth. For it is perfect. The men and women there are fair and free and noble. Justice and honor and dignity abound, and peace. It is the country of the heart.

TWO

LAND OF DREAMS

13

Keeping to the fields and guiding, as they often had in Africa, by the heavens, they set course southwards. The star Polaris at their backs, they marched until they had covered, Matthe estimated, fifteen or more kilometers.

America's riches lodged them for the day like potentates. As the night washed they came to a narrow lane lined with tall Aleppo pines, at the end of which was an iron gate, a gatehouse and light, and a low adobe wall around a composition of whitewashed adobe buildings of oriental design, the largest surmounted by a dome similar to that of the Taj Mahal. It was a hotel-resort for the wealthy who fled the East and Middle West, even during the war, to escape the horrors of ice and snow. POWs from No. 80 had repainted it during the summer, Albert recalled. It was closed now till the autumn, and in its luxury, he declared, they would stay. The gatehouse light went out. They stepped behind a pine as a car, presumably that of the night watchman, passed them, then went round to the side of the resort, listened, and hearing nothing, pitched cases and shinnied over the wall.

In the dawn they sauntered along ornate walks and fine lawns set with orange, lemon, and grapefruit trees. They gazed into shopwindows stocked for the season with Indian silverwork and into the clear blue depths of a swimming pool. They had never before seen such a place, and it was theirs. Albert found an unlocked window in one of the dwellings and opened a spacious, carpeted room for them. They stripped and, whooping, ran naked over the lawns and plunged into the pool, splashing, racing, floating, snorting enjoyment. Returning to the room, they took sheets from a cupboard, made up the two beds, and breakfasted on grapefruit and Baby Ruth candy bars.

"We will sleep till dark," Richter said. "These beds, this room—I should pinch myself that I am not asleep now."

"Land of *Milch* and *Honig*—so I told you," Albert asserted. "Here are we, two lost lambs, and it is so rich, a whole hotel it gives to us." He sighed. "*Gott* bless *Amerika*."

Like shahs, khans, grand nabobs, they lounged against their pillows and digested regally. "Albert, if we are not caught, if we stay and are safe, what do you wish to be?"

"A cowboy. The Silver Six-Shooter. Also a millionaire."

"I am sober."

"I also." Albert ran a hand over his damp head and pressed water down his nose. "I worry which to be. Like Old Shatterhand a hero or like Rockefeller. I see myself going back one day to Taplacken for a visit, riding down and up in a Cadillac and married to Rita Hayworth. It is a *verdammt* decision—to be poor but honest and buried to be on the lone prairie or rich and corrupt." He grinned out of his buck teeth. "But maybe I shall be both. A *kolossal* ranch I will have and the dogies produce like sedans. Why should I not? Lucky I have always been, lucky always."

For Hampelmann anything was conceivable. If, in the wilderness, he had need of a swim and a soft bed, a palace out of the Arabian Nights was provided. If, as a boy, he doted on tales of derring-do, the library in Taplacken was well supplied with Karl May's novels. He could even ride, for his father was the village blacksmith, and it was a son's chore to bring in for shoeing and return to the junker estates about Taplacken not only the big Belgian horses which, harnessed eight or ten to a plow, turned the thick gray soil of East Prussia, but the swift Hanovers as well, on whose bare backs a youngster might gallop into and out of every imaginable hazard. When he was inducted at fourteen into the Hitler Jugend and desired to make himself heard in the Troop, there was an opening for a tuba player in the band.

But it was after he was drafted into the Wehrmacht at eighteen —he never volunteered for anything—that his natural talent for flowering in dunghills began to manifest itself. Trained as an engineer at the Dessau-Rossler sapper school, destined surely for extinction on the Russian front, he talked himself instead into a cookhouse company which was sent in 1941 to join the Afrika Korps. There, by turns a cook, a clerk, a motorcyclist, he prospered, he survived. Even in surrender Hampelmann was lucky, which is to say that he turned adversity into opportunity. He was quite aware which way the wind of battle was blowing in Tunisia those last chaotic days in May, 1943. Fifteen fat and belligerent American and British divisions were shoving the bits and pieces of nine German into a sack. He loaded his sidecar, he appointed himself a messenger from Colonel-General von Arnim's HQ. He wound himself about his machine, sped south, and during the night of May eleventh found the remains of the Hermann Goering Division in hand-to-hand combat with the Free French. To engage himself in anything as barbaric and as dangerous, or to deliver himself up a prisoner to vengeful Frenchmen, was unthinkable. The next day he dashed north along the crumbling front to the gates of Tunis, contacting grenadiers of the Fifteenth Panzer. But they were being wiped out by the Eleventh Hussars of Montgomery's First Army, and the food in a British POW camp was bound to be abominable. *Ach du lieber*, where were the amiable, protein-conscious *Amerikaner*? His luck and gasoline held out. After a final, full-throttle race with disaster, he joined the 164th Light Afrika Division on May thirteenth, just in time to surrender with them to Eisenhower's Second Corps. "Thank you, thank you!" he greeted them joyfully, uncovering his sidecar to display his wares of Scotch whiskey, Aussie tinned fruit, American cigars and cigarettes, English chocolate and marmalade, Italian bully beef, German blood sausage and Löwenbräu Export beer. "I thank you!" the GIs cried.

So grateful were they that their Government paid his passage to America, and once there, his keep. A grand show his twenty-three years had been, it was not yet over, and the best, he was convinced, was still to come. Why in *Hölle*, he would ask, should Albert Pomtow return to Deutschland? Like his father to hammer and heave when he was frail by constitution? Around the hind ends of horses to hang when he was sensitive by temperament? To heat himself white-hot in efforts to amass sufficient dowry his ugly sisters, Erna and Maria, to marry off? Most *idiotisch* of all, to sail away from the land of the Film and the home of the Ford to ask the *Russen*, who had occupied East Prussia, for a one-way ticket to Siberia?

Through a window sunlight warned that it was morning, time to sleep. Hampelmann let his big feet dangle voluptuously over the end of the bed. He sighed. "But I think of Willi."

"Yes."

"In the Fatherland, he had seen only one movie in his whole life, he told me. Do you know which one?"

"Which?"

"Der Schwarze Adler."

" 'The Black Eagle.' "

"Tom Mix."

Matthe arranged his pillow. "Albert, did you ever kill an American, in Africa?"

"Nein."

"The truth."

Albert walked a finger along the ladder of his ribs. *"Nein.* Never did I shoot a weapon. At anyone. I would not, *Kamerad,* for then they might shoot at me. I think there must be many such, on both sides, who never. Did you?" Matthe was silent. "Did you?"

"Yes."

Then Albert was silent. Finally he said, innocently, as though from sleep, "Richter, would you again soldier, for the Americans?"

"Yes."

"Against Germans?"

"Ja."

14

They left the pool and gardens and the pleasure dome that evening and marched through a second night cross-country, south. They passed from the agricultural environs of Phoenix. Houses were infrequent now, and lights. An occasional dog barked at them. Hampelmann barked back.

His feet hurt, his tuba case grew heavy. He was not accustomed to hiking like mere infantry. It was beneath the dignity of the Afrika Korps to hike, he claimed. They should be clanking and grinding grandly in Matthe's Tiger, or snarling along on his own motorcycle. Or better yet, prancing on beautiful horses, decked out with silver and jewels like the Valientes, those cowboy-gods in the show at the stadium.

They speculated about the Apaches, the new friends they were on their way to meet. Richter warned that they must be prepared for changes. The Indians could not be in this time what they had been in the old days, or as they were still in books and movies. Then they no longer went out on war parties, Albert asked, to burn and loot and avenge themselves on the white man? Matthe doubted it. Probably they lived a kind of uneasy truce, he guessed, staying themselves on the reservation and guarding it against the white man's trespass. What puzzled him was why the whore-girl from whom he had bought information had fallen into such evil ways. Perhaps she was an outcast from her tribe, or perhaps stolen from it as a child and debauched by the whites. *Wohl,* soon they would see how it was with the Apaches.

By the first faint signs of morning they had come a hundred kilometers according to Albert, though closer to forty according to Matthe. They were out in the open. Risking a change of course for higher ground from which they might survey the terrain for a place to sleep the day, they climbed a ridge. They stopped.

They looked below, then at each other. In America, wonders never ceased. Below and before them, across a highway on a sandy plain, their shapes exotic, their fins motionless and eyes protuberant, school upon school of tropical fish were suspended in the dim aquarium of dawn. There must have been a thousand. There were huge four-engined and two-engined bombers; stubby fighter planes and sleek fighter-bombers; carrier fighters with fractured, folded wings; transports; bloated seaplanes perched on tiny wheels. They had stumbled upon a depot of warplanes for which there was now no war. Ferried in from the four corners of the earth for storage in the dry atmosphere of Arizona, skyworn, scarred and riveted over, a billion dollars' worth of aircraft was parked in impotent tier upon impotent tier to the horizon, there to rest and reminisce in aluminum. Only the sun would construe the orange symbols on their sides. Winds would be their only solace, dust their compensation. It was an unforgettable sight. The squander mocked man's very sanity. As it grew lighter, Matthe and Albert could see a landing strip in the distance, and a control tower, but the junkyard, the mausoleum, whatever it was, seemed unguarded. They had the idea simultaneously.

They slept that day in the whale-belly of a four-engined Navy seaplane marked XP4Y-1, entering it through a door in the nose under a ball turret, climbing through the cockpit, stepping down into the maw of the fuselage and making pallets of life jackets.

They wakened in the evening, dined on Butterfingers and cheese, and, as night enveloped the depot, went forward into the cockpit to leave. They drew back, then crouched. From the highway a car turned onto the flat and, shutting off its headlights, pulled under the wing of the seaplane. Car doors were opened, then a door into the fuselage below them. There was thumping about and swearing and laughter. In the cockpit, the two Germans sat down in the pilot's and copilot's seats. They had no choice but to stay.

They listened. Three very drunk soldiers, men of the Air Corps, evidently from one of the nearby bases, continued to drink. They had earlier picked up a woman on a street in Phoenix. All three had enjoyed her sexually in the car and had brought her here, into the aircraft which, appropriately enough, they had used before, to enjoy her further. But the woman had, as they put it, "conked stinkin' out."

It was an impasse. In the dark cockpit the Germans waited for the soldiers to leave, while under them in darkness the soldiers waited for the woman to sober up sufficiently to be responsive. She did not. The Air Corpsmen drained their bottle. Lolling on life jackets, soddenly they compared cultural experiences overseas, which seemed to consist of an appreciation not of architecture or painting or sculpture but of the performing arts in the European Theater. So contortionist were the Ay-rab whores, they agreed, that you overlooked their dirt, but they were generally critical of prophylactic conditions in North Africa. Tripoli, one said, was the natural habitat of the crotch cricket; Cairo, another insisted, was the clap capital of the world. The whores of Piccadilly they dismissed as amateur, the Frogs, or French, as mercenary. They approved the guinea girls, the Italians. All three regretted not being in on the finish in Germany. The kraut dames, so the hot poop had it, would break your back for a candy bar and shack up for a week for a carton of cigarettes.

Albert put a hand before Matthe's nose and made it into a fist. Matthe shook his head. They listened.

"Well," one airman philosophized, "in the end it's only ass."

"You lay one, you lay 'em all."

"I get home my wife'll say honey, where at did you pick up all them tricks, I'll say baby, on the GI Bill."

"I am Christ-on-a-crutch drunk."

"Over here, though, I tell you."

"What?"

"We better damn soon haul."

"Well, over here, stateside, I've had jigs and Mex an' Indian an' the jigs are the best but there's something about Indian tail."

"Something what?"

"I mean, like this skinny little bitch here. No goddam good, really, but American an' Indian, there's something special about it."

"I know what you mean."

"What do I mean?"

"Damn if I know."

"What in hell we talkin' about?"

"Indians."

"Indians?"

"American an' Indians."

"Oh. Yeah. Well."

"Well what?"

"Well, it gets you where the hair is short."

"Oh. White man and squaw you mean."

"That's it. Like old times."

"I know what you mean. American lay an Indian, it's like in the movies, and you're winning the West all the hell over again, you're back in the saddle and the bugle's blowing and you're laying her for Old Glory."

"You said it."

"What a crock. You guys don't know shit from Shinola. She ain't comin' to. Indians never could handle whiskey an' I'm due back at base ten P.M."

"Me too."

"We leave 'er here, shall we?"

"Why not. Save us dumpin' the bag out somewhere."

"What about the money? We told her five bucks apiece."

"Screw 'er."

"She got a free drunk, didn' she?"

"I don't know."

"They're used to it, the Indians. Gettin' screwed."

"Hey le's take off."

"You right, buddy. Into the wil' blue yonder."

The airmen staggered and cursed and fell out of the fuselage. Car doors were opened and slammed, a motor roared. The car lurched out onto the highway.

They went below. Matthe struck a match.

"I knew," he said. "*Ach,* I knew."

Hampelmann looked, made a face.

But she would be useful, Matthe said. Take her with them and they would have a guide, she could save them time and blisters. Together they dragged the girl outside, over the float, and stood her against the seaplane. Before she slid downward he slapped her twice, sharply. "Shameless, shameless," he said.

It required perhaps half an hour, alternately slapping her and letting her sag to the ground, to sober her enough so that she could stand. They brought the horn cases from the XP4Y-1 then, and taking her elbows, pausing till the highway was clear of traffic, scuttled her across it between them, up the ridge, and resumed their journey.

After a kilometer or two she reeled a few steps from them, fell onto her hands and knees, and was sick. When she had crawled away from her sickness, Matthe squatted by her and struck a match in order to reveal his face to her.

"Do you remember me?"

She would not speak.

"I remember you. We have escaped and we are going to the Apache reservation. You will go with us. As our guide, to show us direct the route. Because you have lied to me. I gave you much money not to be *Hure* with soldiers, and to shame your people, which you have accepted. They will discipline you. And thank us also. Rise now."

The match went out. "Rise now," he repeated.

Taking her balky time, she got up and turned her back on him.

"*Marsch!*" he ordered.

She folded her arms and rooted herself.

"*Marsch!*" So small was she that his angry swat on the rump sent her skipping.

15

Under half a moon they made a strange and comic caravan. Out in front a sloven girl led two soldiers like an evil spirit, swiftly, as though to walk them into the ground, or like a small but venomous serpent, gliding. She did not speak, did not pause, and seemed to carry her own compass. In the center Matthe Teege, sweating and marching grimly, ordering her now and then to slow. Next, scuffing and grumbling at the marathon and shifting the clumsy tuba case and yodeling, mogged Albert Pomtow. Last, behind and above them, the star Polaris.

Kilometer after kilometer, over a treeless, soundless tableland of greasewood and sage and creosote bush she sped. In the middle of this third night Richter halted them to rest and eat. She sulked. She would neither sit with them nor acknowledge his offer of a Baby Ruth. When they set out again her pace was as tireless and unerring as before, and there was in her walk something innate, not acquired, Matthe noticed, a stealth, a grace, an elusiveness, something which was Indian.

She wore them out. Toward morning, by his estimate they had made nearer fifty kilometers than forty. They reentered an irrigated area, traversing fields of young cotton, of alfalfa, of sorghum, and of melons too heavy to pick and carry. When they crossed a dirt road along which was a ditch of running water, he halted them again. They drank from the ditch, and groaning, Hampelmann waded knee-deep into it, shoes and all. The sky paled. Across the ditch was a vineyard. In it they would stay the day, Matthe said, hidden in the vine-rows, and told the girl to lead them. She crawled

73

under the vines. The grapes were not yet ripe. Eight or ten rows
from the ditch and road he stopped her. Seated against posts they
ate again, and this time when she was offered food she took everything they gave her, four candy bars and a tin of sardines, wolfing
more, really, than they could spare. "Where are we?" Matthe asked.

She licked her fingers.

"You will answer me."

"Arizona, *Dummkopf*."

Albert laughed. Matthe raised his hand.

"Taft's over there, down the road," she said. "A town."

"Tell us, sweetheart," Hampelmann asked, "to the reservation
how many kilometers yet to walk?"

She shrugged. "Four, five hours."

"We will watch over you," Matthe said. "In order that you will
not run away. Do you lie down and sleep now."

"Killer."

"Friend."

"Friend, crap." Her lips curled as though at something vile. "You
killed Tony."

"Who?"

"Go to hell."

They made their own stockade between vine-rows, a case at one
end, then long Albert, then the girl, stretched lengthwise in the soft
loam, then Matthe sitting up in the morning sun at her head, back
against his own case. After two hours he waked Albert, slept himself, and was waked in turn.

He had the last watch in the late afternoon. In the vines, a breeze
investigated. Albert snored. Several cars, more than Matthe would
have expected, passed along the dirt road beyond the vineyard.
Tansie Scout slept with her mouth open. Her den look and animal
smell disgusted him. She was little more than skin and bones. Besides discipline and feeding, she needed soap and water. There was
sand in her tangled hair, a smear of chocolate on her brown cheek,
sardine oil stains on her blouse, the hem of her skirt was unsewn,
her bobby sox were filthy. Over the instep of each low shoe, in a
pocket between seams, she had stuck a copper penny. They made
him pity her. Leaving her people, being cast out by them for some
reason and coming to the city, drinking and lying with soldiers, and
this was what it had gained her: two pennies for her shoes. It was

74

the fault of the war. There must be many maidens like this one, he thought, vagabond and misbegotten, and everywhere, including America. He recalled the remarks of the soldiers in the seaplane about kraut girls. Even in Deutschland, too. But how anyone could find Tansie Scout desirable he could not conceive. Unless it truly was as the one airman had theorized: that for an American to subdue an Indian female physically was tantamount to subduing the West all over again. He looked for her identification bracelet, but she had lost even that.

A racket startled him, a sudden dissonant chorus of automobile horns and church bells so loud that it reached the vineyard. It must come from the town, Taft. It was sustained. It waked Albert and the girl. For their question he had no answer. More cars dusted along the road. Richter stood and raised his head out of vines. Bells and horns continued to ring and blow from the town and some intuition told him he should have the intelligence. Crawling under vines to the last, he peered out. Down the road a boy appeared on a bicycle, his legs pedaling a blur. Deciding to chance his English, he crawled from the vineyard and stepped out roadside. "Hello!" he called.

The boy skidded to a stop.

"What is happening in the town?" He spoke deliberately. "Is there perhaps a festival?"

"Festival?"

"Or a fire?"

The boy frowned scorn and as he began pedaling again, shouted back over his shoulder. "War's over!"

Matthe turned. Spread in a grin from ear to ear, Hampelmann's face rose up out of vines like a periscope. "Matthe, war's over!"

Matthe stiffened. "The girl! The girl!"

The grin vanished, the head swiveled. She was gone.

75

16

They decamped at once. To hunt her in a vineyard would be futile. She would undoubtedly be in Taft in a few minutes, informing on them.

And then, as they headed south, putting distance between them and the town, suddenly it did not matter that she had given them the slip. Who would heed her now, who would care this night of final victory for the USA? For the war with Japan was over, the guns were muted everywhere, soon No. 80 Camp must close, and the fact that two insignificant German prisoners were still at large would be filed and forgotten. They had only to lie low, to find shelter for a few weeks while the dust of war was swept up and thrown away. And in four hours, only four hours, they would be among friends.

Into the declining day they marched elated, swinging the tuba cases smartly, as though on parade. Peace!

While marching they ate the last of their provisions, and even with his mouth stuffed Hampelmann managed to praise in song that home on the range he would soon have, where seldom was heard a discouraging word, and *der Himmel* was not cloudy all day. The Apaches!

In an hour they entered the uninhabitable land. In southernmost Arizona, it was a region of infernal sun and identical days. From it every living thing would have fled had it been able, and every dead. Red sundown made it lurid. Low black mountains crawled toward Mexico, their scales and tails on fire. These must be the Lagartos, or Lizards. To the far floor of the furnace were chained varieties of cactus, small tormented trees and, like saints at stakes, their arms upraised in fiery hopelessness, stands of great saguaro cacti. Dumb stones ached. Limbs were consumed. Mouths opened

76

in beggary. Nostrils dried. And for relief from fever, the desert awaited feverish night.

This inquisition of rock and parch and heat the two boys entered with misgiving. They were awed. This was the land much photographed, the land read about round the world, the real American *Wilden Westen*. But neither photograph nor page could tell it as it really was. To cheer his companion, Matthe said that it was here, in the booting and breaking of such reaches, that what was finest in the American character had been hammered out. From this harsh brow of the earth the cowboy-hero, the man of the Wild West, had burst forth with yahoo and blazing six-gun, and the literature to match him. Even Karl May had never seen it. Now they had.

Night came. Through a moonscape they trudged. All was black and pale and stark and pitiless. Against horn cases cactus needles scratched. Shoes crunched. When suddenly, quite near, a coyote howled, the hairs walked on their heads.

"Are we on the reservation of the Apaches?" Albert asked in lowered, apprehensive voice.

"We must be."

"And not a *verdammt* popgun even. Partner, I hope you were *korrekt*."

"Regarding?"

"That they are no more savage." He paused to settle his Stetson tighter on his head. "Perhaps they have never taken a scalp from a squarehead."

They hiked another hour, bearing toward the somber bulk of a mountain. They were hungry again, and thirsty. They neared the tail of the mountain, slipped down into a cobbled, empty watercourse, mounted its opposite bank, and picked their way along the lower slope, Matthe leading. He stopped. Bumping into him, Hampelmann jumped.

"What's that?"

"Sssssh."

Fifty meters ahead of them, on a ledge, a flickering glow lit lava rock.

"I think we are here," Matthe whispered. "Any light in this place must be Indian, a campfire. So now, let us change."

Furtively they opened the cases. Clumsily they fumbled themselves into their Afrika Korps uniforms, similar except that through the third buttonhole of Matthe's tunic was the ribbon of the Iron Cross. They were nervous and calm and determined and timid. Albert tried to occupy one trouser leg with both of his. Finally they were ready. Tilting their caps, they squared shoulders. They climbed. They could hear their hearts drumrolling. They reached the ledge, halted.

The wan light on the ledge was produced by several dozen *luminarias*. These were tiny lanterns made from open brown paper sacks weighted with a layer of sand in which candles were set and lit. Between the graves the luminarias twinkled. Since the mountainside would not permit deep digging, the graves, possibly forty in number, were smoothed and rounded mounds of earth with wooden crosses painted white and red and yellow and blue, over which were hung wreaths of tattered paper flowers. There were neither names nor dates nor inscriptions on the crosses. On the very small mounds, those of infants, food ready to eat had been placed, partial loaves of bread, dishes of canned fruit, bowls of beans, bananas and apples, plates of tortillas, and bottles of soft drinks, uncapped and ready to drink.

By this humble, haunting scene the Germans were transfixed. It was as though they had wandered into a Walpurgisnacht, a Witches' Sabbath. They could not have been more dumbfounded had thunder issued from the mountain, had lightning flashed, had shrieks and apparitions torn the hot night high above them. They could not know that instead, they had chanced upon an observance of Small Souls' Night. So inordinate was the infant death toll here that most grandmothers had lost several grandchildren, and among them it was a common superstition that at certain times they could hear the babies crying out upon the desert for nourishment. Food was therefore set out upon their mounds on Small Souls' Night, and light provided, and the elders withdrew in order that the small departed souls might eat in private.

The two boys stood in staggered silence. Then Matthe Teege touched Albert Pomtow's arm. Albert looked across the cemetery, then to the right, the left, and behind him. His face white as a ghost's despite his tan, he swallowed audibly.

They were no longer alone. Their pilgrimage was ended. They were surrounded by the *Indianer*.

17

They were surrounded not by warriors with painted cheeks and looks like lances but by old people and very young children with soft round brownish faces and round black astonished eyes. By the eerie flicker of the luminarias they issued out of the rock around the cemetery. Curiosity drew them in, as though to a show.

And curiously enough, the confrontation was indeed similar to that during the show in No. 80 Camp. Where that had been dramatic, however, this was upside-down, absurd. Now it was not Indians in war-dress who were on display but two bewildered boys in jaunty caps and khaki, silver-trimmed uniforms whose turn it was to be gawked at and in turn to gawk. It would have been impossible to say which side was more surprised.

Feeling foolish, unable to think of any other greeting, Matthe raised an arm in the classic gesture. "Peace," he said.

Fascinated, the Indians came closer. There were perhaps a score of them, half old men and women and half children.

Hampelmann raised his hand. "How," he said.

A small boy giggled.

An old man stepped forward. His black hair was in braids. He had white earlocks. He wore a faded denim shirt and trousers with a purple sash and on his feet, sandals cut from tire inner tubes and tied with string. He considered, then spoke. "I'm one hundred and eight years old and have my own teeth." He showed them.

"That is good," Matthe said. Growing bolder, the children had hemmed him in. A little girl touched the silver palm tree on his sleeve. "We are German soldiers," he said anxiously. "We have escaped the prison camp near Phoenix and here we have come with our blood brothers, the Apaches, to stay."

"Apaches?" The old man looked grave. "They were the enemy. In the long years I fought them. Now they are cowboys."

"What tribe is this?"

"We are the Moencopa."

Matthe and Albert looked at each other. "Is there a village here?" Matthe asked.

"This is Mouse Sits."

"You are the chief?"

"We don't have chiefs. Say some German."

"*Ich heisse* Matthe Teege."

"*Ich heisse* Albert Pomtow. *Sehr angenehm*, pleased to meet you."

"OK."

"We bring gifts," Hampelmann said.

"I like gifts."

An old woman interrupted. Her hair was gray and she was tattooed with four vertical blue lines from her lips to the point of her chin. "My name is Alice Walkingstick," she said. "That old man wants to marry up with me but he's too damn old. We call him Lies About His Age. You can give us the gifts later. Now we've got to eat this food before the young people come. Now everybody help."

Children and old folk all busied themselves snuffing out the luminarias and gathering bowls and plates of food and the fruit from the small souls' graves and forming a kind of procession after which, down a path, the Germans tagged. The procession made its quiet way along the bank of the dried-up watercourse perhaps a hundred meters and into what seemed a sprawl of low structures among and under trees. Unexpectedly, two light bulbs were snapped on, and the soldiers blinked not only at the electricity but in efforts to see around them. They could not, except that each moth-clouded bulb hung over a table spread with oilcloth in a separate structure open on four sides, its roof supported at the corners by crooked tree trunks. The food was placed on the tables, the adults seated themselves on benches, leaving space for the uninvited guests, and the banquet began. Not a word was spoken. Everyone ate ravenously, the children gobbling their portions while hunkered down on the bare earth and laughing at the peculiar manner in which the guests used their cutlery, knife in the right hand, fork in the left. The instant the dishes were clean, old women snatched them up and hurried into the darkness to splash and clatter domestically. Soon they returned to cluck the reluctant children off to bed somewhere, only to return again and take seats on the benches with sighs of relief.

It made a strange tableau, five old men and four old women and two uniformed Germans silent and polite about the tables, the wrinkled faces impassive, the smooth uncertain. No one looked at anyone else. One old man fanned himself with his hat. Alice Walkingstick took out a plug of Red Man tobacco, gnawed a cheekful, then spat delicately over several heads. Hampelmann twiddled bony thumbs. What in *Hölle*, he asked Matthe in German, were they waiting for, the second coming of Sitting Bull? Matthe did not know. It occurred to him that all they had witnessed in Mouse Sits since their arrival—the observance of Small Souls' Night, the hasty feast, the rushing off to bed of the young—had been surreptitious. It was as though these old people, like froward children, had misbehaved, had knowingly been naughty, and now sat about in self-congratulation that they had not been caught. Caught by whom? Not by their own elders, surely. And then he realized. There were only very old people and very young here. A generation was missing. And not until that middle generation was present could they plead their case or could any decision about them be made.

It soon appeared. The old people stirred. A distant hum, a nearer squeak of springs and muffle of exhausts and by some bumpy access two automobiles, one large and infirm, the other small and infirm, wheeled importantly in to spill out ten more Indians, men and women in their thirties and forties and one youth. There was much unloading of groceries and greeting and reference to the newcomers, probably, but most of it in the Moencopa tongue, a low mumble and sibilance. From the English spoken, the soldiers gathered that these were the workers of the village, the wage earners, and that they had been absent for two weeks picking the first cotton of the season near Tucson. After a time the two sexes separated, and the old men brought the younger to a table under the light bulb. Lies About His Age introduced the Germans to Victor Scout, his brother Manuel Scout, to Grover Jones and Ramon Walkingstick, who nodded but did not shake hands. By all the rights of film and fiction, these should have been the braves in eagle-bonnets, gaunt and haughty, the fearless bowmen and horsemen, but they

81

were men of medium height and inclined to girth, with small feet and hands, who wore straw field hats and the usual denim and khaki. They let the old men sit down and stood behind them, but it was a deference to age, not to authority.

"They bring gifts," Lies announced. "I like gifts."

At the hint, the soldiers opened the tuba cases and made their offerings. They had brought things which, they believed, would most impress their Indian allies: a large German swastika flag, a carved model of a Tiger Panzer and one of the battleship *Gneisenau*. From hand to hand the men passed them.

"No cigarettes? asked Lies.

They were embarrassed.

"These you can one day sell to the Americans," Albert assured them. "For much money, because they are made by real German prisoners."

"You're real Germans? asked Grover Jones. "From over the ocean?"

They nodded.

An old man spoke up. "My name is Wesley Scout. I was a scout for General Crook. In the long years. We caught Geronimo, a very bad man, but he beat the Americans many times. I don't remember much of that. Did you beat the Americans?"

"Twice," Matthe said.

"Where?"

"At the Faid and Kasserine Pass, in North Africa. We were of the Afrika Korps."

"I saw that in a movie. But I don't remember much. In Vaca. So you beat them." Wesley Scout smiled maliciously. "It's good for everyone to lose sometimes."

"Soldiers always lose," Matthe said. "Americans or Germans or Indians. I do not like to discuss these things."

"I wish they'd brought cigarettes," said Lies About His Age. "My friend's son," he said to Victor Scout, "shouldn't we be sitting in the Council smoking?"

"No, that takes too long. What do they want?"

Everyone looked at Richter. He rose and speaking precisely, explained how long they had been prisoners of war and how they had escaped the camp and traveled overland from Phoenix. "It was to find the Indians that we came. Because we have read many books

82

about them when we were young in Germany. By a German. In the stories the Indians were brave and free and to their own ways maintained and—how do you say—their dignity. Germans and Indians have been friends always, blood brothers. They have much together. And now they have more."

Victor Scout put the question again. "What do you want? Guns? Horses? We're not goin' to help you over to Mexico or anything like that."

"No, no," Matthe protested. "Now that the war is over, we escape to stay in the USA."

Murmurs interrupted him. The news had not yet reached the village. "Yes, we heard comin' tonight from Tucson," Ramon Walkingstick told the old men. "She's over. Bitter Boy'll be home soon."

"So that the prison camp will soon now be closed," Matthe resumed. "No one will hunt for us. If we may stay here till it is closed, that is what we ask of our friends. Then we will leave. We have money, we will pay for our expense."

He sat down. He assumed that, old and middle-aged, the men around the table were considering his appeal, yet they gave no sign. Those seated watched moths flutter about the light bulb. Those standing glanced idly upwards at the night as though making a guess about the morrow's weather. The soldiers dropped their elbows glumly on the table and their chins in their hands. Matthe might have been more eloquent, more persuasive, he knew and Albert knew, but both were confused, both found it difficult to hide their disappointment in this place, these people, their reception.

"I'm ninety-one years old," Lies About His Age remarked at length, "and I don't care if they stay. Maybe they can help us with the farmin'."

Manuel Scout spoke for the first time. "My relatives, I don't think we better. They better go. They could bring us a lot of trouble."

Everyone stirred uncomfortably. A difference of opinion, particularly one between generations, the Moencopa would avoid at any cost. Ramon Walkingstick changed the subject. "How'd you find this village?" he asked Matthe.

"A girl led us. I believe her name was Tansie Scout."

"That's my girl," said Victor Scout. "She's here?"

"No. From us she escaped."

"From us, too. Every time we take her out to work, she won't

83

work, she just goes. She went to school too much and now she's gone to hell. Where did she leave you?"

Matthe would have replied, but Hampelmann prevented him. In German he said they must bargain, that was what you did with Indians.

"Meine Herren," he addressed them, rubbing his hands and rising, "let us make a trade. If we will tell you where the girl is, you will permit that we remain." He smiled commercially. *"Ist das nicht* a damn good deal?"

"You could go get her, my son," said Wesley Scout to her father. "She's pretty sick."

The four men standing withdrew a few paces, conversed, and came back. "OK," said Victor Scout. "You tell us and you can stay here till we get home next time from workin'. Then we'll have Council on this thing. Where is she?"

At the reprieve, Albert expelled a long breath. "OK, partners. Near a town from here four hours marching. Taft, it was."

Manuel Scout nudged his brother. "That's where she'd go. The war over, they're havin' a big time there tonight."

So the compromise was made. The four fathers drove away at once in the bigger sedan and the five old men took charge of the visitors. There was some discussion about where they might sleep, some reflection which seemed instead to be an examination of the wooden models and the German flag, and another decision. Lies About His Age yawned and on his inner-tube sandals shuffled the soldiers among trees until, through a doorway which had no door, he preceded them into something walled and roofed. Locating another light bulb, he snapped it on. What he had brought them into was not a wigwam or tepee of hides, but a one-room, windowless dwelling called a wattle-and-daub house, its walls laid up of cactus ribs plastered with dried mud, its low roof lathed by ribs covered with dirt. It was furnished only with a double bed, a set of rusty springs, and a rain-stained mattress on the earthen floor rather than the manly buffalo robes in which Winnetou and Old Shatterhand had bunked. This had been General and Josie Miles's house, he said, but now they lived in a better one, that of their children, who had abandoned them to go to California to work in the fields. They, the children, sent no money home. It was a disgrace, such treatment of parents by offspring. It would never have been permitted by the Moencopa in the long years.

He looked steadily at the two soldiers, who had put down their cases. "You thought you were comin' to the Apaches?" They nodded. "Want to see an Apache?" They nodded.

The old man went to the bed corner and took down a small woven basket hung by a string from the roof. He brought it to them. In the open basket, on a cloth, was a dusty little doll made of human hair. It was a scalp. The doll was dressed in tiny deerskin shirt and moccasins and had a feather in its own hair.

"This is my child," he said, cradling the basket fondly. "I took it in the long years. The Apaches would come down here and steal and kill and we'd go out and fight them, sometimes with our brothers, the Pima and Papago. Every house has one. They bring power. We call them 'prisoners.'"

Lies About His Age replaced the basket. At the door he wagged a finger. "Be careful. These prisoners are still bad. Sometimes they jump out in the night and run around."

In silence Matthe Teege and Albert Pomtow turned out the light bulb, undressed, and folded away their uniforms. In silence they lay down on the mattress. They were not sleepy, for they had slept most of that day in the vineyard near Taft. They lay on their backs in the pitch-black heat. Whenever one moved, the springs twanged. Above them hung the basket with its prisoner. They were as cheated and lonely and chagrined and forlorn and disabused as they had ever been in their lives. The war was over, the journey was over, and they were speechless. To come so far. To come by tank and motorcycle and truck and ship and train and march and all the magical conveyances of fantasy. To come to join a proud and valiant tribe in its lair and discover it a hank of hair cribbed in a costume. To come instead to bare electric light bulbs and a cemetery called Mouse Sits, to a motley of old folk and children and lowly laborers called Moencopa. To come to a reception as casual as though veterans of the Afrika Korps in dress uniform materialized nightly in the southwestern deserts of the United States. To come to only temporary refuge, and that granted only by barter. Their hearts hurt. At that hour, in that paltry place, they were all boys everywhere who had ever run away to find the runaway not

85

worth it. The cave not worth the exploration. The river not worth the raft. The game, its rules changed by time and circumstance and adults, not worth the playing.

"*Ach*, how I wish," sighed Hampelmann finally.

"For?"

"That here I had Karl May. In his own *verdammt* ink I would drown him." He turned on his side and the bed springs whined. "Maybe it is well he could not accompany us. Willi, I mean."

"*Jawohl*."

They stiffened. A scurry on the roof. Perhaps the hair-prisoner was out. But it was only mice.

"Maybe we should leave. Now. And to the devil with these pickers of cotton."

"And go where, *Kamerad?*"

They stewed in heat and their own hoax. They tried to sleep and could not. Though neither would admit it, they were homesick. When he was young, Hampelmann said, sometimes there would be several horses to return to their stable after shoeing, and he would enlist two or three of his friends to help. Down the roads out of Taplacken they would trot the lumbering Belgians bareback, pretending to be Buck Jones or Hoot Gibson and a Prussian posse in chase of a gang of desperadoes which had just robbed a stagecoach and carried off a virgin damsel. It was great sport, though a hardship on the backsides. His pastimes, Matthe reminisced, were not too different, although horses were not available to city boys. Streetcars were, however, and he and his playmates would ride one to the Duisburger Wald, an extensive woods between Duisburg and Mülheim/Ruhr in which they might reenact as loudly and realistically as they wished the historic contests between Napoleon and the Cossacks, between the Fox of Glenavon and the British, between Frederick the First and the Saracens during the Crusades. Their most exciting game, of course, was White Man versus Indian. But those Indians, he added ruefully, had been the Apache or the Sioux. They had never heard of the Moencopa.

18

If German boys at games in the Duisburger Wald had not heard of them, neither had most Americans for that matter, nor of the Pima, Papago, Yuma, Cocopah, Yavapai, Maricopa, Hualpai, Chemehuevi, Mohave or any of the smaller tribes native to those deserts. One man, exploring the West obscurely in the eighteen-fifties, had described the Moencopa as "more deserving of the attention of philanthropists than any other Indians. None exhibit a more peaceful disposition, or greater simplicity of character; and certainly none excel them in virtue and honesty." In this lay their fault. They had committed the grave historical sin of welcoming the white man to their lands rather than defending them, of offering him sustenance and friendship, of helping him to help himself, and thus had won his undying indifference. Since then they had languished. Novelists and film makers and the Government of the United States had overlooked them, pouring out prose and footage and public monies instead on tribes more colorful and homicidal, dramatizing and subsidizing them in direct proportion to the blood they had spilled. In modern times several expeditions sponsored by universities had trekked to the area to study the ethnology, sociology, and economy of the Moencopa. These studied a tribe of approximately two thousand scattered in villages across a reservation of arid, alkali wasteland which would not, under present conditions, support half that number. They wrote reports; like pinches of symbolic dust dropped upon the casket of the deceased, they dropped in terms such as "subsistence," "malnutrition," "adaptation," "group responsibility," "exploitation," "illiteracy," "family-centered," "irremediable," "destitution," "patriarchal," "adjustment," and "tragedy"; they rewrote the reports to effect a more scientific, less funereal tone; they edited the reports for publication; and they departed gladly. The scholars, fortunately, had an alternative. Now two had come who could not go, and their opportuniy to study the Moencopa was at hand.

Big eyes waked them late in the morning, black eyes peering through cracks and holes in the mud walls by their bed, delighted eyes. Before this audience Matthe and Albert rose, dressed in their escape clothes, and went outside. A whole covey of children, six boys and two girls, aged four to nine, clasped their hands and led them through trees up the mountain a few meters to what was evidently their most prized civic possession. It was a well-built wooden outhouse with stenciled lettering on the door: CIVILIAN CONSERVATION CORPS 1938. From a staff on the corrugated tin roof flew the rags of an American flag. The visitors came to attention, saluted, and with what military aplomb they could muster, entered and used the accommodation. When they emerged, the waiting children took them next to the village water supply. It was an iron tank holding perhaps a thousand gallons and mounted on a rickety horse-drawn wagon. At the spigot they washed hands and faces, then followed their guides to the wattle-and-daub house of Alice Walkingstick. Under her *wato,* the open-sided, roofed shelter detached from the house and similar to those under which they had feasted the night before, she served them beans and coffee. Alice said she was damn busy that day, and they agreed she was. On the table a small radio blared recorded music from the station in Taft. Beside the table a washing machine humped and sloshed. Alice was chewing Red Man and listening to the radio and doing a washing and making a close-coil basket of bear grass and devil's-claw, inset with a green swastika design, which she hoped to sell in town. Tattooed, widowed and profane, she was the only woman in the village still doing basketry, she told them. The fingers of the other old ladies were too stiff and the younger women wouldn't sit on their asses long enough.

They were joined by Lies About His Age and Wesley Scout and the other three old gentlemen who, less reserved today, introduced themselves as General Nelson Miles, Joe John Jones and Duncan Walkingstick. The latter's nickname was Uncle Rumbles because he was always hungry and his stomach proclaimed it. It was difficult for newcomers to make sense out of the Moencopa system of names. Each had at least three, an Indian name, a legal, and a nickname, all three used interchangeably. Since to American ears the Indian names were unintelligible, for census purposes the heads of families had been christened by government officials when the reservation was established in 1914—Miles in honor of the general who had imprisoned Geronimo, Scout since Wesley had served under General Crook, Walkingstick because Duncan had then affected one, and Jones for obvious reasons.

Finished eating, Matthe and Albert were taken on a tour of the entire village by the old men, the children trooping before and after. None of the latter spoke English. None attended school. From house to house the group moved, meeting Josie Miles, the General's wife, Julia Jones, Joe John's wife, and Duchess Walkingstick, Uncle Rumbles' wife and elder sister of Alice, all three in their seventies or eighties and all three occupied in listening to their radios, carrying water in buckets from the wagon, grinding corn, baking in adobe ovens, sweeping, and calling gossip from wato to wato. In addition to Lies and the Miles couple, there were three extended and interrelated family groups in the village, the Scouts, the Joneses and the Walkingsticks. Excluding several dogs too flea-flayed to multiply, its population at this moment numbered twenty —two escaped prisoners of war, nine elders, and eight children. But two and nine and eight were nineteen, not twenty, Hampelmann pointed out. Cleaning his teeth with the end of his purple sash, Lies About His Age explained that the girl, Tansie, had been located in Taft during the night and brought back and put in the sickness hut. When Matthe asked about the workers, Joe John Jones said that all ten of them, Manuel and Antonia Scout, Victor and Ethel Scout, Ramon and Betty Walkingstick, Grover and Lupe Jones, and Lupe's sister Rita, or Peppertail, and Charles Lindbergh Scout, who at eleven was old enough to pick cotton, were already on their way to Tucson and the fields in the two cars. They came home every week or so to bring food and see their families, but they couldn't afford to miss more than a day's wages. During their absence, it was the grandparents' duty to maintain the village and rear the children and be good. That meant, added General Miles with toothless cynicism, not to quarrel and not to eat too much and not to practice any of the old-fashioned Moencopa customs such as Small Souls' Night and Evil-Spitting.

Mouse Sits clung to the skirts of a basalt mountain. Ancient tamarisk trees sequestered it. They were like low-hovering clouds of green moss. Under the clouds the village hid. There were five one-room adobe houses, each with its wato, and five of wattle and daub, including that where the soldiers had slept, and the Council, into which they were not taken, and one very small one, little more than a hut. A tour of the dwellings concluded, the committee of old men and children escorted their guests to every other point of municipal interest.

By night, the twinkling luminarias and paper garlands and multi-colored crosses had lent the cemetery a kind of nursery charm. By day, it was a cheerless, impoverished place, a place in which bones might endure but never rest.

The junkpile was magnificent. In the center of the village near the Council and the well, it rivaled the tamarisks, it rose in an untidy temple to progress which would offer the mechanic, the dealer in scrap metal, and the archaeologist of the future riches beyond compare. Make even the most cursory inspection of its outsides and one could identify car bodies, beds and springs, destitution, oil drums, car motors, old refrigerators, wheels, derelict washing machines, malnutrition, soft-drink bottles, illiteracy, kerosene stoves, axles and chassis, rubber tires, exploitation, tin cans, tools, harness, beer bottles, baby carriages, pots, kettles, pans, adjustment, wash-tubs, magazines, lumber, newspapers, the carcass of a truck, wine jugs, cardboard boxes, adaptation, furniture frames, live lizards, and tragedy. Delve into it and what other trinkets of blunder, what other artifacts of futility it might hold no man could say.

The well, of the windlass-and-bucket type, had been dug for the village by the government in 1939, according to the date in the cement rim. It had gone dry two years ago.

The log corral enclosed five spare-ribbed, melancholy horses, two of which were hitched each morning to the water wagon and driven by the old men two miles to the reservation line and two more into Vaca, where the tank was filled from the town system under government contract.

The last stop was the village farm, more properly a garden, a level acre or two along and a little lower than the dry wash. Here was a stand of wheat, of corn, and patches of beans, squash, pumpkins, and melons, planted and tended by the elders and made to grow in this desert by what was known as flash-flood irrigation.

When summer rains filled the wash, ditches along its banks diverted water into the garden, flooding it to a depth of several inches. The more rain, the fuller the flood, the better the crop. Skilled at irrigation, for three hundred years the Moencopa had farmed and flourished along this river, the Sonoita, the life-giver. The Germans were perplexed. What river? This was only a pebbled, sandy watercourse. The old men were embarrassed. Well, that was the trouble, Uncle Rumbles admitted presently; they were dependent on rain now, for as soon as the reservation was established, the whites up around Phoenix had dammed the Sonoita there, using the impounded water for their own fields. That was a thing the Moencopa had never understood—why, when they had always been hospitable to the white man, the Spaniards and priests and settlers, they had been placed on land worthless without water while the Apaches had been given well-watered grazing range up north upon which they might become as fat as their cattle. It was a mystery.

Meandering back into the village, they passed the sickness hut in which Tansie Scout was confined. It was not high enough to stand up in, it had a hole for a door and cracks in the mud plaster for windows. In the long years, Wesley Scout, her grandfather, explained with some diffidence, all females were segregated for several days each month, since their touch or even the sight of them during this period was harmful to males. The people no longer believed that, he said, and the hut was used now as a place of punishment. She had the necessities, food was brought her, and inside she would stay until they, the elders, could rid her of evil one of these evenings before her parents returned. The old gentlemen shook their heads. What young people were coming to, they dreaded to imagine.

In her hut of shame Tansie must have heard them, but to show her disdain she went on humming "I'm Gonna Buy a Paper Doll" and, as they left, with her arm through a crack thrust a scrap of paper at Matthe. She had penciled on it the most spiteful epithet she could think of: "Notsi."

It was the habit of the old people and children, their day's work done, to turn off the radios and climb up the mountain and there, just above the tops of the tamarisks, to rest and watch the sun go down. There was little else to do. Matthe and Albert joined them that evening. Men and women, the nine elders smoked one ceremonious cigarette from the pack of Wings each had been brought by their children, the workers, and only one, for the ration must last until they came home again with another pack. From this height the prospect was splendid. The black Lagartos slithered in whitish air. To the south they could almost see, six and eight miles away, two other Moencopa villages, Too Many Ants and Goat Drink. The nearest village, on the opposite side of the mountain behind them, they called Opposite. Four miles to the west, beyond the fiery red-lands over which the soldiers had marched to Mouse Sits, lay the town of Vaca, the sun glistering its water tower, the square fields about it dark in the distance with cotton irrigated by deep-well pumping, cotton which, before winter came, must be picked. From Vaca a road with electric power poles unrolled across the desert, tarvia to the reservation line, gravel then to the dry bed of the Sonoita below them, and the tamarisks. Around Hampelmann the children clustered. He was teaching them to sing "A Penny and a Dollar" in German. Around his baritone their shrill, inconstant voices clustered:

> "The penny went to water,
> The dollar went to wine.
> *Hei di, hei do, hei da,*
> *Hei di, hei do, hei da!*"

Matthe Teege looked at the old folk smoking blissfully, the men in patched denim, the women in shapeless cotton dresses, with black scarves covering their heads, at the broad, brick-brown, care-cut faces, as innocent almost as those of their grandchildren. Mouse Sits, he thought. *Gewiss,* of course. On a mountainside Mouse Sits waiting for its day to end. They are a body without a spine. How they are lonely, these old ones, for their own children who must be away. How they are glad two strong young men to have here with them. Of them shelter we have asked, but it is we who give them shelter. Their warriors are we.

The sun rim sank. The flare of light was extinguished. Between day and dusk there was an instant like a heartbeat intermitted. It was for this the Moencopa waited. Then, as they gazed, their land

92

was beautiful, green and sand and various, and to it they were reconciled. The instant was a benediction.

Shadow ensued. Duchess Walkingstick had something to ask Matthe. "My old man told me. He said you said Indians are in books."

"They are."

"And people, they're readin' about us?"

"Everywhere."

"That's nice," said Duchess. "I'd like to read about them but it's too late to learn how. Did you read about us?"

"Yes. That is why we came."

Hampelmann put in his *pfennig*-worth. "Also we would play games when we were boys. Indians against white men."

"Who won?" Julia Jones wanted to know.

"Indians always," he assured her.

The old people sat in gratified silence. When it was dark, they indulged themselves in a second cigarette.

"We have made many plans to come here," Matthe dared to say. "We wish very much to remain and be of service."

"If it was up to us," said General Miles. "But it isn't. In the long years it was."

After everyone had pondered that, Lies About His Age told a story. "When I was young we'd go to the ocean to get salt. It was four days ridin' from here and four days comin' back. We'd find big stones of salt on the beach because the ocean ate something bad in the winter and got sick and spit them up. We'd pack it on horses and trade with it. We'd walk into the ocean up to our chins and throw cornmeal around on the waves, I don't know why but we did. One year we went all the way to the ocean and there wasn't any salt. I don't know why. That's how it is sometimes."

Before they went to bed that night under the prisoner, Matthe and Albert sat side by side for a few minutes in the government outhouse. The door was open. Out on the desert a coyote howled. In the village a dog defied him. Richter confessed he had been mistaken, he had once again judged too soon. He was glad now that they had been duped by the girl into throwing themselves on the mercy of the Moencopa. They were simple, uncorrupted people who had been robbed of their birthright by the whites as they, the

Germans, had been of their honor by the Nazis, and who were also prisoners, but in their own land rather than a foreign.

"We must help them, Albert," he said. "It is our chance to deserve. To be Americans we must earn. We must something do before the workers come again and decide, we must succeed something. What, what?" Of course Albert had an idea. A cook, a clerk, a motorcyclist he might have been, but at the Dessau-Rossler school he had been trained as a *Pionier*, or engineer.

19

Hampelmann the engineer began work in the morning. First he rigged a wooden slat from the junkpile to replace the bucket and seated on it, had Matthe windlass him down the well shaft, then up again. The depth was approximately fifty meters, and at the bottom, he reported, there was much caved-in earth which would have to come out. In the junkpile he unearthed a shovel with a broken handle and a washtub in a fine state of preservation except for a few small holes. From the children he recruited a bucket brigade. Digging in shifts with Matthe, filling the washtub, hoisting it, filling the buckets, the old men superintending the children toting the buckets to the dry wash and emptying them while the old ladies superintended the old men, in two days he was down in the shaft to solid rock. Mouse Sits was busier than it had been in years.

Hampelmann took a day off, then, to delve in his *wunderbar* junkpile. Layer after layer he went down, civilization after civilization, until he turned up what he needed: a sledgehammer and a crowbar which, though slightly bent, would serve his purpose. If such a junkpile, he asserted, had been available to the Afrika Korps, short as it always was of parts, it might have rolled all the way to Bombay.

By turns the young men commenced the strenuous process of

driving the crowbar into the rock. Hour after hour, changing places when the sledgeman could no longer lift the hammer, unable in the narrow shaft to swing freely, they banged away at short, inept range. No one could assist them now. It was a matter of muscle and sheer squarehead obstinacy, and it would come to *nichts* if there were not a second subterranean stream within detonating distance below the one which had given out. In two days they had a hole in the rock nineteen inches deep.

Dusty and cramped, Matthe would sometimes during his relief stroll down to the sickness hut. Tansie Scout would converse with him only in writing.

"How many women did you rayp in the war?" she scrawled, poking paper and pencil out a crack in her mud wall.

"Many," he printed in reply.

"I went six years to school ha," she bragged.

It was difficult for him to think in English through the pencil. "Then you should better spell," he chided.

"Bull. Did you have a girl?"

"Yes."

"Whats her name?"

"Miss Germany."

"Go to hell notsi."

Alice Walkingstick happened along, and Matthe inquired why Tansie would not talk. "Because she's mean and stuck-up," sniffed Alice, addressing the hut. "She and Peppertail are the only ones can read and write and she shows off. She went to school six years and now she's too damn smart to work in the fields so she runs off to Phoenix and spreads her legs for soldiers. Indians—send them to school and they get stuck-up and go to hell. They're too good to be Indians and not good enough to be white." She rambled on that what Tansie needed was to marry and settle down, and maybe Tony's gettin' killed was also to blame, but if it was her girl she'd beat her till she behaved, but the old fool men were sure one of their doll-baby prisoners had got out of its basket and made her evil, so tomorrow they were going to spit it out of her, they were crazy but that would be a sight to see, the old fools, and they had to do it before her father, Victor, and the workers came home because they didn't believe in those damn ceremonies. "I don't either," she said, "but it gives the old men somethin' to do, so let them rattle around if they want. Now you hear me, girl." She bent to the hut and raised her quaver. "Tomorrow afternoon I'm takin' you out and you're goin' to get washed up and dressed up and then you're goin' back in there till they're through and then you're comin' out lookin' and actin' nice so they'll think they're young bucks again and they've done somethin' big, do you hear?"

For a response Tansie hummed "Praise the Lord and Pass the Ammunition!"

Alice accompanied Matthe to the well. She stopped and put her hand on his arm. Her face was furrowed as a washboard. "My mouth works by itself," she said. "Us old ones, we can smoke and keep a garden and make a basket and wait to die. Our own chil‑ dren can pick cotton and feed us. It's the young ones I'm sorry for. So many dumb girls, they've gone to Phoenix and made a lot of bad money. The white soldiers, they like to lie with Indian girls, I don't know why. Tansie I have to be grandmother to. Wesley's wife, she died a long while back. I'm sorry for this girl, but our people don't cry. I don't know how they will turn out, her and the little ones." Her fingers hooked into his arms like talons. "I hope they let you stay here," the old woman whispered. "I hope to hell you hit wa‑ ter."

They persevered. Hampelmann yodelled up the well shaft in rhythm with his hammer, Matthe swung tirelessly away, and the next day they drove the crowbar down another ten inches.

That evening the village did not assemble on the mountainside to watch the sun set. Instead, it gathered to attend the Evil-Spitting. From the Council the five old men came solemnly to ring the sick‑ ness hut. They were dressed as shamans, medicine men, doctors. Naked from the waist up, they wore eagle feathers in their hair and armlets of eagle down. Three seated themselves. The ceremony began. Joe John Jones shook a gourd rattle. Uncle Rumbles thumped a drum which was merely an inverted basket. Wesley Scout played the scraping sticks, one of them notched and slightly curved, over which the other was rubbed with rapid motion to make a sharp, incessant clicking. Since they were the eldest, Lies About His Age and General Miles shuffled about the hut in tempo with the scraping and the thumping and the rattle. In one hand they held a stalk of ocotillo, a thorny cactus, and with these stalks they struck the walls of the hut in order to rout the evil spirits which had first tempted, then compelled the girl inside to dishonor her tribe and kind. Once routed, the spirits fled down the cactus stalks to take refuge in the bodies of Lies and General Miles, who expelled them in the end by spitting, with great gusto, into baking-powder cans. Round and round the hut the dancers shuffled and flailed and spat until their wattles flapped and their old sides heaved, until they staggered from exertion. When they were quite out, both of breath and saliva, they ceased, puffing, and everyone waited.

Whether their medicine was responsible, or Alice Walkingstick's secret ministrations, the Tansie Scout who crawled from the hut was a different person. She was scrubbed, her hair was combed, the chipped lacquer had been removed from her fingernails, sandals replaced her penny loafers, and she had been put into a plain mus-lin dress. Everyone murmured approval, and for a moment she played her new role well, standing demurely before them, eyes downcast, the shy village virgin of sixteen. But she could not play it long. All at once she tossed her head in rebellion, thumbed her nose, and darting round the hut ran away again, this time up a tree. That nearest tamarisk had grown on a slant. It was easy to walk or run up the huge trunk and disappear into the green cloud. Sometimes, almost at the top, the little children frisked like squirrels. The old women looked I-told-you-so at one another.

Night came like a curtain now for it was September, the Month of Dry Grass, as the Moencopa called it. In their daub house, Matthe lay awake staring at the doll of hair in its basket and think-ing about the girl in the tree and wondering if she were still there. He was sorry for her. All she had achieved was to exchange one confinement for another, that of a childish insurgence. Easing out of bed, he drew on his trousers and went to see. Walking the tama-risk, pulling limb by limb, was like going up an inverted, even darker well shaft. He could be sure only of the radium hands on his wristwatch. Then a sharp kick on the head by a sandal almost made him lose his balance. He retreated to a lower limb and ad-vised her to come down and begin to deport herself like an adult, not a spoiled, willful brat. She would say nothing.

"I forgive that you lied to us, Albert and me," he said, "to bring us here to this reservation and it was not that of the Apache as we believed. For we are content and we will if we can aid these people, who are good and, and, considering." He waited. "Who was Tony?" he asked. She would say nothing. He settled himself against the broad back of the tree. "How it is with you I understand," he said gently. "So was it with me when I was young. I come from Duisburg, on a big river, the Rhine. Our harbor was full always with ships and tugs and barges of all nations, and I would for hours sit and study the flags and wish to run away and to see those far, idyll places. I talked to the captains and with their children played on the boats and learned words of Dutch and French. Also I had a bicycle and later went on a holiday through Bavaria. And also a Klepper Faltboot and tent. Up the Rhine we would go by train and down again paddle in our little boats and camp. I was happy. Duisburg is destroyed now by one-half, bombed." It was as though he were speaking to himself. "But I was exciting to go to Africa and most of all, to America. It is not wrong to want when you are young to see the world and live. It is—how do you say—humane."

The mass of the tamarisk muffled a wind. Curiosity got the better of the girl somewhere above him. "What was her name?"

"Erika. I met her at the Panzer school where I was trained, at Krampnitz. She was of the Red Cross and we were betrothed."

"Where is she?"

"I do not know. I had a letter in Africa. She would be married to another."

"Tough."

"For her also. He was going to the Russian front."

"How old are you?"

"Twenty-one."

"You got a family?"

"I had. Father, mother, two small brothers, Klaus and Wolfgang."

"What's their trouble?"

"They are dead. All. The bombing."

"Oh."

Richter changed the subject. "Do you have an Indian name?"

"Laughing Corn."

"Laughing Corn?"

"How d'you say it in kraut?"

"Lachender Mais."

She repeated it. Then Matthe heard movement, and felt, on the crown of his head, a hand. The fingers spread and were still. The hand which lay upon his head did not offer, did not claim. It asked. It asked perception and tenderness and support and above all, deliverance. It obliged him. And when, high in the ancient tree, he recalled the color of the hand he could not see, the source and texture of its blood, when he remembered that the hand was Indian, the touch of it dizzied him. He went down the tree immediately.

They labored ten hours the following day, deepening the hole in the rock by eighteen inches. Another foot and they would reach the end of the crowbar. They were as anxious to be done as the old men had been to have the mischief of their ceremony finished, for the workers were expected back in Mouse Sits any day; they must come soon or the village would have little to eat except melons and nothing to smoke. Whether or not the Germans would be allowed to remain depended on the men of that middle generation, and with them, the find of a new water supply might tip the scales. Whether or not he would really find it, Albert confessed he did not know. Sometimes, down in the shaft, he seemed to hear the trickle of water under him, sometimes he did not. But he was lucky, he would remind Matthe, and they had to lose nothing, to gain everything.

It was the turn of Uncle Rumbles and General Miles to drive the water wagon into Vaca the next morning. Hampelmann gave them twenty dollars and instructions to buy, at the hardware store, a stick of dynamite, a blasting cap, and four feet of fuse.

Three hours later the wagon rattled across the dry wash at a skittish, unprecedented trot. Uncle Rumbles lashed at the nags while General Miles, arms high above his head, held the fuse and blasting cap in one hand and the dynamite in the other as though they were live rattlesnakes. The two old men were terrified. Someone had told them what dynamite would do.

Ten minutes later, as Matthe was at work below, an automobile crossed the dry wash, its rear wheels spraying pebbles. Tongue-tied, waving an alarm, Wesley Scout came as fast as his legs would carry him and Hampelmann, after one look at the car, jumped over the well rim, and spinning the windlass, hurtled down the shaft.

99

20

It was a patrol car of the Taft County Sheriff's Department. When it parked near the well, a tall officer in boots and star and big hat got out and greeted Lies About His Age. "What say, Chief. How old are you today?"

Nodding, the old man cleaned his teeth with the end of his sash. Mouse Sits seemed to draw a blanket of silence about itself. Radios were stilled. Elders and children alike stood or sat where they were, contemplative; not one glance was cast at the well. A tension was set up, an atmosphere not of fear but of alert, as though the village never knew what the white man might do next.

The deputy said he'd heard they'd bought some dynamite. What were the Moencopa about to do, he smiled, go on the warpath against the Apaches? This was reservation land, it was their business, but when anyone around Vaca bought dynamite he made it his business.

Lies About His Age replied that Ramon and Victor and the others were trying to reopen the well.

"Don't like our water, huh?" Jack Thode picked up a stone and tossed it over the well rim and listened for the click. "Chief, do me a favor, will you? I got word a while back, three more German prisoners took off from the Phoenix camp, two together and one on his own. Keep an eye out, will you?"

"The war's over, we heard."

"You heard right. But they took off anyway. Didn't care to go back to krautland and face the music, I guess. How I figure it, they'll head down this way to make South America if they can, like the others. They cross that border and we can't touch them with the war over."

Lies About His Age twisted an earlock. "Is that prisoner camp goin' to close now?"

"Sometime. Not till we've squeezed as much elbow grease out of them as we can." Thode pushed up his hat. Any prisoners who escaped now, he explained, were bound to be the meanest kind of Nazis, men who were desperate to avoid going home and being called to account for their crimes. "Chief, now listen." He spoke slowly, in short sentences. "They are worse than Apaches. They murdered millions. Men, women, and kids. Shooting and poison gas and cutting on them. Or they put them in concentration camps and worked them to death or starved them. Then you know what they did with their skin? They made lampshades and purses out of it, like animal hide." The deputy let that sink in. "We can't let them get away with that. So start a lookout, and send me word like before, savvy?"

He got back into the car, started it, and smiling, added a reminder out the window. "One more thing, Chief. We're going to have a lot of cotton to pick around Vaca come winter. If your people don't pick it, somebody else will. Remember that."

Around the well the patrol car slewed, disappointing a village dog which, after sniffing one of the wheels, had just lifted a decrepit leg.

21

That afternoon, when the two carloads of Scouts and Joneses and Walkingsticks arrived from the cottonfields near Tucson with groceries and cigarettes and surprises of candy for their children, the elders had a surprise for them. Collecting about the well, the entire village peered below, where two young strangers were tamping the charge of dynamite, blasting cap and fuse attached, down the crowbar hole in the rock. Together, Joe John Jones and Wesley Scout windlassed Matthe aboveground, while Hampelmann the engineer remained to light the fuse.

Matthe had everyone move back. He laid hold of the windlass crank. They heard the snap of the match.

"*Schnell!* Quick!" Hampelmann yelled.

Matthe cranked furiously and Albert rose up pale as a shade from the underworld, scrambled his arms and legs out of the shaft and in polyglot English and German commanded everyone to move back still further, there would be a *gigantisch* explosion!

Faces squinched and black eyes widened and the old ladies stuck fingers in their ears. Like the fuse below, time hissed.

An ignominious thud. A twirl of dust.

Everyone concealed smiles. Hampelmann gaped, and looking more the hapless clown than ever, in disgust and disbelief went to the well and slammed in a small boulder.

Splash!

Boys and girls squealed and the populace crowded about Albert and the well and the bucket was tied on and lowered and cranked up full of muddy water which, the beaming Pionier assured them, would soon run clear. Middle-aged and old, the men lit cigarettes and smoked in gratified serenity. Mothers decided to do a washing. Grandmothers decided the children ought to bathe.

After a festive evening meal Matthe Teege and Albert Pomtow were admitted for the first time to the Council, a wattle-and-daub structure larger than any of the ten houses of the village. Lies About His Age took them inside and turned on a light bulb. The sanctum of Mouse Sits was a single room with the usual bare-earth floor, in the center of which the frayed, sprung, upholstered seats from junked automobiles had been arranged in a square. The chamber served not only as a place for conference but as a repository for the most precious and hallowed possessions of the community, and these the old man showed the Germans with the utmost reverence. From the ceiling hung several Apache prisoner-scalps in their baskets. In one corner were stacked three Springfield rifles, relics of an earlier World War. To the walls were fixed a number of warped, primitive bows without strings, a deerskin quiver empty of arrows, the eagle feathers and armlets of down and sticks and rattles used in Evil-Spitting, the red-black-and-white German flag made in Camp No. 80 and recently presented by the newcomers, and a yellow telegram to Mr. and Mrs. Grover Jones in which the War Department in Washington deeply regretted to inform them that their son, Anthony, age nineteen, had been killed in action in the Pacific. He had been, evidently, the Tony to whom Tansie Scout had referred. In another corner leaned a calendar stick, a length of cactus rib marked for every year with strange red and blue figures which recorded the crucial event in tribal history for that year, such as an Apache raid or a fight with Mexicans or the results of athletic contests between villages. In the long years, Lies said apologetically, he had been able to read the calendar stick from the very top, to the dimmest beginnings of the Moencopa, but now that he was well over a hundred he had forgotten what the figures meant. Only the younger people knew, Tansie and Bitter Boy, and only the vague account they had learned in school from the whites. In a third corner stood a dusty, massive, old-fashioned player piano, its mechanism actuated by two wide foot pedals. How the village had come by this antique he did not explain.

Council convened. After the four old men entered and took places of prestige with Lies on the automobile seats, they were followed by Manuel and Victor Scout and Grover Jones and Ramon Walkingstick, who sat beside them. Matthe and Albert remained standing, not at attention but correctly. Lies About His Age took a cigarette from a new pack of Wings, lit it, puffed once, and passed it on. Each man did likewise. Then, to create an even more deliberative mood, the two oldest boys, Manuel Scout's son Charles Lindbergh, age eleven, and a Walkingstick boy who was nine, slipped into the chamber and kneeling before the player piano since it had no bench, began to pump the pedals with their hands. Chords were struck by unseen fingers, spirits whirred inside, and in obedience either to the spinning paper roll of music or the invisible gods which dwelt within the instrument, it produced a loud, metallic, sentimental rendition of "Where the Shy Little Violets Grow."

The soldiers made their faces as solemn as those of the Indians. With its incoherence of objects old and new, hair and electric, lethal and sacred, the chamber was as preposterous as the pockets of children turned inside out—children who, since they did not know what it would be best to save, saved everything. And with its prelude of music and puffing, its substitution of form for faith, the dilemma of the Council was as pitiable as that of children lost—children who, unable to surname their parents or themselves, could not be helped to find their home.

The roll flapped, the music ceased, and the pumpers edged from the room. Of the two decisions which must be made by the men of Mouse Sits, that of what to do with Tansie Scout was taken up first.

General Miles revealed to the younger men that they, the elders, had spit away her evil, so that she might safely go again to the fields.

But she had run away three times, objected Grover Jones. There was still much temptation for a girl off the reservation, and she was only sixteen.

The nine men were silent. Here again was a difference of opinion which must be resolved, for concord, unanimity in fact, was their tradition. It would be impolite for the workers to discount the magic of the shamans; it would be ungrateful on the other hand for the older generation to thwart the wishes of those who kept it alive. In the silence, Uncle Rumbles' stomach mediated.

It was Victor Scout, her father, who suggested, now that the war was over, that she remain in the village until the spring, until the soldiers in Phoenix, and hence the temptations, were removed.

Wesley Scout, her grandfather, seconded the motion, and heads nodded concurrence.

They smoked again, passing the cigarette, and Lies About His Age opened a discussion of the other matter. Upon this, the elders were of one mind. The young strangers, said General Miles, had earned the hospitality of the Moencopa, whose custom it had been to welcome travelers. They had found water where there had been no water. They had done more for the village in two weeks, asserted Joe John Jones, than the government had done in two years. They deserved to be given shelter until the prisoner camp was closed and they might go their way in peace.

"We've been away, my relatives," said Ramon Walkingstick. "We don't know much about them."

"Ask, my son," said Uncle Rumbles.

Ramon turned on his automobile seat. "Why is it you don't want to go back over there to your people? Everybody needs to go home."

Albert responded. "His family is dead. All in the war *kaputt* by bombs. My father and sisters I do not know, for where they live the *Russen* occupy." He drew a finger across his throat. "So to go home to, we have nothing."

"I understand that," said Grover Jones. "But why is it you want to stay in this country? I don't understand that."

This was a question for Matthe. They had been prisoners in Arizona for almost two years, he said, and in that time they had come to esteem the USA. It was their wish to become citizens, and to prepare themselves they had studied the form of government and the geography of this nation, and also the noble documents upon which it was founded, the Declaration of Independence and the Constitution. In this great country, where all men were created equal, they desired to live and enjoy liberty and happiness to pursue. But they did not intend only to take, but to give, to contribute what they could to the USA, as had so many others of German ancestry. The robes of his judiciousness parted, and Richter's emotions were bared as obviously as the light bulb over the Council. "Therefore," he said, "our hope and ambition is easy. It is to be Americans, as Americans you are."

Inadvertently the men of the Moencopa glanced at one another, then lowered heads and concentrated on the backs of hands, the knees of trousers. After an uncomfortable moment, Wesley Scout mentioned that the deputy sheriff had been in Mouse Sits that morning. Three more prisoners had escaped from the Phoenix camp, and the deputy asked that the village watch for them because they must be very bad men. The war was over but they were afraid to go home.

"We know the Germans been doin' some bad things," Manuel Scout said, addressing the meeting generally. "We don't read, but we go to movies sometimes, down in Vaca, and we've seen them. They've killed a lot of people. I wonder if these two did."

"They showed us films also, in the camp," said Matthe. "And we have heard and read. If these things are true, the guilt we some accept, for we are German. But we have not personally taken part, or even known. This you may trust. My friend and I, we were soldiers, we have not been in Deutschland since being boys. The Afrika Korps did never conduct itself like that." He made a helpless gesture. "I am sorry. We are both captures. You believe that all

105

Germans are Nazis, and we did believe that all Indians are savage Apaches. We are both captures of what we do not know. It is, is, unfortune. Because some good Germans there must be as well as misdoing. Is it not so with Americans, and also among Indians?"

But the Council was uneasy. For several minutes it conferred in Moencopa, the mumble and rustle almost unrecognizable as a language since the final syllables of many words were whispered. Some consensus must have been reached, and Victor Scout chosen to act as spokesman.

"We don't want to do wrong," he said. "We thank you for the water. But if we let you stay here that sher'ff, he'll be comin' back and back. This is our land, not the whites', but they come on it when they want. How we goin' to stop them? With those old guns?" He pointed at the Springfields in the corner. "No, if we want to pick cotton we have to do what they say. We've been good Americans ourselves in the war. Tony we gave to the Army, and Bitter Boy, and when we saw prisoners tryin' to get over to Mexico, we told the sher'ff."

Matthe frowned. "What prisoners?"

"Germans. From the camp up to Phoenix," Victor said. "He asked us to watch out if we saw any strangers goin' south and send him word. So we had a lookout on this mountain, like for the enemy in the long years, and we saw five."

"Five!"

"Sure. Five walkin'."

"Was there one alone, then one, then two, then one more?" Matthe demanded.

"That's right. How do you know?"

"The Krautfange!" Albert blurted.

"What's that?" asked Grover Jones.

The soldiers stared at each other.

"Ehlert!"

"Boehm!"

"Mohrdieck, Fuge!"

"Buchting!"

"*Nein, nein, nein!*" Matthe protested. "And by the Indians!"

"*Grüss Gott!*" groaned Albert.

The revelation sent them striding round the automobile seats, around the Council, shaking their heads in despair. Finally Matthe faced them angrily.

"They had a right to escape! It is the same with all war prisoners of any country. To try is a duty, as it is to fight. They tried, but they were caught after four days marching, by eight men on horses. Did you not see what was done them? *Ach,* how they were beaten, because they were few against many, all so beaten. They were then found by the gate of the camp, hurt, with on their jacket a sign, 'Kraut Ketchers.' The jaw of Fuge was broken. And Leutnant Buchting, a pilot, the last, in the hospital of the camp he is still. He does not walk or see or hear or himself feed. He is a child, so much was he beaten in his head, and always a child will be or die." He turned his face from them. "And of bad Germans you speak to me. Did you not see what was done them?"

"Many times from the Afrika Korps prisoners would escape," Albert accused. "Americans and *Engländer,* and we would not beat them if they were again caught. Did you not know of the Krautfange?"

The Indians were silent. His movements uncertain, Lies About His Age lit another cigarette and forgot to pass it. "We didn't know," he said. "We thought that sher'ff, he'd just take them back to the camp like he was supposed to. He must of got up a posse. That sher'ff," he said to the Council, "the war's over but he wants to have these two who found water and beat up on them."

It was almost a signal. Ramon Walkingstick came to his feet. "No, we didn't know what that sher'ff would do. My relatives, we made a mistake and I'm changin' my mind. The war's over and Thode, he can go to hell. I say, let them stay with us till the camp's closed up to Phoenix."

"We like them," said General Miles. "They could be sons to us. Our sons are gone away all the time."

"I just remembered," Wesley Scout said. "The Germans beat the Americans over the ocean, two times. That's why that sher'ff is mean. He looks you in the eye, you don't see anything."

"We're sorry about those others," Uncle Rumbles apologized. "We better not tell that," he said to his relatives, "we better keep that here in Council."

Victor and Manuel Scout and Grover Jones stood up with Ramon

107

Walkingstick, and then the elders. "OK, we invite you to stay," Victor Scout said to the soldiers. "We've lost one in the war and that's enough. In the days of these old men, our fathers, when the Papago came to us for help against the Apaches, we helped. We gave our word and fought with them and saved our families. That's what our fathers tell us anyway. We have shame about this thing and we give you our word. We don't have power any more, that's all over, but you'll be sons to us and we can still take care of our own." He put out his hand. "I'd like to shake hands."

So alien and alone and from so far away, the two young men hesitated, incredulous at the sudden turn of feeling in their favor. It was difficult to comprehend that now, finally, they had friends, and that mischance had given them a place and a people to whom they might belong. They were ashamed themselves, of their earlier amusement at this museum of mud and its tinny invocation, of their underestimate of these simple, unheroic laborers with their steady eyes and stoicism. And they hesitated for another reason. Accept the offered hand of Victor Scout and they shed the romantic skin of their boyhood. They burned the books and said *Auf Wiedersehen* to Winnetou and let the screens go dark. Accept that hand, and the country of the heart, the land of *Milch* and *Honig*, the America in which all men were brave and free and equal—these they renounced, and took an oath to fact.

Both Matthe Teege and Albert Pomtow extended hands at once, and smiling, tried to take all nine.

22

"*Eins! Zwei! Drei! Vier! Eins! Eins!* Eyes right!" Brown faces split with grins, arms swinging, they chirped the cadence. Up to the outhouse, round the junkpile, down to the riverbed, up to the cemetery Feldmarschall Pomtow marched his troops in columns of twos

—three Scout boys and a girl, two Jones boys and a girl, and a Walkingstick boy. He called them the Moenkopa Korps. He drilled them daily. They adored him. His mechanical genius also saved them the bother of scampering up and down the mountainside to shoo away the mourning doves which threatened to devour the stand of wheat. Rummaging in the junkpile he located rope, twine, and an assortment of glass bottles, and rigged through the trees an alarm system. One tug at the rope end in the village, one tinkling of bottles down near the wheat, and away flapped the doves. Most fun of all, he built them a play Panzer. Collecting odds and ends from the junkpile, four wheels and panels of tin for sides and a washtub for a turret and a length of stovepipe for an .88 gun, he put together somehow a fine toy Tiger big enough to ride in, painted gray with a martial black-and-white cross on its turret. For locomotive power a push sufficed, or the bare feet of the cannoneer.

Drift the days away upon the slow current of their new life, make themselves completely at home in their new home, the German youths could not. It was a village betwixt and between. It was an anachronism with radios. Even for America, it was too fantastic. And when the workers had gone again, the foster-sons of Mouse Sits did whatever they might to merit their adoption. They forced a few dollars upon their hosts each week. They helped water the squash and pumpkins. The old men they enlightened with travelogues of Europe and Africa. For the old ladies they ground corn and tinkered appliances and gathered wood. Hampelmann beguiled the children. Richter tutored them. Each morning he held class under a wato, his eight charming, illiterate pupils seated decorously about the table. Like most Moencopa children they had never attended the government school at Casa Buena, the reservation headquarters, because it was forty miles away and they would have had to live there in a dormitory, banished from their families. Unlike most, they were near a public school, that in Vaca, but white youngsters there, cruel as only the young can be, would not tolerate Indians as classmates. And they had a tribal characteristic which maddened their German master: while they would try, they would not try to excel. To excel was unseemly. To learn as much as everyone else, exactly that and no more, was perfection. Richter frowned and fumed and taught them the English alphabet and how to write their names and some simple arithmetic and to recite in chorus the states of the USA and their capitals and the names of the baseball teams in the major leagues, and freed them to Hampelmann, their Pied Piper.

He enlisted Tansie Scout as an assistant, but she was little help. She was impatient both with the children and with her sentence by the Council to the village till spring. She kept house for her grandfather Wesley and her small brother and sister in the adobe of her parents, Victor and Ethel; cooking and washing and teaching drove her, she said, "nuts." She wanted Matthe to walk and talk with her. "You slapped my butt and made me bring you to this dump," she reminded him, "so you be nice."

One day she led him up a path behind the village to the ridge line of the black mountain. The view was even more breathtaking than that from above the trees where the village rested of an evening. Through sparkling air one could see deceptive miles in every direction. Here, Matthe realized, was where Mouse Sits, doing its duty to its country, had picked out Ehlert, Boehm, Mohrdieck, Fuge, and Leutnant Buchting tramping toward Mexico. And down there somewhere on that arid, vicious plain, out of sight in a wash perhaps, they had been captured and abused. He said nothing of this to Tansie, who wanted only to talk about herself.

In a sense, she had been a hostage of the village to the future. Sent to government grammar school in Casa Buena, homesick for parents and friends, she had run away three times in four years. But since she was bright and apt, Victor and Ethel had chanced placing her in the Phoenix Indian School, another government institution, when she was fourteen. They could not have been more reckless. She was thrown together with young people from other tribes, with Apaches, for example, who fought as ruthlessly for high marks as they had once raided for horses. And she was galled by the contradictions inherent in the society for which she was being educated.

"The damn whites," she said, sitting on a rock and facing him and drawing up her knees under her chin and biting at a fingernail. "They try to turn you white so's you can make money and be somebody. You cross-eye yourself studyin' and you know what? They give you two, three dollars a day to pick or'nges or scrub their floors. I see London, I see France, I see someone's underpants." He blushed. "You're cute. Back East, I hear the whites they're so sad!

for the poor Indian. Out here they hate us because they got to look at us every day and see what bastards they are. Not the soldiers, though." She winked. Having observed that the American criterion of ability and success was money, some Indian girls, like their Negro and Mexican sisters, had set out to earn it in and around Phoenix, which fairly panted with soldiers and sailors and prisoners. "You can make a hundred a week easy. So you do and the whites, they're jealous, they throw you in jail. I've been in Juvie twice—that's what we call Juv'nile Detention. I wouldn't of, but after I heard Tony was killed, I sort of went crazy. Oh, how I loved that kid! And you killed him." Matthe corrected her. Anthony Jones had fallen in the Pacific area. "Japs, krauts, what's the difference? So did Tony's folks, Grover and Lupe and her sister Peppertail, go crazy. They got that ten thousand insur'nce from the gover'ment for him—it's funny, every soldier's worth the same thing, ten thousand—and took off for Tucson and bought that car and blew it all in six months and Peppertail, she got knocked up again. That's the third time for her, three kids and no name for a one and she's been to school, too." After Tony's loss Tansie ran away from school with an older girl, a Navajo, and they rented a room and learned to drink and smoke and go to movies and buy clothes and have fun with soldiers like white girls, except that they were paid for it. "A girl can get rich from the war, she's smart. I didn't yet but I would of. And I'd be right up in Phoenix makin' money right now wasn't for you, krauthead. So where am I? In this dump that's almost as dead as Juvie and all I've got is the pennies I came here with in my shoes."

"You are better here," Richter said.

"Up your. Don't you preach. I remember you in that date grove —what a *Dummkopf.*"

"What does Moencopa mean?"

"The People."

"*Volk!*" Matthe was startled. "With us it is also an important word. *Volk.* What do they believe in, the Moencopa? I mean to say, what is their religion?"

"Beats me. Oh, you saw some of it, those ol' men jumpin' around and spittin'," she sniffed. "We had a god once, Tohi-i'itoi, or somethin' like that, I can't even speak my own language very good. Anyways, we called him Elder Brother. He brought the People

111

here, to this damn desert. Then he got mean, so we killed him. Then the priests came along later and gave us some others, God and Jesus and a bunch of saints. Then they went away and now we don't have anybody but the gover'ment, and that's too busy fightin' wars so we're in bad shape. Hey, I just remembered from school!" She jumped down from her rock. "You know how the sky's streaky white in the east early in the mornin'? Well, those streaks are s'posed to be Elder Brother's hairs. He pulled them out of his head to show us day was comin'."

Richter was silent. He could not keep up with her. She was vulgar and selfish and vindictive and impulsive and vain and quicksilver. And captivating. And also, he thought, a little *verrückt*, a little cracked.

"Shut up," she said.

"*Reden ist Silber, schweigen ist Gold.*"

"No capeesh."

"Speech is silver, silence is gold."

"Oh. What's your problem, soldier?"

"It is that—that you, the Indians, are not as I thought."

"Who'n hell is?" Tansie Scout demanded. "Grow up, Adolf, get wise. You can't just hang around waitin' for things to happen, you have to get on the stick. Every time my mom and pop dragged me back to the fields I'd take off again. Next time I'm goin' so far they'll never find me, California maybe." She clapped her hands to her hips. "Anyways, I'm through pickin' cotton and I'm never goin' to be maid to some ol' white bag and clean her toilets. This papoose got heap big plans. What you lookin' at?"

"I am not."

She wiggled her hips. "You are so. You're not like I thought either. You're no Nazi superman, you're sort of a sad sack. Cute, though. I wish you smoked."

At night Matthe Teege and Albert Pomtow would talk themselves to sleep. They murmured conjecture about the Fourth Reich and No. 80 POW Camp, about how soon its two thousand stateless, defeated men would take the long train and the slow ship to the smoking chaos that was Deutschland. They would lie staring up at the basket. Sometimes it seemed to descend, to hang only inches above them; sometimes the daub walls of the house seemed to shrink, to draw close; and it would occur to them that they were

112

captive in Mouse Sits as surely as the doll made from a scalp, that they belonged to the Moencopa as incongruously as the player piano. Since Hampelmann was more gregarious, he had learned, in conversation particularly with the old ladies, Josie Miles and Duchess Walkingstick and Alice, her sister, and Julia Jones, more about the tribe than Matthe, but bit by piece the pair added to the junk-pile of their information. Rather than the warrior, the trader, the builder, the Moencopa had always exalted the songmaker, the dreamer, the mystic. Cooperation within family, village, and tribe, and with their neighbors white and Indian, had been their ideal, not competition. No *Volk* on earth was therefore less prepared by tradition and temperament to adapt to the American culture and economy than these humble dwellers in the desert. And what had the Americans practiced upon them? A trickery so consummate that it could only have been conceived by the well-intentioned. Generously it gave the Indians their own land, then by diverting their water forced them to leave it. Generously it provided schools, then asked as tuition the dismemberment of the family. For songs it gave them the radio, for visions the bottle, for freedom the automobile, for gods the dollar, and for sanctuary an outhouse. It dispossessed them of their past. It displaced them in the present. It offered them a future conditional upon a deal. Change the color of your skin and the contours of your face you cannot, it granted. But if you would be Americans, it propositioned, you must trade in your dances for stoop labor in our fields, your heritage for our soap operas, your philosophy for our laxatives, your Elder Brother for our Uncle Sam, your being for our getting. If you would be Americans, it smiled agreeably, you must be like us. And when the Moencopa replied that they had thought they were Americans, it said: the hell you are.

"They are like us," Albert concluded one night. "They are prisoners, but of peace prisoners, not war, because they have not fought. *Ist das nicht* a dirty trick?"

"And to be citizens is what they wish also," Matthe added.

"*Oui, oui.* And like us, who they are they do not know."

"What?"

"*Wohl,* who are we? We have not a country. Now we are not Germans or Americans either. And they, now they are not Americans or Indians either."

113

Richter folded his arms for a pillow. "The American democracy I do not understand. Why do the Indians not elect, elect—how do you say—politicals, who will help them?"

"Because in Arizona they have no vote."

"You are sober?"

"Howgh, howgh. Julia Jones has told me."

"But they are taxed. And taken into the Army. And die."

"And they cannot *Alkohol* buy. *Ach,* if I could not buy beer I would pull out *Da Tomahawken* and take many scalps."

Matthe was not listening. "Even prisoners rights have. And dignity, if they have fought well." His lips moved. To himself he was repeating the words he had memorized so long ago in the latrine where Willi Loffelbein had contributed himself, hearing them in his heart: ". . . that among these are life, liberty and the pursuit of happiness. . . . Neither slavery nor involuntary servitude . . . shall exist within the United States, or any place subject to their jurisdiction." The words were as majestic as before, the ideas as elevated, but now there was no echo in his mind.

Hampelmann yawned. "Do you think that *verdammt* sheriff will again come?"

"I do not know. But something I begin to see. How much we have asked that they do for us, these people."

That they, the young Germans, would in turn be asked, Matthe Teege was presently to discover. He was weeding the pumpkin patch one afternoon when Tansie Scout took him away again from his work, this time for a stroll down the sandy, smooth-stoned course of what had been the Sonoita. Ever inconsistent, Tansie on this occasion was quiet, walking beside him barefoot. She'd been dumb the other time, up on the mountain, she realized afterward. A girl could catch more flies with sugar than with vinegar, and this day she wanted him to do the talking. Cottonwood trees were spaced along the banks of the dry wash, their gnarled roots exposed and yearning for the water which had ceased to flow. Their green leaves were turning now to gold, for it was October, the Month of Little Rain. In Arizona the movement of season from summer to autumn was oblique rather than obvious, a subtle modification rather than a change. The nights cooled. The air dried, tanged. From the mountain slopes were heard the long farewells of quail. Rabbits rested.

114

Artfully she questioned him. He had been four years in Volks-schule, four in Mittelschule, three in Gymnasium, majoring in English and Latin. What did his father do? He had been a *Polizei-wachtmeister,* a police officer, not of the state but of Duisburg, concerned with civil crimes rather than with politics. Was he a Nazi? Yes and no; he joined the Reichsparty for the sake of appearances as he had joined the Stahlhelm, the league of frontline German soldiers after the First World War, in which he had been wounded at the Somme. In his official capacity, he was expected to. But his father was too much the skeptical veteran to swallow the exhortations of men such as Goering and Goebbels, riffraff clearly his intellectual inferiors, and too keen a student of the criminal mentality. To distrust emotion was reason's duty besides, and the most emotional of all Germans was Hitler himself. What about his mother? Matthe trudged along grimly, head down. His mother, he replied after a while, was the Nazi in the family. She had mortified both his father and himself by producing, in her late thirties, a new litter of young, his two brothers, for the Führer, and not incidentally in order to qualify her for the motherhood ring with its detachable center number recording her donations to the Reich. "Use Eye and Hand for the Fatherland" had been a slogan of that earlier war, now, his father told him with private sarcasm, his mother had volunteered her womb as well. Had he himself been a Nazi? Not a Nazi perhaps, but at least an ardent patriot, at least during his *Jugend* period, he admitted. Matthe searched for phrases. He wanted very much to explain himself to someone. Adolescent and romantic, he said, his world-vision had not been that of a world prostrate before a conqueror, or even a Europe, but of a kind of Pan-European union under the benign German aegis—an arrangement as logical and convenient as the commercial sharing of the Rhine by the vessels of many nations. History he saw then as a German tide on which a truly international ship of state might be borne. For him, at seventeen, it was Deutschland *und,* not *über alles.* And when at eighteen he was drafted into the Wehrmacht, it was not as Siegfried that he posed, quaffing potions and playing with matches and setting off in the end a Götterdämmerung, but as Parsifal, pure and guileless, healing wounds, a white dove hovering above his head as he knelt before the Grail of war. It was too ridiculous to recall. It was impossible to believe he had been that naïve. He glanced at Tansie

Scout. Her hand was in her hair. She was bored, she had not understood a word. What did he do as a soldier? He had driven a tank in the Afrika Korps. Did he shoot any Americans? He would prefer that, he said curtly, not to discuss.

"How d'you say whore in German?"

"*Hure.*"

Without his notice, she had led him to the bank. She sprang up and sat down in cottonwood shade. The grass was dry and soft. He lay on his side in it, at arm's length from her.

"How d'you say sweetheart?"

"*Schätzlein.*"

"I love you."

"*Ich liebe dich.*"

"Ugh."

"How do you in Moencopa say it?"

"Damn if I know."

"Your language you should know."

"Nazi."

"You see? You have not understood what I said. Even those Germans of us who were boys and—and—ignorance, to you Nazis we will be always. Always you will hate us."

Tansie Scout placed her hands behind her for support. Slowly she extended one small, sandy foot. His sleeve was rolled up, and against his bare forearm she put her bare foot, brown against white, and cleansed it of sand with his blond hair, back and forth in friction. "I don't hate you," she said.

His skin smoked.

"I bet we could be in love."

"*Nein.*"

The foot stopped. Suddenly she bounced forward and wriggled down beside him in the grass, on her back, looking up, her face near his. Tansie was very small. She had a kind of truant beauty. The river-brown skin. The blue-black violence of her hair. The snub nose. The great black eyes.

"Hey, how long since you kissed anybody?"

"Three years."

She smiled, teasing. Her teeth were white and sharp. She frightened him. "You're scared."

"*Nein.*"

"Then kiss me, you kraut."

Her breath was hot and musky. He faltered. To kiss an Indian girl. To touch, with his lips, time itself. *"Lachender Mais,"* he murmured. He closed his eyes, sought. And then.

She opened his kiss, whispered into him. "When you goin'?"

"When the camp it is closed."

"Take me with you."

"I could not."

"I love you."

"No."

"You can have it," she breathed into his anguish. "You paid for it, remember?"

"No."

She pushed him away and leaped to her feet. "You go to hell, then! Go on back and play with the ol' ladies!"

Matthe rose, and turning his back on her walked from under the cottonwoods, jumped into the dry wash, and started toward the village. After a moment Tansie chased after him, swearing, snapping at his heels like a small wild animal. Matthe had kissed her, but it was Richter who retreated now, shoulders squared against her fury. He had not scorned her. He pitied her. And he mistrusted himself. She was a cactus needle festering under his skin. She was a strange squawling creature being torn into life by breech birth. She was child of sorrow and woman of rut, savage and schoolgirl, Indian and white, one bare foot in another time, one shoe in this, with a penny in it. She was her people, the Moencopa, who did not know what they were or what they should be.

"Make me bring you here," she raged, "then be a dirty Nazi!"

"You pretended Apache to be," he said.

She scooped up a handful of stones and pelted him. "You wanted Indians, you got Indians!"

"You lied."

She hit him in the nape of the neck with another stone. "I'll lie, I'll steal, I'll screw the whole US Army! But I'll get out of this damn cemetery, you Hitler!"

He thought of seizing her, bending her, spanking her shameless little rump raw, but she was not to blame. She was sixteen. And she really was *verrückt,* mad.

23

Thode was not. He was calm and reasoned, even amiable, as he spoke with Victor and Manuel Scout, Grover Jones, and Ramon Walkingstick near the Council, one boot cocked up on the running board of his patrol car. He wore his uniform, khaki breeches and shirt and wide black belt. So slowly had he driven over the dry wash this day that there had been scarcely any warning of his entry into the village. He'd waited till the workers were home, he said, because on his trip out to the Mouse from Vaca two weeks ago the old men must not have understood him. He nodded at them, Lies and Uncle Rumbles and Joe John Jones and General Miles and Wesley Scout, who lounged against the water wagon preoccupied with the sunshine. Those three German prisoners were still on the loose. He wanted them. The only reason they'd have jumped No. 80 Camp was to hightail it across the border to beat paying the freight for what they'd done in the old country to innocent men, women, and children. Now the Moencopa, he said, were good, patriotic Americans, he knew that; they'd located him five other krauts trying to escape. But here were three more who had to pass this way, under a mountain from which you could see a scorpion yawn ten miles off, yet the Moencopa claimed to have seen neither hide nor hair of them. He wasn't accusing anyone, but he intended to have those Nazis. Reservation land was out of his authority, but there would soon be a lot of cotton to pick around Vaca and he expected cooperation. Was he making himself clear? Victor and the others nodded. The deputy sheriff got into his car, then got out again at the sound of the parade.

"*Eins! Zwei! Drei! Vier! Eins! Eins! Eins!*" It was the Moenkopa Korps. Past the car they marched proudly, arms swinging, pushing in the center of their column the toy Panzer with its German cross

118

on the turret, past the well, around the junkpile and into the trees. The old men leaned against the water wagon.

The workers examined their shoes.

Jack Thode watched the parade out of sight and hearing. He turned to the workers, towering a foot above the crowns of their straw hats. He rested a palm on the pearl handle of his Smith & Wesson revolver. "Victor," he said, "I ask the Moencopa one thing. You for the United States or against it?"

"For."

"Then I want the Nazis."

"Why? The war's over."

"To take them back to their camp."

"Like the others?"

"What's that mean?"

"What did you do to those other five?"

The deputy's eyes went opaque. "Indian," he said, "do you know what'd happen I was to tell the government you're hiding prisoners of war? You'd wind up in jail, old folks and all."

Ramon Walkingstick spoke. "Sher'ff, what if we was to tell the gover'ment down to Casa Buena about those others?"

Thode looked at the brown, impenetrable faces. "I don't know where you've got them," he said quietly. "I know if you want, you can hide them out on this reservation so nobody can find them. But think it over. You don't produce them damn soon, I'll see to it you come crawling to me to take them off your hands. Crawling."

The tall man stooped as though to enter his car, then noticed an indigent dog lifting its hind leg beside a rear wheel. He took one graceful step and with the pointed toe of his right boot caught the dog in its exposed belly. He kicked the animal fifteen feet. It lay without moving. He started the patrol car then and drove slowly around the well and out of the village.

Matthe Teege and Albert Pomtow climbed out of the opening at the top of the tank on the water wagon, which had been the nearest hiding place when the deputy's car appeared. The old men and their sons were gathered thoughtfully about the dog. It was dead. Like a knife, the boot toe had split open its belly. Purple entrails distended in loops, still pulsing. Lies About His Age said that they had better have the children keep a lookout on the mountain again, as during the war, from morning-stands-up until night, a lookout this time for the sheriff. He would come again, surely, and not by car but like a snake. They knew what he had done to the other five, and he knew they knew. Uncle Rumbles' stomach concurred. That was how it was with the whites, said Wesley Scout: when they began a thing, good or bad, they finished it. That was how it was with Geronimo, he seemed to remember. Lies About His Age twined his braids reflectively. There was something wrong with that one, that sheriff, he added, something wrong.

24

To be certain they knew the prodigal son was coming and would assemble to greet him Bitter Boy pushed on the horn button a mile out of the village and held it down across the dry wash as he roared and blared and rattled into Mouse Sits. But when he released the button the horn continued to blow, a stricken, tremulous moo like that of a cow separated from her calf, and while he tried both to steer and unstick the button he bawled past the well and the Council and drove bumper-deep into the junkpile, which shuddered at the impact and erupted a sewing machine, an oil drum, and a cascade of pop bottles. Frenziedly he jumped out of the car and threw up the hood and yanked at every wire he could see, cutting both horn and engine. He stood erect and at bay, challenging anyone to smile, then smiled himself. He had created a sensation. Mouse Sits was agog. And Staff Sergeant Claude Walkingstick was home from the war.

No one could decide which to marvel at first, his appearance or his transportation. Bitter Boy's battle jacket was a spectrum of achievement—a Distinguished Service Cross, a Silver Star, a Bronze Star, a Good Conduct Medal, the European Theater ribbon with four campaign stars, the Combat Infantry badge, the stripes of a staff sergeant, hash marks for his length of service, the Thirteenth Infantry Division patch, and over his shoulder the golden rope of the Croix de Guerre. His cap with its blue piping was a halo over one ear and he wore gleaming paratrooper boots. Equally as remarkable as his car was the fact that a Moencopa youth of twenty had one. It was a 1933 Ford convertible coupe with a V-8 engine and splayed wire wheels and recapped tires. It had the frame for a top although the fabric was missing, as were three hubcaps and a rear fender. Its color was purple and green and black and rust. But it ran, he had demonstrated that, and they marveled at him and then at it and then at him again and all at once he threw his cap in the air and let out a war whoop:

"Hello goddammit!"

The tension broke in laughter. He shook hands with the old men and squeezed the old ladies and patted the children on their heads. He asked after his parents, Ramon and Betty Walkingstick, and was told they were working in the fields near Chandler but would return next week. He asked after Tony Jones, and was informed of Tony's death. In his three years' absence Bitter Boy had never had a letter from Mouse Sits and had never written one, but they had known he was alive for no telegram had come from Washington, nor any ten thousand dollars. From a barracks bag he distributed presents—candy bars and packs of cigarettes and spools of thread, and as a joke for Peppertail, bright red panties emblazoned with a sinking battleship and the motto "Remember Pearl Harbor!" He looked about him eagerly. He was amazed to find Tansie Scout a young lady. He was glad to see the outhouse standing firm, to learn the well was usable again. How healthy and happy everyone looked, he said, grinning at them. So did he. At twenty he was no taller than the older men, but he was lean and fit and soldierly, and unlike their round faces his was sharp-boned. His hair was the same weapon-black but he swept a comb through it frequently and nervously. And he smoked and swore. He wanted to shock them, to show how much the Army had Americanized him. "Hey, you know where I been? It'ly!"

Bitter Boy installed himself on the top of his car seat and propped his boots on the dashboard and while the children perched on the three fenders and the old ones made an audience on the junkpile he recounted his war experiences, from his assignment as a rifleman with the Thirteenth Infantry to the landing at Salerno in southern Italy to the taking of Naples and Rome and Florence to the crossing of the Po River. He stilled the children. He engrossed the ears of his elders. No one from Mouse Sits had ever ventured farther than Los Angeles.

"Did you see the salt?" Lies About His Age inquired. "On the beach?"

"All I saw was blood," said Bitter Boy. "Blood and bodies and the guns goin' boom! Boom! Boom!" Everyone jumped. He lit a cigarette and blew a stream of epic smoke. "I'm a hero," he said modestly. "See these ribbons? You should of seen me in Vaca this morning. I bought this car there, cost me a hundred and fifty dollars cash. I'm rich—look at this!" He pulled out a wallet and spread it to display the bills inside. "I've still got a hundred and seventy-five left, you get three hundred dollars musterin'-out pay. I walked up and down the street in Vaca and the whites shook hands with me and the sher'ff, he took me right into Coye's bar and right up to the bar and bought me a drink of whiskey—goddam, white man buyin' an Indian a drink! My relatives," said Staff Sergeant Claude Walkingstick, "I am on the GI ball. I'm a vet'ran now, I can get a real job with a sal'ry like the whites. This soldier's never goin' to pick cotton, he's never goin' back to the blanket—who in hell's that?"

Tansie Scout had slipped away and brought from somewhere two strangers with blond hair and blue eyes, two youths his own age. It seemed to be great fun for her to push them up beside the car. "Say, hero," she said, "how 'bout you meetin' the enemy? Here's a couple German prisoners."

Bitter Boy shot to his feet.

"No BS," she said. "They escaped from their camp up to Phoenix and they're stayin' here."

"Krauts? Krauts!" Claude Walkingstick did not know how to act. The swagger went out of him. His face worked. He leaped out of his car and backed away from the enemy, around the junkpile where no one could see him. "That's a goddam swell thing!" he shouted over the appliances and auto parts. "I been shootin' at krauts for two years and they been shootin' at me and I get home and Jesus Christ!"

He heard Duchess, his grandmother, tell the Germans not to mind him, and he glimpsed Alice Walkingstick give Tansie a whack on the backside, but his homecoming was spoiled and the villagers dispersed while Bitter Boy, a gaping wound in his vanity, stalked away to the house of his parents. He spent part of the afternoon trying to get his car started, unsuccessfully since he had no more mechanical knack than his tribesmen, and the rest of it listening to mystical, long-winded explanations and justifications of the Germans' presence from his elders. In the end he understood the how of their coming, but he gave up on the why. To be Americans, his achin' back! Either they were crazy in the head or it was some kind of plot to make a fool of him.

That evening Bitter Boy was persuaded to go up on the mountain to watch the sun set. He sulked. And when the rasp of a car starter pierced him, he dashed down again. He approached the coupe as though it were booby-trapped. He peered under the hood. Someone had reconnected the ignition wires and he knew who. He started the engine himself, raced it, backed away from the junkpile, and parked under a tamarisk. After dark he took a bottle of wine out of his trunk and sat in the car drinking and building up compression. Tamper with his property, would they; try to be asshole buddies with a US sergeant, would they. When he had polished off half the bottle he went to the daub house where they bunked, walked around it several times, loudly, then stood in the doorway. They were awake in there and he was tight. "I must of shot fifty krauts in It'ly," he announced. He waited. "I know you're in there, I can smell krauts. OK, sons of the Moencopa, what's your name?"

"Teege, Matthe."

"Pomtow, Albert."

"Who's been foolin' with my car?"

"Pomtow. Also it is losing oil from the pan. A new *Dichtung* you need—how do you say—a gasket."

Bitter Boy entered the house and sat down on the earthen floor away from them. "They snowed me good in Vaca, sellin' me that car, didn't they?"

"*Jawohl*, partner."

"But you thought you were goin' to the Apaches, didn' you? So we both got snowed." He drank, sloshing the bottle so that they would know what he had and was not sharing.

123

"We are not sorry now. Your people we—we esteem. This is a fine village. Teege."

"The Mouse? Don' crap me, buddy. This place is jus' as piss-poor-pitiful as when I left three years ago. More dust on the player piano, bigger junkpile, that's all. Ol' Tohi-i'itoi's gone AWOL, I guess. I'm pullin' out myself any day. When you guys?"

"When the prisoner camp it is closed."

"An' doin' what?"

"I will a cowboy be. Pomtow."

"I do not know. But for a time work here, a man of the West. The mountains I like and the space. It is mighty country. It is the most ex—expectant of all countries. Teege."

"You guys are shell-shocked. No wonder you lost the goddam war. What outfit were you?"

"Afrika Korps."

Bitter Boy lit a cigarette and inhaled to his paratrooper boots. "I started pickin' cotton when I was ten. My folks, they still are, always will be. Not this soldier. Day I was seventeen I signed up for the Army and got the hell out. I'm a GI now, and I'm not goin' back to the blanket."

"That saying, what is its meaning?"

"They send you to school, then they won't hire you because you're a stinkin' Indian. So you go back to the reservation, to the blanket, the whites say. That's what they really want anyway—good for the tourist bus'ness." He came to his haunches. "You guys like to hear how I got this DSC? For killin' krauts. I was point on my squad, near Velletri goin' up to Rome, an' aroun' the corner of a house I ran into five krauts. I shot three from the hip an' broke one's head with my M1 butt an' stuck a bayonet into one's guts up to the front sight. An' the other medals I got the same way so don't try buddyin' up to me! I hate krauts but I thank those dead ones—they're my ticket out of here!"

He let that sink in, enjoying their silence, then sat back again with his wine. "Gasket for the oil pan, Pomtow, you said?"

"Yes."

"I get one, you'll put it on?"

"Gladly."

"You guys want some wine?"

"No, *danke schön.*"

Bitter Boy groaned. "Why'd you have to be here when I came home? Why'n hell don't you go back where you came from?"

Albert answered for them. "For us, there is nothing. As it is here for you, *Kamerad*."

"Christ on a crutch, what's for you here?" Bitter Boy shouted at them. "Or any of these cigar-store Indians? Mouse Sits—where the shy little violets grow in shit!" Claude Walkingstick's mouth was foul with profanity. His heart was tainted with despair and insult and boast and the cheap wine of hatred. His voice thickened. "OK, OK, I'll tell you. It's the truth. Why I killed so many Germans was because—because they looked like Americans. Because they were white. And if you shot up some Americans yourselves, you know what that makes us. Brothers. Bloody goddam brothers."

25

The wheat was cut with sickles and carried by the armload to a flat place and heaped about a sturdy upright post. Hitched abreast, the inside animal tied to the post by a rope, three horses plodded round and round and as the rope shortened, the grain was threshed from the outer edge of the circle to the center. One old man walked behind the horses to drive them while another raked the wheat stalks evenly over the ground. Winnowing waited on a windy day. Then the grain was placed in large open baskets and tossed until the chaff had blown away. The old ladies whipped the beans to shell them, and sifted out the husks. They cut the squash and pumpkins into long strips and hung them up to dry. Corn they roasted in the ear and later shelled and stored in ollas. Between the deaths of these moons it was November, the Month of Pleasant Cold, the proudest, happiest time of the year, the harvest time. What they threshed and shelled and roasted and put away for the winter would not sustain them two weeks, but the symbolism of the harvest cheered them. The whites could not steal the sun, they smiled. They could not put a stopper in a rainy sky. And for a moment it was with the Moencopa as it had been in the long years. They toiled in the manner of their ancestors, reaping what they had sown in their own harsh soil. They were freedmen.

There were many things to do besides. The children kept a lookout from the mountain against surprise by the deputy sheriff. The old women cooked and baked in preparation for the fiesta which would celebrate completion of the harvest. And it was well they had a modest harvest, for the middle-generation Walkingsticks and Scouts and Joneses came more often now from the fields around Phoenix where they worked less and at lower wages, since prisoners from the camp there, Germans by the hundreds, they said, were available to employers. It was unfair. The war with them had been over almost seven months, yet no one seemed to know when they would go. Matthe taught the children, sometimes with Tansie's help, usually without. Hampelmann worked on Bitter Boy's runs-by-itself. He replaced the leaky gasket, he patched the muffler; he adjusted the timing, cleaned the points and spark plugs; he unearthed in the junkpile three tires with better tread than those already on the car. Bitter Boy lurked about, uncertain whether to envy or deprecate or thank. A hero, he took no hand in the harvest or the repairs. He had more important missions. Spinning his wheels and bellowing exhaust fumes he drove off first to hire a fiddler from Goat Drink and a guitar player from Too Many Ants, and later to buy from a bootlegger in Taft several gallons of wine at three times the store price, an extortion to be endured since even the possession of liquor by Indians was a jailable offense. The night of the fiesta neared.

Wato posts were wound with crepe-paper streamers. A dance ground was swept, and benches placed around it.

The foster sons of the village had their blond hair cut by Josie Miles.

In the afternoon the workers returned. Children were bathed and dressed in their best. The men, even the old men, appeared in rainbow western shirts, their boots polished. The ladies, even those of advanced years, made entrances in bright calico and percale and head scarves of daring colors. At dark, lights were snapped on under the watos and the tables set to sagging with the most lavish

126

banquet of the year—chili, tamales, bananas and apples and bologna, tortillas, chick-peas, beans, soda pop and meat stew and wheat buns and ice cream on a stick.

Soon, out of the desert on foot, the fiddler and guitar player arrived, took places, tuned up and struck up "You Are My Sunshine," two little girls pulled two little boys onto the dance ground, and the fiesta began. There was a pattern of revelry. You had some wine, you danced, you ate for once all you wanted, you had more wine, you danced, you ate again. The fiddler stamped his foot and sawed out polkas and schottisches and reels, but whatever the music the Indians danced their own adapted fox-trot, heads close together, faces intent, the man's arm grasping his partner tightly round the neck. The old folk were spry, their sons and daughters vigorous, the children hugged each other and bobbed about between the adult couples, the music was merry, the lights bright, the streamers gay, the wine warming, and Mouse Sits was happy. Tansie Scout wanted Matthe to dance with her. He was diffident, he said he did not know how. It was not easy to refuse her. That she wear only the plain muslin dress her mother had insisted, but either she had fattened up or the dress had shrunk, for it was skintight. She had sneaked some lipstick, too, and drawn her hair into a tail with a strip of Hopi beadwork. To make him jealous she danced with Bitter Boy and wiggled her behind at Matthe, who went stiff-backed to have some wine. Bitter Boy, who had drunk more than anyone, and who was aware that she had asked the German first, was rough with her. Still in uniform he danced Army, his arm about her waist, and pulled her hips to his. He was high and taut.

"I saw you. You won't get him, Tans. I know what you want, to run off with him when he goes, but he won't take you. You're Copa, he's white." Joe John Jones was dancing with Duchess Walkingstick.

"You speakin' to me, soldier?"

"Say, you're a big girl now, Tans. I can feel."

"I can kick. I'm goin' by myself someday, all the way to California. I'll swim in the ocean and see where they make movies." Wesley Scout was dancing strenuously with Josie Miles, who flirted, and General Miles disapproved.

"Go with me? I got a car and money and the whites'll give me a job. I'm a hero."

"That'll be the day, they give you a job." Uncle Rumbles was eating.

"Hell they won't. I got the ribbons. I could drive into Vaca or Taft or anywhere and get one. Gover'ment'll pay while I'm learnin' it, that's what they do for vet'rans. On-the-job trainin' it's called or somethin'."

"Seein's believin'. Take your hand off my fanny." He stuck his tongue in her ear.

"How 'bout shackin' up with me, Tans?" The fiddler bowed into "Don't Fence Me In."

"Blow it out your B-bag. I can read and write and I'm not goin' back to the blanket either. Pickin' cotton and havin' babies and slappin' tortillas."

"S'pos'n I love you, goddammit?"

"S'pos'n they give this country back to the Indians?"

"Listen, Tans, I need somebody to talk to. Tony's dead and you and me, we're the only Americans around here now. Those Germans are OK krauts, I guess, but you kill them for two years, how can you be friends? Tans, I'm lonesome. I bet we could make it. Love, I mean."

"Bed, you mean."

"Don't be so stuck-up. I heard what you been doin' up in Phoenix. But I don't mind. Somebody else does the threshin', I'll eat the wheat." Charles Lindbergh Scout, age eleven, had been made to dance with his sister, age five.

"I wouldn't sleep with you or marry you, Claude Walkingstick, you were the last thing in pants!"

"Oh yeah? They weren't so goddam choosy in It'ly!"

"Who?"

"The whores!" She brought her knee up between his legs, into his groin, fiercely. Bitter Boy let go of her and bent over in pain.

When, having had some wine and willing now to try the dancing, Matthe returned to look for Tansie Scout, she was nowhere to be seen. But to the lilt and strain of "Roll Out the Barrel," the fiesta was at full blast. Two couples were the center of attention, Lies About His Age and Alice Walkingstick, Hampelmann and Rita, or Peppertail, Jones. They were doing a gavotte. So lightly did Lies foot it that Alice could not chew. Hampelmann's arms and legs were inspired. With such abandon did he twirl the Peppertail that her skirts were raised upon the bright red panties and the debacle at Pearl Harbor.

Richter left the dance ground. Among the houses, alone with his thoughts he wandered. How fortunate that these people could forget their cares for a night, their hand-to-mouth subsistence, and celebrate a meager harvest. There was a certain wisdom in it, he decided. They might one day inherit the earth, but against that vague pledge it was prudent of them to store up such simple pleasures as they could. Away from the dancing and feasting the night was chill. He thrust his hands into his pockets, yet they did not warm. It was not the night but something else which chilled him. He was passing the mud house in which he and Albert were billeted when something suggested that he go inside.

He did. He was not alone. As he tensed and reached for the light bulb, someone rushed past him out the door, running. It was Tansie Scout.

He found the light, turned it on, and as the bulb swung saw that his tuba case was open, his belongings strewn. Quickly he went through them. The square black box was open. It was gone—the jewel of shame he had purchased at Sidi bou Zid, the coal of hell he had carried smoldering halfway round the world. She had stolen his Iron Cross.

He ran outside, knowing even in his wrath where she would hide, ducking between the trees to the base of the slanting tree. Up the great tamarisk he climbed, hauling himself limb by limb. Near the top he slowed, recalling what she could do to his head with her sandal. He paused, turned, planted his feet on two diverging limbs, and leaning back groped above him.

Nothing. Light from the village suffused the improbable play-world of the tree. Child-music serenaded.

Then she was on him. Tiring of the hide-and-seek, she sprang along one of the limbs on which he stood and pounced upon him and bore him back against the trunk. She kissed him on the mouth, the chin, the nose.

"Give me," he ordered.

"Find it!"

She took his hands and teased them up and down her breasts, her ribs, her back, as though to hint that she had pinned the medal somewhere underneath her dress. "Here. Here. No, here!"

129

Then it was not a dress. It was not coarse muslin but a fairy fabric, heated, living, precious. Her skin. For she slid the dress above her bare hips.

"German, German," she purred.

"Do not, *ach*, do not," he groaned.

But her hands fluttered, opening his trousers, tugging down his shorts. It was a disgrace, and dangerous in a tree, and impossible. He would lose balance. They would fall. She had no right. He fought her. Bracing himself against the tree, he remembered the other tree.

That he had put his arms about the night they escaped. Being weary to his soul of playing the superman, infallible and pure. Of waiting and weighing and reserving judgment, of being Richter. Of saying no.

For the second time, Matthe Teege surrendered.

To her flesh she grafted him. About his neck her arms notched. A thigh curved about his hip.

Truth might be in the reassurance of a tree.

His hands lifted and close-coiled her.

Let me be young as my years.

His loins drummed.

Let me say yes, not no. Let me kill no more, but instead love.

Her small supple body was a notched, curved scraping stick drawn over his with rapid, primitive motion.

Let me to *Amerika* myself give.

She made magic. His body became the tree, hers the lightning.

He was riven.

Tansie clung to him. And as he let her down he made a basket of his arms and cradled her high in their tree because she was so small, so wanton, so savage and so dear. He pressed his face into the wing of her hair.

"*Ach Gott*, my Miss America."

"Told you so," she whispered. "Told you we could be in love. Love me?"

"It may be. I am so, so gratitude."

"I'm crazy for you, no crap." She kissed his mouth, his chin, his nose, making little chirps with her lips. "Want to Indian-marry me?"

"What is that?"

"We don't have weddings and that stuff. I guess they used to, when the priests were around, but not now, costs money. Like in the old days I just take you to my house and screw you silly for three nights and then everybody knows we're married and I go live with you."

"I would not."

"How come?"

"When I marry it will be in a church, and official."

"I'd like that." Tansie hugged him. "Oh I'm so crazy-mad-crazy for you. When you leave, take me with you?"

"How may I, *Liebchen?* Do you not love me, or make me love you. I am no one, I have nothing, not even a country."

"You take me, dammit. Don't you see I don't have a prayer here?"

"Yes."

"Well then?"

Pitying her, Matthe despised himself for his weakness. They had made magic in a tree, but he could not spit the evil voices from his confusion. White man and squaw. Lay an Indian it's like you're winnin' the West all over again. You're back in the saddle an' the bugle's blowin' an' you're layin' her for Old Glory.

"How 'bout it?"

The voices he must still, must refute. "I will try," he said.

"Promise?"

"I promise."

"Prove it."

"How?"

"Let me keep it, 'stead of a ring. That medal."

"Where is it?"

"Here." She brought his hands to the hollow of her bosom. The Iron Cross was pinned there, under the muslin.

"Why did you take it?"

"I lost my 'dentification bracelet. Some sailor gave it to me, I don't even know his name. So I wanted somethin' all my own. Know what I mean?"

"Yes. As do I want something."

"And now you got me. So can I keep it?"

"Yes."

His touch whetted her again. The nipples of her breasts were arrow points. "You sexy kraut."

"*Tanslein, Tanslein.*"

To take the village unawares, they had walked the horses up the bed of the Sonoita, heading toward the lights fitful through the tamarisks and toward the music of the fiesta. He gathered them there—Coye, Buster, Doc, Hamp, Lloyd, Joe Mack, Tate—and recapitulated what he'd said earlier that evening in Coye's bar. It was the principle of the thing. When you sprayed a field for bollworm, you sprayed all of it. When you got on the pot, you used it or got off. He knew they felt likewise. As far as he could find out from the FBI, every POW in the country was accounted for but these three from No. 80 Camp. The war with Germany was supposed to have ended six months ago, but as far as he was concerned, it wasn't over as long as a single Nazi was running around loose. He knew they felt likewise. They'd got the five, which left three to go. The Moencopa were hiding them out, he knew it, and he intended to push them a little. When you got an Indian down you'd better keep him there, in his place, the white men in Arizona had learned that quite a while back. So get ready to ride. Remember, no one was to be hurt. The Council was what they were after. He had no idea what was in it, but get the Council and you took the tucker out of them. No use trying to flush the POWs either, there wouldn't be time. All he wanted was for them to step on the Mouse's tail a little. Then it would know for sure it had damn well better do what it was told or next time have its balls under a boot. So let's go, boys, let's make the Mouse squeak.

They masked faces with bandannas, they lit the torches, which were rags wound upon sticks and drenched with gasoline. They mounted up and spurred the animals out of the riverbed into the village. When the eight riders reached the well, hooves cracking on the rocky ground, they pulled revolvers and began firing in the air and yelling. Circling the Council according to plan, they threw torches at it from all sides, onto the roof and through the doorway. The tinder-dry cactus ribs of the walls, exposed for years where the daub had crumbled away, and of the roof where earth had washed, caught at once, and within moments the structure blazed.

But accident altered the plan. Backing from the fire, one horse struck a corner of the house of Lies About His Age and a section of the wall caved in. So flimsy were the wattle-and-daub dwellings that the weight of a horse would bring them down. The discovery meant that they might test their horsemanship at a new sport—better yet, that they might take out the revenge the guilty always wreak upon the innocent. And boys, they would later laugh, would be boys. Shouting excitement, the riders gigged their mounts sideways into the other walls until the entire house collapsed, walls crashing into debris and roof down upon the debris. Next they destroyed Alice Walkingstick's house nearby. The adobe houses they could not damage, but in any case, the horses were by now unmanageable. Gunfire and bruising and the cries of women and children terrorized them. Out of control the maddened beasts bolted. One galloped across the dance ground and tore down two watos, smashing tables and benches and dishes and sending food flying. Masked men hanging on, the horses charged in several directions, trampling over the edges of the junkpile, bucking into trees, scattering the villagers in panic. The storm passed, the raid was over, the fiesta finished, in four or five minutes.

Mouse Sits did not squeak. Emerging silently from the adobe houses and the tamarisks, children clinging to their parents, the population converged upon the Council. Miraculously, no one had been injured. The fiddler from Goat Drink examined the splintered shell of his instrument. The Indians stood in groups and watched as flames consumed the Council and with it all the sacred things it held—scalp trophies, bows and eagle feathers, swastika flag, calendar stick, telegram from Washington, player piano, and perhaps most fittingly, the three old rifles, the last means of defense. With them stood the tall, disheveled youth who had crawled out of the ruins of Alice Walkingstick's house, out from beneath the bed where she had hidden him, and his sturdy, reticent companion, who had come down out of a tree. The Germans waited. From the women they expected sorrow, even lamentation perhaps; from the men the natural reaction of anger at such an outrage. Wrecking houses had been spur-of-the-moment sport. Putting the Council to the torch, however, was an uprooting, an emasculation, a deliberate plunder of identity itself.

Victor Scout raised another relic Springfield. "My relatives, when

133

they came I went into my house for this, but I couldn't find the cartridges. I've got some somewhere." Everyone understood. "My father got this gun after the other war," he added. "To hunt deer. Now the deer, they're gone. They don't have enough water."

Everyone understood except the German and Bitter Boy. He paced up and down hitting a fist into his palm, his ribbons gleaming martially. He wanted to berate the people for cowardice, to describe what he, a hero, a warrior, would do in their place, but one of his elders was about to speak.

"This is how the Apaches used to come in the long years," Wesley Scout said. "By the moon. I don't remember much about it, but they wanted food and horses and our women."

"These men are sick. They have to show us who's boss," said Ramon Walkingstick. "We know who is, but they have to show us and show us. I'm sorry for them."

The foster sons of the village could not believe their ears. The roof of the Council sank with a sigh and a lovely display of sparks.

"I'm ninety-eight years old," complained Lies About His Age, "and now I don't even have a house."

"Me either," Alice Walkingstick reminded him. She pulled one of his braids. "It must be a sign from Elder Brother. Old man, we better marry up, I guess, and live with the General and Josie. I'll cook for you and you can keep me warm at night. I damn near freeze at night."

Everyone smiled. Matthe Teege and Albert Pomtow finally understood. The talking, the reminiscence, the smiles—these were the masks the Indians put on as the horsemen had been masked. Dejection and fear they covered with chatter, resolution with a joke. It was the Moencopa way. Catastrophe and abuse were kin to them, domination like drought their natural lot, but if their forebears had survived these things, they in their turn would. Underneath the brown firelit faces they hid an amulet of fortitude uniquely their own. It made them indomitable. It was the iron cross of character.

"*Meine Damen und Herren,* I am sorry," Hampelmann said impulsively. "But damn fine *Soldaten* are you all."

Richter addressed himself to the men of the middle generation. "I also am sorry. For this we have the blame. You are absolute friends, but we cannot ask any more. We will go away now. When we are absent, they will not again harm this village. We will go tonight."

Victor and Manuel Scout and Ramon Walkingstick and Grover Jones shook their heads. "No," said Grover Jones. "We gave our word."

"That'd be worse than losin' a piano," said Victor Scout. "They can go to hell."

"If we have to, we'll keep you in a cave," said Ramon Walkingstick. "We can still take care of our own."

"They better not come back here," warned Manuel Scout. "I've got another gun somewhere. And I'll buy some cartridges."

Emotions were too close to the surface. Everyone was embarrassed. "There's still plenty of that food left," Uncle Rumbles announced, breaking indefatigable wind.

Toward morning, when the village was fast asleep, the two Germans climbed the mountain to the lookout. Here the children kept vigil during the day, here Matthe and Tansie Scout had come one afternoon. It was a good place for perspective. Neither had rested well. In his dreams, Hampelmann had danced a gavotte to the caterwauling of a splintered violin. Talking in his sleep, Richter had waked them both with a discourse upon responsibility and obligation. Up here, even the stars reproved them. To the north, below Polaris, the sky seemed phenomenally pale with what might have been the glow of Phoenix, intensified by the wall of light about the perimeter of No. 80 Camp. "When will it close?" Matthe muttered, "when?"

Vaca they could tell by a feeble lambency along what must have been its main street. "Verdammt town," Albert growled. "Ach, if here we had that Mark IV, and shells, and you would drive and I would the cannoneer be and into that town the desert foxes would again roll!"

Matthe wondered why the villagers could not go to Casa Buena, to the government, and report their ill-treatment. He had himself asked Bitter Boy about that, Albert said. The trip would not be worth the gasoline. No one could identify the riders, and in a local court it would be the white man's oath against the Indian's. "The Krautfange," he reflected. "The same ones tonight, only now it is our necks they will have. What monsters they must be."

Matthe said he had given them much thought. "Not monsters, or at the first they were not. Men too old to be soldiers, I think they are. So they played to be soldiers. When they caught Buchting and Ehlert and the others and gave the Holy Ghost, they were here, in Arizona, helping fight the war. Now the atrocities they enjoy, the being soldiers, and they cannot stop. They must always have war, and violence always. You have seen it with the SS in the camp. It is so with some men in every country."

To thaw himself, Hampelmann galloped in place and wrapped his arms about himself. "And back they will come for us again, riding and shooting and everything smashing until nothing is there left of the Mouse but the outhouse." He stopped. "*Ist das nicht* a land of dreams?" he said to himself, breathing hard. "Matthe?"

"What?"

"Have we made a mistake? To be Americans?" he appealed.

"Do not ask."

"And to the Indians coming?"

"Please do not ask. But if we cause, if we one more thing bring upon these people, we will go from them. A harmless dog is dead, and this wrong tonight. There must not be more."

26

But there was more. Two weeks blurred by, unintelligible markings on a calendar stick. Then a little girl on afternoon lookout raced pell-mell down the mountain calling in Moencopa. By the time someone had translated for the Germans, Staff Sergeant Claude Walkingstick had found Victor Scout's old rifle, bridled a horse, and with as much commotion as a troop of cavalry charged out of the corral toward the south end of the mountain.

A man walking in the desert, the child said breathlessly, a man walking toward Mexico!

The Germans started at once down the dry wash. Who the man

might be, who he had to be, Matthe knew in his bowels. They were to be punished for overstaying their leave. Sins they had never committed were to be visited upon them as they had imposed themselves upon the compassion of the Indians.

They met near the cottonwoods. Riding triumphant, Bitter Boy herded his quarry before him. Except for sunburn and gray smatters in the red bristle of his hair the Nuremberger had changed little. Out of the bulk of him, out of a sweat-stained sport shirt and gray civilian trousers extruded that square head without a neck, that block of stubbled face and the tight ears, blistered by sun. His eyes recognized them, took from files certain military data, checked it, returned it to the files, went blank. Once an Oberfeldwebel, always an Oberfeldwebel.

"Attention!" he demanded.

The order seemed to derange Albert Pomtow. He hurled himself at the man like a comic acrobat.

One paw, one formidable forearm swung and slapped him across the face and tumbled him into a welter of arms and legs over the sand. It was rather like a bear cuffing a giraffe.

Sniffing blood from the nose, crying, "Murderer! Willi you killed!" Hampelmann scrambled up and would have attacked again had Matthe not prevented him.

Otto Skubovius frowned. "Let the clown keep his hands off an NCO. Well, well. Teege and Pomtow."

"You know each other!" Bitter Boy exclaimed. "Old buddies!"

"No, buddies not," Matthe said. "This is a Nazi, by name Otto Skubovius, and was in the camp our master sergeant. He killed our friend."

"What do you say?" Skubovius asked.

"That you killed Willi Loffelbein, our friend," Matthe said in German.

"Eighteen he was, eighteen!" Albert howled. "To him we were *alles!*"

The Oberfeldwebel ignored the outburst. "Loffelbein? Loffelbein. *Ja,* that good, brave, stupid boy. But I have not harmed him. He was escaping from the camp with someone, and I needed also to go, I wanted only *Kameraden.* Therefore I asked him who and to where and he would not say, in a most friendly way I asked him. So I escaped by myself, through the wire. A very close scrape it was, bullets like flies because some guard in the tower opened up with his machine gun. You say he is dead? What a pity. What happened?"

"He was hung by the neck in the latrine, you murderer!" Albert screamed at him.

"And this is where you would come, of course. The foxes of the desert to the desert, and young foxes to the *Indianer*, as in the storybooks. How logical. The camp—have you heard, is it closed?"

"No."

"*Verdammt Amerikaner!* To keep our boys so long. *Wohl,* we will one day repay them, eh?"

"I've had enough kraut talk," Bitter Boy interrupted. "I'm taking this joker into Vaca. Might be a reward on him."

"You cannot," Matthe said.

"Why the hell not?"

"Because he would inform. At the camp he would inform that we are here and the Government would come, not the Army, the Government."

"*Mein Gott,* yes," Albert said, slipping out of Matthe's grasp. "So what can we do but execute him? How logical! Give me the gun!"

Skubovius understood enough English to smile. "That is right, you cannot give me to the police. Very well, we will come to an agreement." In complete command of himself, he addressed them as though they were a formation drawn up in the yard of First Stockade. "I have had a long hike in this wilderness, four nights from Phoenix. Here I must be close to the border. Therefore supply me with water and food and you go your way and I go mine."

"*Nein,*" Matthe said.

"*Nein?* How do you say *nein,* you bastard?" demanded the Oberfeldwebel.

"Somebody make up his goddam mind," said Claude Walkingstick.

"Shoot him! Shoot him!" Albert shouted. "Permit me!"

"We will take him to the village," Richter decided.

"It's your ass in a sling, not mine," Bitter Boy grinned. He pointed the Springfield. "OK, kraut, get the lead out, move it."

Skubovius inspected the gun, scanned the decorations on the rider's jacket.

"*Marsch!*" Albert shouted.

138

They put him in the sickness hut. The workers were gone, but the old folk and the children buzzed excitedly about the hut, peeping through the cracks at the man inside. Some food was brought him, and water, and Bitter Boy stood gallant guard, amazing the children by doing the manual of arms with his weapon. Matthe could do nothing with Albert except to forbid him to come near the hut. The real Reichsführer was *kaputt,* Albert ranted; why should they not purge the world of the Führer of the Fourth Reich? Taking the old men of the Council aside, Matthe had equal difficulty explaining why the Moencopa should not offer their hospitality and protection to this prisoner. He was a German, yes, but an evil German.

General Miles had a suggestion. "We could dance. I feel pretty good. We could spit up his evil."

"You're gettin' so old you forget," Wesley Scout sniffed. "Our sticks and rattles—everything's burned up."

"He is wicked as the sheriff is wicked," Matthe told them. "This we have discussed, how there are in every people some—some, unworthy. But not all."

"All Apaches are," corrected Joe John Jones.

"You want us to take him to Vaca, to that Thode?" asked Lies About His Age.

"No, we cannot do that." And Matthe had to make plain their predicament, why Skubovius did not deserve to be given sanctuary across the border and why, at the same time, he could not be turned over to the authorities. When he was finished, the village elders gazed at the sky, the trees, the ashes of the Council, the ruins of the two daub houses, and since this was a matter upon which no agreement was possible, also examined their bare, horny toes.

"I'd shoot him," advised Uncle Rumbles. "Can we watch?"

"We cannot either do that."

"Then I guess we don't know," said Lies. "Anything you do is OK with us. Does he have any cigarettes?"

Matthe went to the sickness hut, relieved Bitter Boy, and crawled inside, keeping the old rifle at the ready. In German he asked the Oberfeldwebel, who lay dozing, entirely impervious to the curious stares slanting through the cracked walls, where he had hidden out since his escape. He had lived with a laundress in Phoenix, Skubovius said, a Mexican woman he met in the American officers' laundry at the camp. She kept her mouth shut while his money lasted, then moved out on him five days ago, taking his pistol for good measure, the whore. Why, Matthe wanted to know, unless he had executed Willi and feared reprisal by the Afrika Korps that night of the riot, why had he troubled to escape from No. 80 when, in a few months, he would be shipped back to the *Heimatland?*

"I am going to *Südamerika.*"

"Why?"

"It is pleasant there, they tell me. Beautiful women, good beer, and many *Deutscher.*"

"Besides Willi, what were your other crimes in the Wehrmacht, your other atrocities? In the SS, the SD?"

"I have been a good soldier, nothing more."

"I do not believe you."

The master sergeant shrugged. "Why are you not over the border yourself? Why do you live with these barbarians, these Indians? Surely you would not remain in the United States?"

"We—we like it here."

"Among the Jews? I do not believe you." The Bavarian sat up. "So we are even. You cannot give me to the *Amerikaner,* I would inform. You will not kill me, you are too pure. Therefore give me supplies, Teege, and let me get to Mexico."

"No."

"Why not?"

"To let you go into the world? One like you? To this country it would be a crime, and to Deutschland, to all people. And I have already been enough criminal." He began to crawl backward out of the hut.

"Teege, I swear it. I did not hang Loffelbein."

"It may be."

"What will you do with me?"

"I do not know."

"*Verdammt* Afrika Korps!"

The old men idled outside the hut listening to Bitter Boy relate how he had rounded up the kraut. He would not stand guard any more, he told Matthe, the kraut was no longer his sweat. When the elders asked Matthe what he had decided, he scowled. Lies About His Age advised him to fast that evening and think about it through the night; that was how the Moencopa had solved their problems, individual and tribal, in the long years. Hungry, sleepless, they waited for a dream, they had a vision, they made songs. Coyote would come to them with instructions, or Owl, or Bear, and whisper in their ear.

"We'll guard that enemy for you," offered Joe John Jones.

"Sometimes in the long years they'd catch an Apache," Wesley Scout recalled. "He'd be wounded and they'd help him heal before they killed him. They'd put him in a house and watch him. I believe that's what they did."

"I could not ask that," Matthe objected.

Lies About His Age put a hand on his shoulder. "My second son, let us do this. While we watch him you can be listening to Coyote."

"I'd like to guard him," General Miles said. "I'm up a lot nights anyways. I have to pee."

"Me too," said Uncle Rumbles. "My guts are very busy."

Matthe humored them. He had already determined to sleep on the disposition of Otto Skubovius. That evening he did not eat, and when it was dark, and the five old men had drawn lots for watches, the first sentry, Wesley Scout, took up proud vigil outside the entrance to the sickness hut, blanket wrapped about him as he sat cross-legged, rifle over his knees. Matthe himself lay under blankets beside Hampelmann on the mattress in their house. Albert racked himself out, rigid and obdurate. "Shoot him, shoot him," had been his sole response to Matthe's equivocation. "Willi he hung, Dreschler he killed like a pig, by bleeding, remember? *Herr im Himmel,* will you set free this Nazi murderer, others to slaughter? In all things I have followed you, Matthe, but this not. Shoot him, shoot him." Finally he would not utter another word. It was the first breach in their friendship. To assist Matthe's thought processes, Lies About His Age had brought to their house and spaced on the earthen floor several more Apache scalp-dolls. These, he asserted, might jump out of their baskets in the night and run about and summon up in the brain a lot of power.

A bit light-headed, Matthe Teege lay waiting in cold darkness, receptive. What was he to do with this Nazi, this black but human soul, Otto Skubovius? The evidence in, history's jury charged and having handed down its verdict, was the judge incapable of passing sentence? Richter twisted. He would for respite think of other things. It had been two weeks since the raid on the fiesta, two more weeks of siege. Tansie Scout tormented him with his promise

141

to take her off the reservation, bribing him with invitations to walk to the cottonwoods or to meet her in their tamarisk at night. When he refused, she pouted that he did not love her and called him Adolf and threatened to run away by herself to California as he had run away from his prison camp and sell his Iron Cross and make heap big money he knew damn well how. He could not blame her. Bitter Boy was alternately vindictive and cordial, taunting them with his exploits against the krauts and laying claim to their companionship. What was he to do with Skubovius? The two carloads of workers brought them one day from Phoenix a rumor that the POW camp would be abandoned by Christmas, and a few days later a second that the first was false. Feldmarschall Pomtow had mustered out his Moenkopa Korps. He moped about whistling "Bury Me Not on the Lone Prairie" through his buck teeth and drawing in the sand scale maps of Europe and the Atlantic Ocean and the USA which illustrated the remoteness of Arizona from East Prussia. Like poor damned-if-they-did-damned-if-they-didn't Indians they had begun to look and act themselves, observed Alice Walkingstick. Their hands and faces were brown as deer dung. They said little. They walked warily. Essaying humor, Hampelmann compared their plight to that of the Armee Gruppe Afrika during those last doomed days about Tunis, the sea at its back, the Allies before it in their might. The comparison did not amuse. To Matthe they were like the horses threshing. Round and round they plodded in an ever smaller circle, tethered by an ever shorter rope. What was he to do with Otto Skubovius?

They had sat on their hind ends in Mouse Sits for three months. Still they could not go. Yet they could not stay much longer. They had put their hosts, their friends, the villagers, in an intolerable position: between a patriotism which decreed that they hand over escaped prisoners to a justice which was unjust, and a humanity which pleaded that they violate the law by giving escaped prisoners refuge. It opposed duty and tradition. It perjured for the sake of truth. It exacted an eye of the sightless. Those in need of bread it required to become samaritans. Now they, or rather he, was ground upon the stone of a dilemma. He must decide what to do with Otto Skubovius. It was one thing to seek truth, but another to elect right action. Shoot him, shoot him. His mind made up, Albert snored. Anything you do is OK with us. Before the sickness hut an aged

Indian drowsed watch as he had done in the long years, secure in the faith that having fasted, having listened to the birds and animals, having been endowed with power by spirits of hair, the foster son of the Moencopa would rise in the morning with a solution. On your shoulders it is once more, said Matthe to himself, trying to meditate in English, once more the responsible. Like us, Skubovius cannot go yet cannot stay. If you grant him to cross the border, a pestilence upon the world you do, and unto this country, to which you would belong. You commit a treason. Yet if you to the law apprehend him, he will apprehend you, and they will come for us and take us away and the objective we have, free Americans to be, citizens, forever is lost.

What was that! The scalps?

I am hearing things. A little cracked I am also. As Tans*lein*. As the Bitter Boy.

Skubovius may have hung Willi, but it was you who killed him. With a wish. Two deaths are yours now, a boy's and a dog's. And more elsewhere. Will you, Richter, a murderer, judgment pass upon a murderer?

What would Parsifal do—dine on white dove? What would Siegfried do—start a fire?

Too old am I to be twenty-one.

Who is prisoner of whom? We Germans are prisoners of the Americans, and also of the Indians. The Indians are prisoners of the whites. Of their guilt the Americans are prisoners, and so of the Indians. Skubovius is a prisoner of the Americans, and now also of us Germans. But we also now are prisoners of Skubovius. And of our hope.

Teege, the Panzer Plato.

If Owl or Bear or Coyote appear, will they whisper in Bavarian? Land of dreams not. Land of nightmares.

We are soon coming to the sea, Matthe Karl Teege and Albert Anton Pomtow. May there be salt.

America, in the name of God, may you not betray us.

Dawn, and streaks of day which were the hairs pulled from Elder Brother's head, and from outside the mud house a long, long wail, piercing as an arrow, a single wail of grief and accusation.

27

It was Alice Walkingstick who stunned the village awake. From daub and adobe houses everyone rushed through the dawn to the sickness hut. Skubovius was gone. He had taken the rifle.

Tongue black, his eyeballs bulging in their sockets, Lies About His Age lay on his back. He had been strangled from the rear with his own braids, garroted rather, with such ferocity that the coils of hair were still crushed into the skin of his throat. Probably, having the last watch, the old man had fallen asleep. His death-visage did not become one so full of years and kindness. It was strangely similar to that of Willi Loffelbein when he had been discovered.

Between those standing about the body no words were exchanged, and there were no tears.

Alice Walkingstick, his wife, took Matthe by both arms and put her graven face close to his. "I made a sound!" she hissed. "We don't cry and we're not supposed to make a sound!" She trembled with grief and blasphemy and with the effort at self-control, the claws of her fingers digging into his arms. "Now I'll be cold!"

Even Bitter Boy stood mute. Matthe asked him to get the other rifle in the village, that of Manuel Scout, and cartridges. "He will go toward the border," he said quietly. "He is ahead of us, but we will ride and track him."

"I'm goin'. These are my people."

"But I have caused it. This is mine."

They made a burlesque war party, two German youths and a young Indian, silent and grim and riding southward down the sand and gravel path of the Sonoita on three spindleshanked nags they had bridled in the log corral. They rode bareback because there were no saddles. The horses they could neither incite nor rebuke beyond a trot. In Army uniform and cap and paratrooper boots and

144

carrying the ramshackle rifle, Staff Sergeant Claude Walkingstick took the lead, alert, following the shoeprints in the sand as though he were point man on an infantry patrol. So long were Hampelmann's legs that his feet locked under the belly of his mount. He did not reproach Matthe. Perhaps he was recalling other days and other rides, on cumbersome Belgian plowhorses along the road about Taplacken, with his boyhood friends pretending to be a Prussian posse in chase of a gang of desperadoes. And as for Matthe, he had never before except in imagination, except on knightly steeds in the Duisburger Wald, been on horseback. He clutched the reins. The gait of the malevolent beast under him seemed intended to jog him head over heels.

They rode to the end of the basalt mountain. Here the shoeprints left the dry wash, which angled to the southwest, and kept a compass course south across the desert, around saguaro cacti and staghorn and the paddle wheel. Butterflies sparkled. Ground squirrels, which had no trees to climb, whisked into their burrows. On the horizon an irregularity became a mound, then a small hill, and as they approached, they could see straight horizontal lines on this, the northern slope. Matthe inquired what they were. *Trincheras,* or entrenchments, was the Mexican word, said Bitter Boy; he didn't know the Indian. They were like fortifications, hand-heaped terraces of rock built on the sides of hills two or three hundred years ago by the ancestors of the Moencopa to defend themselves against the Apaches, who swooped down always from what was now northern Arizona and New Mexico.

"We better lead the horses," he warned. "If that kraut wants to see if anybody's followin' him, that's the place to look from. I know, some of us kids used to play up there. And if he sees us, he'll know we're gainin' and that's where he'll dig in. So watch it. From here on he could shoot our ass off."

They dismounted. They picked a tortuous way among the cactus until they were within four hundred meters of the hill, until they heard the report and Matthe's horse fell heavily, kicking, then relaxed, sighed almost blissfully, and was dead. They squatted by it. Bitter Boy lit a cigarette. The bullet had entered the animal diagonally, ripping entirely through its body from the left shoulder out the right ribs.

"You goddam krauts," said Bitter Boy, "you just can't stop killin'."

145

Matthe asked how many cartridges he had. "Two. One in the slot and this." He tossed the brass cylinder, caught it. "And this old cannon, Jesus. Barrel's fouled, prob'ly hasn't been fired in ten years. I wish I had a good old M1. Well, that's the Copa—one outhouse, one gun." Matthe asked how much ammunition the killer had. "Christ knows. These Springfields can be clip-fed, five rounds. Maybe he's got a clip, maybe not. Anyway, he's got one less now." He inhaled deeply and disposed of the cigarette with a mock-heroic flick. "Well, men, this is it, here I go."

"No," Matthe said. "I am going. If I had executed him yesterday this would not be."

"Blow it."

"Look!" Pointing suddenly, Hampelmann spoke his first word that morning.

They looked. But it was a ruse. Hampelmann reached, pushed them both off-balance, seized the rifle and catapulted toward the hill before they could react. They sprang to their feet, yelling at him, but he would not break lope.

"One round, that's all he's got!" cried Bitter Boy.

Matthe shouted to head for the left side of the hill, he would take the right—to draw fire, if they could, away from Hampelmann! Both ran.

Concentration on a sailor dangling from a noose in Kriegsmarine uniform with white cap and ribbons propelled Albert Pomtow half the distance to the hill, two hundred meters. Then his legs rubberized with fright. Careening behind a thick saguaro cactus, he almost impaled himself on its spikes. He stood gulping air, dumbfounded equally by his courage and his stupidity. It was cool, but he broke out in sacrificial damps. He saw the shapes of Matthe on his right and Bitter Boy on his left as they ducked and rushed, ducked and rushed infantry-fashion toward opposite sides of the hill. He peeked round the saguaro. There were two trincheras, two breastworks of rock. He would be behind one of them, the lower or upper, waiting, secure in a perfect Wehrmacht position, waiting, his rifle loaded with one, two, three, or four rounds. Albert stared at his own weapon. He could not know that it was a 1903 model 30.06 caliber Springfield of the type used by the Americans in the First World War, with a mulish fifteen foot-pounds of recoil per square inch. He knew only that it was a *verdammt* blunderbuss, a Bear-

146

Killer such as Old Shatterhand must have used—certainly not a weapon with which Tom Mix or Hoot Gibson could be presumed to be expert. He raised the leaf-type sight, aimed at another cactus for practice. The sight was calibrated for 100-200-300-500 yards, with a lock-knob on the right. Yards—*ach du lieber Gott!* Only in meters could he calculate! And he, a veteran of the Afrika Korps—but a cook, a dustmaker, a pencil pusher in the paper war, a motorcycle cowboy—had not since training at the Pionier school, not for five years fired a rifle! And that had been a 7 mm. Mauser! And but one bullet he had, but one!

Donner!

He jumped as though at the crack and whoosh of an .88 gun. But the shot had been at Bitter Boy, not at him, and the Indian was down and already up again, running. It infuriated him. Jamming the Stetson over his big ears, he pulled back the bolt, checked the round in the chamber, slammed home the bolt, stepped around the saguaro, and began to march with long strides and in a straight inexorable line toward the hill, muzzle forward.

Shouts. Matthe and Bitter Boy were ordering him to get down, get down!

Adieu, dear Albert.

A hundred meters. A hundred more.

My sisters. May they find husbands.

If he does not shoot at me I will not at him but only make him prisoner and ask Matthe what to do.

Sweat splashed down the end of his nose.

The Silver Six-Shooter may be only by a silver bullet killed.

Fifty meters to the first trinchera.

Adios, cruel world!

He does not shoot, out of bullets he must be!

Albert galloped the last few meters and plunged into the protection of the crumbling stonework, hitting the ground with a crash. He sat up, careful not to raise his head above the terrace. For a minute he savored little things—the warrant of his breathing, the tidbits of grit upon his lips, the blue illimitable sky of Arizona.

"Pomtow?"

Albert did not answer.

"Hampelmann, the clown, that is what you were called, *nein?* Hampelmann, I have no more ammunition. But I would not have shot you. And surely, you would not shoot a fellow *Deutscher*, would you?"

The voice was mild, almost gentle. It came from the trinchera above, perhaps twenty paces above.

"I did not hang Loffelbein. Pomtow, speak to me."

"Skubovius."

"*Danke, danke.* Hampelmann, I am so near to the border. Let me go. You were a good businessman in the camp, a born trader. I have no money, but I have a ring, a gold ring from the finger of an *Amerikaner* in Sicily. It is yours. Hampelmann?"

"*Jawohl.*"

"Hitler I despised, it is the truth, and I used the *Reichspartei*. I have been a good soldier, obeying orders only. What is an old man, who would soon die anyway?"

On hands and knees, inching the rifle, Albert crawled along the trinchera so that he would not be where the Oberfeldwebel expected him to be. He must not speak again.

"Hampelmann, listen to me." The voice grew guttural, importunate. "I was an orphan. I had no father or mother or home, such a *tragisch* life. Do you hear me? I am now coming down to you, Hampelmann, my hands high. I have no more ammunition. To you I entrust myself. You will not shoot? You will not kill me in this godforsaken place? If I am to die, *Kamerad*, may it be in the Reich!"

Albert came to his knees. How deathly still it was, there on the hillside. Wherever Matthe and Bitter Boy were, they were not moving, they could only watch. To his shoulder Albert fitted the butt plate of his howitzer. He prepared to rise. Above him a rock rolled. He would not fire first.

Suddenly he stood.

The reports of the guns were nearly simultaneous. Spread-legged on the upper trinchera, surprised that his target had moved, Otto Skubovius swung his rifle and fired. The Stetson sailed from Albert's head.

But he too had fired, sighting over the end of the barrel. The recoil of the old Springfield knocked him flat, so that he did not see what ensued.

Even more surprised, both by the fact that he had missed and by the impact of the slug in his chest, the Oberfeldwebel stepped from the rockwork. He marched a dozen paces down the hillside, rifle at hip-level, working the bolt and pulling the trigger of the empty weapon reflexively, the expression on his square, red face one of annoyance. Had he had cartridges, he would have killed his antagonist several times over.

But Otto Skubovius was dead on his feet. He dropped like a boulder.

A dazed Albert Pomtow picked himself up to see what he had done. One look, and swaying, white-faced, he walked away to another place, sat down again, covered his face with his hands and began to cry uncontrollably.

Matthe and Bitter Boy reached him. "A cryin' kraut," said Bitter Boy. "Now I've seen everything."

Out of deference to his feelings they moved on to the body. The Nazi lay over the lower trinchera, a gaping, imploded wound in his chest. His eyes were open and opaque. They slid him down, and after the Indian removed the gold ring from his finger, built over him a structure of rocks against the depredation of coyotes and vultures. It was what they used to do with their dead in Africa, both sides, Matthe remarked, where there were jackals. Bitter Boy indicated with a shoe. A line of ants, already formed, led under the rocks to the body and out again, hurrying and salvaging. "I'll tell you something funny as hell," he said. "That over there a couple miles is Mexico. You can't tell any difference, it's just like this. There isn't a goddam thing over that line—a town, a house, water, anything, for another forty miles." He grinned. "So even if he'd made it, he wouldn't of."

Saying he wished to be alone with his friend for a minute, Matthe picked up the Stetson hat, noted the hole in the crown, and taking it to Albert, who was still crying, put it on his head. Tears smeared Albert's face, misery made him ugly. If Skubovius had not at him fired first, he sobbed, he would not himself have fired, truly, he would have made him again prisoner, and asked Matthe what to do. But it was not Skubovius, it was the killing, of anyone. Only once in his twenty-three years had he fired, and then a life taken. In all his soldiering he had not, but now see what he had done, see, see. He was inconsolable.

Richter stood over him. Concussion of the rifles seemed still to linger in the clear, disinterested air. Perhaps the war had ended not in Europe, not in Asia, but here, just now, upon this apathetic desert. Perhaps that echo would forever mark the place. Perhaps this hovel of rock would serve as makeshift shrine to man's last seizure, the final epilepsy of the world. Two shots fired far from every battlefield. Two shots from two archaic weapons long after every greater gun was cold. Two shots exchanged by unknown soldiers near an undenoted border. A fratricide to gratify an audience of ants. *Amen,* he thought, *so sei es.*

He looked toward Mexico, and toward the invisible line that Ehlert, Boehm, Mohrdieck, Fuge, Buchting, and Skubovius had tried so desperately to cross until their interception. *Ja,* how funny. For there was nothing on the other side. Had they survived this trek, they could not have survived that. But now there were two who could, by taking the horses, if they wished. Or do what he had too long delayed to do, and at too terrible a toll. A boy hung. A dog kicked to death. A village partially destroyed. An old man murdered. And a horse. And someone named Skubovius buried. The adventure was *kaputt.* And this was what it had come to: a young man sitting in the sand and sobbing. *Amen,* he thought, *so sei es.*

He went to Claude Walkingstick, who sat on the trinchera smoking. It was time for them to leave Mouse Sits, he said, and take their chances off the reservation.

They were OK krauts, said the Indian, trying the gold ring on various of his fingers, but he agreed, it was overtime.

What they needed, Richter continued, was some means to support themselves, some kind of job, any kind. He, Bitter Boy, drove into Vaca frequently, and to Taft. They had only a few dollars left, but they would gladly pay him if he would inquire for them, offering the services of two able-bodied men willing to work hard and cheaply, for food and lodging even. It was a favor, but would he do it for the sake of the Moencopa, to be rid of them? And not to his people speak of it, in order that they might not say good-bye but disappear merely?

Sure, *paisan,* said Bitter Boy. He had white buddies all over the place. With his war record he could have had himself a job like that, flipping the cigarette, but after three years in service he owed himself a vacation. But he could fix them up for sure.

The ring was too large. He put it into his pocket, touching by chance the Iron Cross that Tansie had given him to take, if he ever made up his mind, into Vaca. Quickly he withdrew the hand. Goddam right, he said, he'd reconnoiter.

28

From Jackrabbit Falls Down and Opposite and Owl Hoot and Big Bush and Turtle Caught in a Crack and Goat Drink and Much Mud and Skunks Hanging and Too Many Ants they came, by rattletrap car and wagon and on foot, pots and pans and bedding and older children, because it was December, the Month of Animals Thin, and time to pick the cotton around Vaca. Most of the Moencopa set up housekeeping in the tar-paper shacks of a labor camp on one of the ranches, but the workers from Mouse Sits were more fortunate. They were near their own village, could drive back and forth to the fields daily, could sleep in their own houses with their own children and old folk, could use their own well and outhouse rather than the single spigot and one privy provided the camp. But no one complained as the Indians fanned out across the field that first day at morning-stands-up. There was much cotton to be picked, and everyone had many presents to buy before Christmas. Together with their tribesmen, Manuel and Antonia Scout, Victor and Ethel Scout and Tansie (since she could be watched over here), Ramon and Betty Walkingstick, Grover and Lupe and Peppertail Jones moved along the rows of cotton picking each white boll individually and pushing it backward into the canvas sacks suspended from their shoulders by wide straps and dragging the sacks along the ground behind them. Indians, the growers agreed, made good hands. They might not pick as rapidly as Mexicans and Negroes and no-good whites, but they picked cleaner cotton, with less trash in it, leaves and dirt, and they were not as prone to pack their sacks with stones to make a heavier weigh-in. When the sack was full they carried it to the field edge where a scale was hung from a wooden tripod; the sack was weighed by the grower or his assistant, the figure noted in a book, and the picker climbed a ladder and dumped his sack into a four-wheeled wire-mesh trailer. Inside the trailer Charles Lindbergh Scout, at eleven the youngest worker, tramped down the fluff to make a tight load. The trailer filled, it was pulled by truck or tractor to the gin at Vaca. The Moencopa men picked approximately 200 pounds of cotton per day, the women 150, and the rate of pay was $3 per hundred, so that a husband and wife, working steadily for eight to ten hours, might together earn $10.50. In most areas, near larger towns or a city, they were paid in cash, but here they were given "cotton tickets," punched coupons honored by all the merchants in Vaca. This medium of exchange was better all the way around, according to the merchants. It kept the Indians from patronizing the bootleggers in Taft. It kept the Indian money in Vaca.

Bitter Boy sat on a fence beside the field, combing his hair and wishing he had cigarettes and wondering if he ought to blow out his brains with one of the old Springfields. But he couldn't even commit suicide because on the way back from burying that kraut he'd shot up the last cartridge in the village. He was going to hell fast. His mustering-out pay was gone. The ribbons on his battle jacket were peeling, the Combat Infantry badge had chipped, the golden fourragère over his left shoulder was turning green, and his paratrooper boots needed new heels. You weren't supposed to wear your uniform more than a month after discharge and he'd been home two, but he had no other clothes except his other uniform and no matter how bad it looked, as long as you wore the flag you were somebody, you were damn near white. Take it off and you were just another Indian. He looked into the field at Tansie Scout. She was dawdling along playing the princess and handling the bolls as though they were turds. She gazed intently at him. What she'd said the other day was, Hey hero, you want to take off with me to California in your car? I know how you can maybe get the money, a lot of it. How? Go into Vaca, ask that sher'ff if there's maybe a big reward from the gover'ment if you could swing it so's he could take in a couple krauts. He'd never believe me. Oh yeah? Say you're a friend of theirs and show him this. She handed him an Iron Cross.

152

Don't forget, she said, they're white too. The medal was burning a hole in his pocket. That Tansie, she was a bitch on wheels. To buy lipstick she'd sell her mother for a whore. But sexy. Some of the Moencopa were staring at him sitting on the fence and he stared right back. They thought he ought to be out there dragging a sack with them and prob'ly he should be and earning his six bucks a day but how many cotton-pickers had seen Vesuvius and the Colosseum and the Leaning Tower of Pisa?

He called to them. "Hey you! I heard somebody invented a cotton-pickin' machine! They put machines in the fields you Indians goin' to be shit out of luck!" He wished he could stop talking dirty and thinking dirty but he couldn't, that was what the Army did to you. His father, Ramon, unhitched his sack and crossed the field to him and told him he'd been a show-off long enough. It was time to wash out his mouth and pick cotton like a man, he said, or leave the field. Bitter Boy hopped off the fence and got into his car and started it and raced the motor till everybody heard him and he had a whole cloud of oil smoke out the pipe. He stood up and shouted. "I'm educated and I'm not goin' back to the blanket!" He sat down again and gunned away not even knowing where he was going.

He headed for Taft in the purple, green, black, and rust car missing a top and three hubcaps and a fender. The other rear fender clunked. It would fall off any day. The car was loud as a truck or tank because the muffler was shot. Maybe Bear or Owl or Coyote'll tell me what to do. It used damned near as much oil as gas. The motor needed a complete overhaul, Pomtow said. Valves ground, new rings, work on the transmission, things he couldn't do because he didn't have the tools.

Bitter Boy made Taft, which was the county seat ten miles north of Vaca on the way to Phoenix, and left his battle jacket in the car and went into the county courthouse to see the government man, the Veterans Administration man, who wanted him to sit down but he wouldn't. He asked about on-the-job training.

Have to have a job first, the man said, then the government will pay part of your wages while you're learning.

He couldn't get a job. He'd tried like hell. Off the reservation they were hiring white boys home from service first. Down at Casa Buena all the government jobs were filled by men with families.

153

College, the man said. The government will pay you while you're studying, so go to college. When did you graduate from high school?

Didn't.

How much school did you have?

Three years at Casa Buena. Two at Phoenix Indian School.

Have to have twelve years, have to graduate to go to college. Go back to high school and graduate.

High school? I'm twenty years old.

I'm sorry.

That's all?

That's all, son, I'm sorry. Here.

The man gave him an eagle button for the lapel of the suit coat he didn't own, a button to show you were a veteran, called a ruptured duck.

Thanks.

Leaving Taft he ran out of gas and pushed the car into a gas station and told the man he had no money but he had this. How much for a gold ring?

Fill your tank.

Quart of oil, too.

OK.

Pack of cigarettes, too.

What the hell you want, Indian, my scalp?

Driving, smoking again, Bitter Boy remembered how, when he was a boy at the government school in Casa Buena, teacher had them make up songs the way the Moencopa did, she said, in the old days. I'll make me up one now, he thought, tapping a rhythm on the steering wheel, which was cracked. He sang in a monotone over the chug of the car:

> "I am a Moencopa
> My name is Ruptured Duck
> I am twenty years old
> I need a new muffler
> Bad
> But a new me
> Worse."

154

He couldn't go back to the fields to eat with the workers and he had no money for food so he fasted and took a nap in the car under a tree. Give me the word, Owl bird. I am in a box.

Waking, he drove on in to Vaca and on out to the Mouse. But the workers were there, in the middle of the afternoon the workers were there when they should have been picking cotton and he'd never seen so many long faces. Everyone just sat around under the watos listening to the radio and pretending everything was okay. Even the kids were quiet. Bitter Boy wasn't speaking to his father so he asked Tansie who died.

Nobody, she said. But at noontime the grower, the boss, they called him Mister Buster, called the hands together and said nobody from the Mouse could pick any more, orders of the sheriff, Jack Thode. Victor Scout asked why and Mister Buster said he didn't know why, everybody from the other villages could pick but nobody from the Mouse, orders of the sheriff. A man from Turtle Caught in a Crack said one work all work, some couldn't nobody could, the Moencopa stuck together, they were the People. Mister Buster said he was sorry, but they'd work or go hungry because if they didn't he'd bring him down some German prisoners from Phoenix to pick his fields and they worked faster and for less anyway. It was up to the People. Christmas was coming. It was presents for the kids or German POWs picking his cotton, which did they want? So Victor and Manuel and Grover and Ramon gave up and weighed in and came home because it wasn't fair to the other villages to keep them from working. And that was why everybody sat around looking like sad sacks, because they'd got tickets for only half a day's work and they couldn't go to the movies tonight.

Brief me, Coyote. I am in a box.

Bitter Boy kept clear of the two krauts but they cornered him and said Please, what about the job he was scouting them, they couldn't stay any longer, the Moencopa would starve if they weren't allowed to work because of them, please, they had to go at once. He told them not to get their asses in an uproar, he was working on it. He ate supper and drove away toward Vaca.

Progress. In the old days they did it with guns. Now they beat us with the buck.

Bitter Boy thought about the Italian whore he'd had in Pozzuoli, near Naples. When he finished and went outside, her kid brother, who pimped for her, told him she'd taken on twenty-seven GIs that day. But that was nothing. Once last year she took on thirty-one *Tedeschi* in one day.

Bear, I don't hear you. I am in a box.

He reached Vaca and parked on the main street and combed his hair and tilted his infantry cap and sauntered up and down under the streetlights past the movie. It was an open-air movie in a vacant lot between the hardware store and a grocery, with a fence along the sidewalk so you couldn't see in for free. There was a regular movie theatre in Vaca on the main street but that was for whites only and cost fifty cents. The same man owned them both, but this one he operated in a vacant lot for Mexican and Indian field workers during the cotton season. You sat on the ground but it was only twenty-five cents, kids a dime. Nearly all the hands within ten miles took their families nearly every night. They were crazy about movies. Bitter Boy made sure no one was watching, then stood on tiptoe and looked over the fence at the screen. The movie was a Western starring Randolph Scott, some crap about building a railroad through Indian territory and white men hiring Scott to fight off the Indians but he was really a friend of theirs because an Indian had once saved his life so he didn't know what the hell to do in Technicolor. The lot was packed with workers and kids and babies, though of course none from the Mouse.

Bitter Boy walked around the corner into the dark alley and banged on the back door of Coye's bar. Pretty soon Coye opened the door enough to see by the light from inside.

"Who?" Coye said, peering. "Oh, Walkin'stick."

"Fifth of wine."

"Got the money?"

"Tomorrow."

"In God we trust, all others pay cash, you know that."

"This worth it?"

"Lessee. What. Where'd you get this?"

"It'ly."

"Well. Might be. Never saw one of these. Hold your water a minute."

The door closed, was opened again, and a hand held out a bottle of muscatel which sold, in the bar or the grocery, for ninety cents. Bitter Boy worked at the cork.

In the bar, Coye was already on the telephone. "Jack? Coye. The Walkin'stick kid, I just sold him a fifth of wine. Thought you'd be int'rested in what he gave me for it. If it's what I think. An Iron Cross. You heard me. Claims he got it overseas. You int'rested?"

"Sure am."

"He's prob'ly out back now, drinkin'."

"I expect."

"Jack, did Buster turn them out of his field today like you told 'im? Those from the Mouse?"

"He did, noontime. He called me."

"Think it'll work?"

"No. They're lazier than pet coons but they stick together, one village'll help another. This kid, though, he's the one I've been waiting on. I had him pegged the day he came home and I bought him a drink in your place."

"Good. You goin' to pick him up now?"

"In a bit. He'll drink fast and I want to see what he does. I'll be by for that thing."

Bitter Boy poured the wine into him as fast as the mechanism of his throat would take it. When he had half the bottle down he stopped, looked both ways. An Indian bought liquor, he had to drink it fast, so he had to get drunk. It was one fine for being drunk, another for having liquor on you, so the faster you drank the less chance of paying double and at least you got a drunk for the price of one fine. Bar owners worked with the police, Indians knew that. They sold it to you, called the police, the police picked you up, fined you, and split the fine with the bar owners. He drank again, put the bottle under his jacket and started out of the alley and around the corner and about when he got to his car it hit him.

Seen the Sistine Chapel. Ceiling of.

In a box barrage. The artillery took a couple batteries of 105s and 155s and laid the shells to make a square, a box, over a kraut emplacement, then cut loose all at once, firing for effect, then lifted it to let the doggies go in with bayonets. Cost a lot but the krauts were out of their goddam minds and begging for the bayonet after that shelling.

Coyote, Bear, Owl, me, we been in a box all our lives.

"I'm a Moencopa
I go in those fields
Pick cotton one day
I'll never come out
Elder goddam you Brother
I need help."

Stumbling over feet and up on a platform and yelling at the People out there in the dark. Not to spend their money watching fake Indians in movies, save it send their kids to school so they can someday see the Sistine Chapel and whores, but also be real Indians and proud of it and keep their own dances, like this. I'm dancin' in a movie! In Technicolor! With Randolph Scott! Ayee, ayee, ayee! In a real movie, me!

29

Slow drunks sobered up slow, fast drunks fast. If you knew how. Thode dragged him into the cage and dropped him on the concrete floor beside the lidless stool. Standing, he urinated into the stool, then taking the prisoner by the hair, pushed his head into the water and held it under till he began to vomit. He let him, then pushed his head under again into what he'd vomited. That did it. The prisoner went into dry heaves which ripped his body like cloth. Thode hoisted him onto the cot, emptied his pockets, removed his belt and paratrooper boots with the long laces, closed the door and took them with him into the office. In case you had to leave him alone you could lose a prisoner letting him hang himself.

He unbuckled his chrome-plated, pearl-handled Smith & Wesson, sat down behind the desk and arranged on it a wallet, a ruptured duck, a comb, a wine bottle and an Iron Cross. Pushing back, he elongated his legs and high-heeled boots over a corner of the desk. The prisoner would sleep. He'd give him a couple hours.

158

Cage and office were actually one room, divided by iron mesh floor to ceiling. The office of the deputy sheriff of Taft County, Arizona, was furnished with a metal desk, two metal chairs, a rack of rifles, filing case, wanted posters on the walls, and on the desk a phone, a bowl of fresh flowers, and a lamp with a green glass shade. Through the downglow from the lamp dust sifted, cotton motes. Jack Thode watched it. They said of the air in a cotton town this time of year that it was too thick to pick and too spread to weigh. He remembered how they'd sat around, the eight of them, in the gin office a year ago now after dumping the German sailor by the POW Camp, sat around drinking and hoping the war would last long enough for them to make another crop. Well, it had and they had. Pickers were in the fields now. The trailers rolled. At the gin, the bale yard was stacked high. And the price was still two hundred dollars a bale for middling. But they'd made it by the fingernails. At the end, Buster and Hamp had pulled water from 370 feet down, Lloyd and Tate from 390. No one would ever make another crop around here. He wondered how long before Vaca dried up and blew away after this season, and how much money, man and bunch, they'd made the last five-six years. Enough, every one of them. Buster, Hamp, Lloyd, Tate, enough to pull out once they had this crop sold. Coye and Doc to let their leased acreage go. He and Joe Mack, his partner in the gin, would get what they could for the machinery, and Joe Mack was moving to the Coast then. Coye might stay on at his bar, Doc in his drugstore might and might not. He himself would stick around if the County installed him radio here and in the car, as they said they would. Or he'd install it himself. Peculiar—a peace officer in a cottoncake town better able to afford police radio than the county he worked for. But the fuzz, you might say, was off the peach. The groundwater was gone and cotton, he'd bet, would be down to a hundred a bale another year. So the Valientes were hanging up their saddles. It was a shame. They'd been a fine bunch of men, they'd ridden in a sight of parades and shows, they'd had them some dandy times.

As the Kraut Ketchers, though, they had one more fence to mend. They wouldn't object. After the first blooding they'd worked up a taste for it. Men and hounds always did. Besides, they owed him. It was he himself Jack Thode who'd blooded them. If cotton had made them comfortable, he'd made them men. Coming to Arizona lardy and short-winded, they'd be leaving it real ringtail Westerners—with hipbones for their pants and backbones to hang their legs on. Thanks to him, and to the German POWs, they knew now just how the old-timers had hobbled this country in the first place. Not with lawjaws and prayer meetings but with vigilantes and rope socials. Not with fancy outfits and trick riding but with fist and boot and bullet and barbed wire. Dudes wrote about how the West was won as though it was a pot in a poker game. It was never won. The West was plain-by-God taken.

The prisoner groaned.

Rest easy, Puking Bull, you'll need it. I been waiting on you a long time.

He had to hand it to the Indians. You couldn't scare them out or burn them out or starve them out. They were like a jackass in a hailstorm—they just hunkered up and took it. You had to get to them in a different way.

Jack Thode slept in his chair without moving. Near two in the morning he woke, put down his legs, stood, stretched. "Walkingstick?"

"Yo."

"How you feel?"

A groan.

"You tied one on, boy. Drunk and intoxicated, possession of liquor, resisting an officer, disturbing the peace. That's twenty-five dollars a count from the judge or a hundred dollars or a hundred and twenty days in the iron wigwam. Know where you were and doing what when I grabbed you?"

"No."

"Dancing. Right up in front of the screen, like you were in the movie. Can your people raise a hundred bucks to get you out?"

"No."

"Well, it's a hundred and twenty days then. Can't accommodate you here that long, I'll move you over to Taft. Walkingstick?"

"Yo."

"Where'd you get this Iron Cross?"

"It'ly."

"How?"

"Off a kraut I killed."

"Indian, you are the biggest hand-stitched copper-plated mutton-

160

butted liar I ever listened to." From his desk the deputy took the manila folder and opened it. "Day you first came home, that day I bought you a drink, wearing all those ribbons. DSC, Silver Star, Bronze Star, staff sergeant, Infantry badge—I smelled you a mile off. So I checked with the Army, I can do that in my line. Boy, you were in the Army confirmed, you were with the Thirteenth Division confirmed, you were in Italy confirmed, and that's it. You were a private, buck. You never saw combat. You were orderly to a Colonel Magruder, G-4 of the Division, Supply. You were his dog-robber. You washed his clothes and shined his shoes and kissed his brass ass and came home and bought yourself every ribbon and badge in the book and walked up and down this street like Audie Murphy." He closed the folder. "Boy, you are in trouble with Taft County and the State of Arizona, four counts. But you are now in trouble with the Great White Father. Wearing those ribbons and stripes is a Federal charge. They'll put you in a Federal pen and many moons will pass before you get out. You are the best liar I ever heard and I am sorry as hell for you."

From the filing case he pulled a bottle of whiskey and filled a tumbler, and opening the cage door, handed it in. "Here, something for what ails you. Whiskey, firewater. You need it."

Jack Thode sat down again at his desk to wait. It would not be as long this time. Whiskey on top of a good degutting on top of wine. The flowers were lovely. How long since they caught the kraut pilot and turned Lloyd loose on him on account of Lloyd's boy? April it was, eight months ago. And now the last three at large in the United States and only four miles from where he sat. It was damn near historical. The last Nazis. What a headline story to bring them in, except that he couldn't bring them in. It was a shame.

"That Colonel Magruder."

The voice was blurry. The whiskey was getting to him. Thode peered. The prisoner sat on the cot, bent over, empty tumbler in his hand. "What about him?"

"From Montana. Crow and Blackfeet tribes up there, he said. His old man fought them for the land and got it, so he hates Indians. The other colonels, they had American Chinks and Japs robbin' for them, but he'd been lookin' for an Indian. Twenty-three months I robbed for him. He gave me one pass, into Naples. He hated Indians."

161

"I got nothing against Indians." Jack Thode took the bottle to the cage again, opened the door and poured the tumbler a quarter full and no more.

When he put up his boots on the desk it was near four in the morning, near time. He yawned. He couldn't bring the Germans in because they knew about the other five being roughed up and they'd told the Moencopa. The Indians knowing meant nothing, for no one believed an Indian in or out of court, but if these Nazis lived and talked, you'd have the Army, the FBI, maybe even the International Red Cross on your tail. No, they must never get off that reservation. It had to be done on Indian land so in case there was ever any fracas there'd be the problem of Federal or State jurisdiction and it might never come to trial. He yawned. No, boy, I got nothing against Indians except I would like to handcuff you arms and legs to that cage and go over you with a fine-tooth comb. He wondered if the prisoner had swallowed the story about going to the Federal pen for wearing those stripes and ribbons. But I won't work you over, boy, I won't do it that way. I'll do it the American way. I'll sell you.

"Walkingstick?"

"What."

"There's three Germans out there at the Mouse."

"Two now."

"Two?"

"One just showed the other day. They shot him."

"How come?"

"He killed Lies. Choked him."

"Lies, old chief? That's too damn bad. Well, that's the Germans for you, every dirty sidewinder one of them. Something rotten in their blood. How come the Copa held the other two out on me all this while?"

"They're not bad, for krauts. They don't want to go home, they plan to stay here, live here."

"In the States? The hell you say. That's all we need, couple of Germans rottening up a clean, decent country like this. Walkingstick, I want those two."

"Why?"

"Some people hate Indians. I hate Nazis. And you're going to help me."

162

"Why should I?"

"Because I'm your friend. Because of all the nice things I'm fixing to do for you."

"Such as."

There were cotton motes on his boots. With a cloth from a desk drawer Jack Thode polished them meticulously as he spoke. "Such as forgetting those four counts tonight. Such as not telling the Government about your duding up to be a hero. And not telling this town and your people either—I can just hear you bragging on yourself to the kids and old folks. Such as letting your people go back to picking. And such as giving you the reward on those Germans."

"How much."

Thode folded and put away the cloth. How much was it worth to ride out with the boys one more time and lay hands on a couple live, walking, talking, honest-to-God enemy? Put another way, since it had to come out of your own pocket, how cheap could you buy an Indian?

"Fifty bucks apiece."

Let him gristle on that. They think slow, the Moencopa. I don't care how poison he is, give me an Apache anytime.

"You see, compadre, I can't go out to the Mouse and search, it's Government land. I have to bait them out somehow, with nobody knowing. All I'm after is to round them up like strays and hustle them back to their camp and let the Army ship them back over the water where they belong. I want to wipe the slate clean. You never fought a lick in the service, and that makes two of us. But we can do our part now. We can wind up the war right here."

The deputy went to the cage. "Walkingstick, you know what you are? You're an Indian. In this country that means you suck on the hind teat. When that uniform wears out and that junkpile car of yours falls apart, you won't have a pot to piss in or a window to throw it out of. One day you'll go out in the fields with the others and drag that cotton sack and then you're done for, for life. But I'm your friend and I'm giving you a chance and you're smart enough to take it, you've been to school. A hundred dollars will fix up your car and get you the hell out of here, all the way to California if you want. You might even amount to something. You might even wake up some morning white."

163

The stench of whiskey and vomit and Indian nauseated him. Jack Thode went back to his desk to wait once more and to be near the counter-fragrance of the flowers.

30

He was high and taut and sick. He gripped the wheel until his knuckles whitened. From Vaca to the reservation line he gave the Ford all the gun it had. But he crossed the dry wash into the village in low gear because he didn't want anyone asking questions about where he'd been last night and doing what. Signals of cooking smoke ascended. Under the watos the families were breakfasting. Parking the car in the usual place by the junkpile, he washed his filthy hands and face at the well and slipped among the tamarisks to the mud house of his foster brothers. They were just dressing when he burst in on them.

He was under such tension and spoke so rapidly that it was difficult for them to follow him. He'd found them a job, so get the lead out, they were supposed to meet the man in a few minutes. He'd been up most of the night with the man, whose name was Buster, drinking and talking him into hiring them. Bunk and keep was all they'd get at first, but they'd learn to ride and work cattle, Buster was a rancher near Vaca. He sat down on their bed and stood up and sat down again and he made them as excited as he was, trying to thank him and ask about the ranch while he said no, goddammit, hurry and get their gear packed, no, for Christ's sake, don't take their Afrika Korps uniforms!

While they tied up their shaving things in a handkerchief he gave them directions: they were to meet Mister Buster down the dry wash south, by the big cottonwoods, where he'd have horses and they could ride cross-desert to his ranch, a short cut. No, they ought not to say good-bye, he'd tell the Moencopa where they'd gone later and why, it would be easier that way and yes, he'd say they'd gone of their own choice and not because the People hadn't done their duty—come on, move it, on the double down the dry wash!

There was a moment.

"*Danke*, Sarge, *danke!*" Albert said fervently.

"No sweat."

"Don't forget you must have new rings for the motor."

"OK, OK."

"For me, will you speak to Tansie?" Matthe asked. "That I am sorry but I will one day return for her soon? And that the Iron Cross she should wear as my—my contract?"

"OK, OK, now take off and keep your tails down!"

As soon as they were gone, Bitter Boy dodged through the trees to the house of his father, Ramon. His parents and brother were eating at Alice Walkingstick's. Snatching, throwing things, he stuffed his barracks bag, and spotting over his head a basket with one of the Apache dolls, he tore it down and tossed the doll in too. Off came his stinking battle jacket with its regalia and his trousers and into the bag. From now on he was risking no Federal prison wearing that store-bought fruit salad. He was just putting on the other uniform the Army had given him at discharge, the unadorned suntan shirt and trousers, and cursing his fingers as he buttoned the shirt, when Tansie Scout entered and wanted to know the score.

Was she still hot to take off for Cal? Was she! OK, move it, he told her, grab her stuff and sneak across the dry wash and he'd pick her up in his car in five minutes and they'd hit the road, he had the money, beaucoup money, so get the lead out of her cute little tail. She hugged him and stuck her tongue in his ear as a promise and started for her house.

Dressed, his pants not even tucked into his paratrooper boots, he had only one thing more to do. He trotted out of the house to his coupe and laid on the horn with one hand and combed his hair with the other. The cow-call, prolonged and blatant among the tamarisks, collected the village better than a bugle. When he had the population assembled around him, wide-eyed children and workers and old folk, Bitter Boy mounted the running board and lit a cigarette and said good morning, goddammit, he had good news for them! He took a long drag and hoped they wouldn't notice his hand shaking. The news was, they could go back to work, to the

165

fields, to Mister Buster's, today, this morning! There'd be plenty of work right through Christmas, no one would have to go without food or presents, and this was his present to them in advance because he was leaving for California!

To his amazement, there were no smiles. The troops just stood there.

"How'd you fix this?" asked Victor Scout.

"With the sher'ff. We're buddies."

"Where are those Germans?" asked Grover Jones.

"Them? Oh, they've gone back to their camp. With the sher'ff." Why did Alice Walkingstick clap a hand over her mouth? "They're goin' back where they belong, to Germany."

Ramon Walkingstick reached and by his belt pulled him off the running board. Father's eyes drilled into son's. "Where's he pickin' them up?"

"What d'you care about those krauts? They brought nothing but trouble. They'll be better off and so'll this town be."

"Where!" Ramon Walkingstick cried.

"Down the wash. By the cottonwoods."

"Let's go!" his father shouted at Grover Jones and Victor and Manuel Scout, who took out in different directions.

"What the hell's wrong?" demanded Bitter Boy.

Something was, but no one took time to answer. Now it was his turn to stand there the way they had, except that his mouth was open because the whole village went nuts. His father Ramon and Grover Jones raced for the corral. Victor and Manuel Scout went into their houses and came out on the run with the two Springfield rifles for which there were no cartridges and headed for the corral. The women and old ladies hoisted their skirts and followed the men and the Moenkopa Korps followed the women helter-skelter. The old men—Wesley Scout and Joe John Jones and Uncle Rumbles—picked up sticks and trundled themselves after the whole damn outfit. And banging the door and shaking a fist and hitching up his trousers, General Miles burst from the government outhouse.

Bitter Boy felt sicker than ever and angry at their ingratitude. That was Mouse Sits for you, a slum of dumb Indians. If they were more interested in a couple of krauts than they were about his maneuver to put food on their tables again he was glad he was pulling

166

out and he was glad anyway. The cigarette singed his fingers. He flipped it. California, here I come!

He strode around the junkpile through the deserted village to his father's house to get his barracks bag and sling it in the car and pick up Tansie and be off like a big-assed bird on the GI ball.

He walked in the door and his B-bag was open. He'd zipped it shut.

Very, very slowly he shoved both hands into the bag, remembering. That the hundred-dollar reward he'd insisted the deputy pay him in advance had been in his OD trousers and he'd changed uniforms and in his hurry forgotten to move the money to his suntans.

His hands weren't shaking now. They seemed paralyzed. It was gone.

He knew who. Who'd taken it and wouldn't be waiting for him by the road but cutting cross-desert by herself.

Claude Walkingstick straightened up and looked at what was in his hands, remembering. That he'd thrown in the prisoner of human hair because in the old days it was supposed to bring you power.

31

They marched beside the black mountain. Down the dry course of what had been a river marched Matthe Teege and Albert Pomtow. They swung their small bundles. All they owned except their youth and hope was knotted in a handkerchief. It was a morning of calm and beauty. Early sun on stone made their path alluvial silver. They were self-conscious. The reprieve had come too suddenly. For the good fortune and the freedom and the beauty they were, for a few minutes, unprepared. Then Hampelmann could no longer contain himself. He swatted Matthe between the shoulder blades and cavorted in circles and fanned his flop-brimmed Stetson hat with the bullet hole, emblem of action, in its crown.

"Cowboys we will be!" he whooped. "Men of the Wild West!"

They grinned at each other. Hampelmann deflated. "*Ach,* if he was with us only. Willi. To live on a real ranch."

Now they could talk. The adventure, they agreed, was not ended, it was just beginning. Seeking out the Indians of Arizona had been an inspiration after all. The Moencopa had done more for them, endured more, in those three months then anyone else might have been expected to. They were *wundervoll* people, as courageous and patient and charming and good and guileless and worthy and true as any in the world, delightful children masquerading as adults or adults reliving their childhood, it was impossible to tell which, and to Mouse Sits they, the Germans, would return often to say thank you and to their friends bring cigarettes and candy. But it was indeed time to steal away without *Auf Wiedersehen,* to go out from that never-never village into enormous America and see what would befall them. Why, Hampelmann muddled, had Bitter Boy been so *nervös,* sitting and standing and swearing at them like a corporal? In Richter's opinion, he had been ashamed. He could find them employment because they were white, but himself he could not, being Indian. That was a thing to regret. They must attempt, when they were citizens, what they could do about that situation. A nation such as the United States it flawed. Albert wondered next how they would fare in this new world. Germans, would they bear always the mark of Cain, be hated always? Richter reassured him. In time, if they earned it, they would win acceptance, they would surely be absolved of crimes they had never committed. If there was room in a land so spacious for oppression and injustice, surely there was place for magnanimity as well, even forgiveness. Hampelmann's chin lifted. He sang softly, as became the morning, "*Ach,* give me a home where *die Büffel* do roam . . ."

Down the unwatered trough of the Sonoita they hiked. A hawk sailed, wings wide and black. No predator he, but a shepherd of the air, watching over them. The quality of the sky was that of quartz or mica. Its blue reminded Albert of the Mediterranean. Once, he said, trying to catch up with Erwin Rommel during one of his slap-dash charges into Egypt, they had looked down from the Via Balbo

168

and there, white boys' bodies antic in the sea, were British soldiers swimming. The *Engländer* had not even been aware the war had passed them by. Hot and dusty, the Germans would have liked nothing better than to join the sport. But they let them be. Its blue reminded Matthe of crystal mornings in Tunisia. And for that matter, how like a wadi was this dead riverbed, how like the djebels of that coast these gaunt and reptile mountains. To ride a fine horse, Hampelmann chortled, to learn to rope and brand and bowlegged to become! And someday he would rig himself out in the same silver and leather and turquoise as the troop of riders they had seen perform in Phoenix the night they had escaped, how were they called? Valientes, Matthe thought. Toward the great gold cottonwoods they moved. Under them he had kissed an Indian girl.

A whistle.

A man stepped down the bank from under the trees and waited for them. He wore boots and denim and a big hat and a gun upon his hip. They met in the middle of the dry wash.

"Howdy, boys," the man said.

"Howdy," Albert grinned.

"You the boys Walkin'stick sent me?"

They nodded.

"You are Mister Buster?" asked Matthe.

"That's the handle."

The man smiled. He was tanned and friendly. From a shirt pocket he took papers and a sack of tobacco and began to roll a cigarette while Albert watched entranced, winking at Matthe. Mister Buster lit the cigarette. "So you want to work cattle?"

"*Ja*. Yes."

"Germans, ain't you?"

They did not know what to say.

"It's OK. Walkin'stick told me. Got some Heinie blood in me myself, from away back. You plannin' to stay on in the States?" They nodded. "Well now, that's dandy."

"We thank you for this—this—occupation," Matthe said.

The man shrugged. "Can of peaches. Say, some friends of mine I'd like you t'meet."

He whistled. Out of the cottonwoods and down the bank two men came to join them. A pebble click. The Germans turned, and from the cottonwoods on the opposite bank two other men appeared. All four were attired in the same denim and boots and big hats and guns. They sauntered.

"These are good ol' boys," said Mister Buster.

Standing in a semicircle, the four newcomers pushed up their hats in greeting. They were middle-aged, and one was short and wore glasses. There was an ease about them that was typically Western and refreshing, a potency and self-control which were admirable.

"You boys skedaddled out of the camp up to Phoenix, didn' you?" one inquired.

Matthe and Albert nodded.

"Didn' you use to play the tuba in the kraut band up there? Oom-pah, oom-pah?"

Albert grinned. "*Jawohl,* oom-pah, oom-pah!"

The five men smiled. Mister Buster whistled.

From the first trees two more men emerged, and stepping into the dry wash approached the group. They were dressed like the others, but one was younger and very tall. Now there were seven men standing about the Germans.

The tall man looked Matthe and Albert up and down. "Real live krauts. Boys," he said to them, "I want to name some names and see if you savvy. Now listen. Dachau. Belsen. Buchenwald."

"Dachau?"

"Belsen? Buchenwald?"

"Mean anything to you?"

They shook their heads. Something about the faces was familiar to Matthe. Recognition went off in his mind with a report like that of a gun. He spoke quietly in German. "Albert, these are the Valientes."

The men caught the word. They looked at each other, squinting in the bright sunlight.

"Understand you boys want to stay in the good old USA," the tall man said. "You figure we got room for Nazis here?"

Albert and Matthe were silent.

The tall man whistled.

Out of the cottonwoods on the opposite bank still another man appeared, the eighth man, and stepping into the wash strode toward them purposefully.

"This here's Lloyd," the tall man said. "He's a good American. Raised a lot of cotton for the war. Back last spring his boy, he's only twenty-two, was in the Army in Germany and got wounded by your Nazi pals. Want to tell them about it, Lloyd?"

The eight men sidled, forming a complete, somber circle about the Germans. Lloyd took off his denim jacket and his hat and unbuckled his gun. He was gray-haired. He faced Albert, spread-legged, and looked up at him.

"He stepped on a mine," Lloyd said, his voice choked. Shockingly, he began to cry. "It's his legs an' spine! He won't never walk again!"

"Albert, the Krautfange," Matthe said.

Something in his tone galvanized the surrounding men. As Albert moved, two of them bent his long arms behind his back. Starting toward him, Matthe himself was seized from the rear by two others.

There was a moment of readying, positioning. It was like the moment of suspension between scenes in a drama, while a stage is being reset and a cast disposed. The faces of the Westerners underwent an abrupt, a drastic change. The guise of ease and self-control was replaced by an expression of gluttony, as though their victims were not male at all, but females naked and voluptuous. Then Lloyd began to bludgeon with both fists.

"He's in a wheelchair!" he shouted, hammering and sobbing. "My boy'll never walk again an' neither'll you! I'm givin' you what he would if he could—I damn you an' your kind to hell, you dirty bastard Nazi!"

Albert Pomtow tried to lower his head, but the blows raised it and battered it into a crimson clown-face with an opening in it crying "Almighty *Gott*, Matthe! Almighty *Gott!*"

Matthe Teege had forgotten a man could scream. But he screamed. "Albert, remember! You swore! To resist not!"

He saw Albert go down. He struggled himself as he saw, too late, uplifted in a man's hands over Albert a water-smooth stone, but arms whirled him like grapples. He heard hooves. Through the ferocity he saw the Indians riding in the distance of the lovely morning and the rifles.

Range of vision closed. The chrome of a revolver flashed, was turned, became a club of costly pearl, descending. An explosion of agony. And the structure of himself which had so long stood, though gutted within, was finally betrayed. It fell with a roar. He ceased to struggle. Matthe Teege surrendered for the last time.

THREE

SILENT NIGHT, HOLY NIGHT

32

A little girl again with something to mother, a bird with a bent wing, a rabbit with a broken leg, she listened for her own mother's voice. But that voice was long ago and over there and her own ears were uncertain. She did hear one thing, the remedy for a wound. She went into the desert and pulled up a greasewood bush and chopped off the roots. In the junkpile she found a shard of beer bottle and with the glass for a razor shaved the blond hair from the left side of his skull. The wound appalled her. She thought of a cracked egg. The greasewood roots she heated and wrapped in a cloth and held against his head as a healing poultice. They offered to fetch a medicine man from Too Many Ants but she said she no longer believed in those damn liars. That day and night he did not move and she let no one else come near and cared for him with savage tenderness.

The next day she heard her father's voice reminding her of what the warriors used to do in the long years to make their horses lively. Going into the desert again she yanked up some dry chufa grass, which grew from tubers under the ground, brought the tubers back to her house, chewed them into little pieces with her excellent teeth, and kneeling over her patient spat the pieces up his nostrils. It did not liven him any. He did not move the second day and she was sure she would lose him.

It was not really her house. It was the adobe into which General and Josie Miles moved when their children abandoned them and into which she and Lies About His Age moved when their own houses were knocked down by the horsemen the night the Council was burned. To keep it quiet now, she would let neither the General nor Josie enter. Neither did she play her radio.

That second night was very cold. He shivered, the first sign that

175

he would live. She was cold, too, and she got right into bed with him and warmed him with her old bones. By the first hairs from Elder Brother's head he stirred. She sat up and looked. His eyes were open and staring at her. He was identifying her by the four vertical blue lines tattooed from her lips to the point of her chin. For several minutes his mouth worked, twitching, shaping, trying speech, before he could create two whispered syllables. She put her face close to his to listen.

"Al-berr," he whispered.

"You're not mad? Sleepin' with an old lady?"

"Al-berr."

"I burned his things, except that pretty uniform. That's what we do."

"Al-berr."

"We don't say their names," she chided softly. "When they go away, we miss them, we grieve, but we don't even put their names on the crosses. Remember when he went away, that old man I married up with? I made one sound, that was all. But I'm damn lonesome. You'll be lonesome, too. Oh, I don't know why they have to go away, but they do, they do!"

His face screwed up as though he understood at last that his friend was dead and he was trying to cry and could not. When laughter is killed, tears often perish with it. Alice Walkingstick was sorrier than ever for him. She put her arms about him and crooned.

She did not know what to feed him. His stomach might not shake hands with tortillas or bologna. That day, however, she was lucky. Her mother spoke to her again. It was an old recipe used both to keep the stomach warm and to make the milk flow after childbirth, but it might also renew his strength. From an olla sealed with mud she took some dried fruit pulp of the saguaro cactus, picked out the seeds, ground them on her metate, mixed them with whole wheat, and boiled the mess to make a porridge. She fed him with a spoon she had got free in a box of cereal. He did not seem to like it but he ate and in a day or two was better. He could not speak properly, it took much effort to form words, and he could not move his right arm or leg. When Alice pricked them with a pin he had no sensation. But she propped him up with a basket and the fifth morning, as she went out, permitted the members of the Council to enter.

The elders, General Miles and Wesley Scout and Joe John Jones and Uncle Rumbles, sat on the earthen floor beside his bed, while the men of the middle generation, Victor and Manuel Scout, Ramon Walkingstick and Grover Jones, stood behind them and took off their straw hats. On the faces of the old men sadness was graven, on those of the middle-aged, shame. Matthe Teege did not see this. He stared at the wall.

Victor Scout had been delegated to speak. He explained why they had reached the cottonwoods too late to save the tall one. They didn't have very fast horses and besides, they didn't know about the trap that Thode had set until Bitter Boy announced that the Germans had gone to meet the sheriff and now they could go back to work in the cottonfields. As soon as he said that, they knew what would happen. They hurried and whipped the horses but they couldn't get there in time to save the tall one who made them laugh and dynamited their well. Those men smashed his head in with a rock. They'd have killed him, too, because Thode was banging his head with a revolver, but the whites saw the rifles and went away. They didn't know there were no cartridges in the rifles.

The Council waited, expecting the young man to say something, but he did not.

Bitter Boy had done it for money, Victor Scout continued. For a hundred dollars from that Thode. Of course, Bitter Boy didn't know what the men would do when they got the Germans because he didn't know anything about those other five prisoners who were caught during the war, the Council had kept that a secret. He thought these two would just be captured and taken back to their camp. But that didn't excuse him. He knew the Moencopa had taken the Germans to be their sons, to shelter and defend them against all enemies. But he'd broken the word of the People, a word always kept in the long years. He must have been drunk or sick or gone crazy. The Army had changed him, and his schooling. His own daughter, Tansie, was just as bad, Victor Scout said. She'd stolen the money from Bitter Boy and now she'd run away again. He wouldn't ever try to find her again. Victor shook his head. If this was the way their young folks behaved nowadays, he didn't know what would become of any Indians.

Still they waited in vain.

"We feel so bad about this we don't know how to say it," said Grover Jones.

"We're all ashamed," admitted Joe John Jones. "The women and children are ashamed, too."

Uncle Rumbles let out some sorrowful gas.

"It's awful. Losin' the tall one and this harm to you," said Wesley Scout. "I don't remember us ever breakin' our word before. We don't have much left to us from those times and now even our word's like smoke."

"We talk about it and talk about it," said General Miles. "We thought of goin' down to Casa Buena and tellin' the Gover'ment. But that sher'ff, he'd say you two put up a fight and he had to do it and they'd trust him, not us. The whites, they stick together."

"We'll do the best we can to make it up to you," offered Manuel Scout. "We'll hide you in a cave we know about till that camp closes, or we'll give you food and our best horse and take you down to Mexico ourselves. You just say."

Matthe Teege said nothing. He lay propped against the swastika basket staring at the blank adobe wall. To the elder Indians, his posture was frighteningly reminiscent of that attitude in which the Moencopa dead were buried in the long years—seated, with folded hands and facing eastward, present yet absent, inviolable. It was as though he had not heard the explanation or the apology or the offer, or if he had, either did not believe them or was indifferent. They knew, although they could not see the left side of his head, that he was hurt, but they could not have been expected to realize how gravely. The pounding of his skull, though less prolonged than that to which the pilot, Leutnant Buchting, had been subjected, had injured the left hemisphere of the brain itself, the speech center. This impaired his oral ability and did permanent motor nerve damage on the opposite, or right side of his body, where his arm and leg were partially paralyzed. But it was more, they did realize, than posture and physical injury. Something internal was altered, or shifted, or removed. Nothing they might say or do could convince or restore him. He was present yet absent. He was inviolable.

Ramon Walkingstick had not yet spoken. "My son did this," he said. "One son did it to another one. That's the worst. So the way we're punishin' him, that's how the Moencopa used to. We waited so you could see what we're doin' to him. We're goin' to carry you outside a minute."

The old men rose and moved aside. Uncovering Matthe Teege,

two men, Ramon Walkingstick and Victor Scout, made a chair of their arms and carried him out the door. Placing his arms over their shoulders, they stood him almost upright so that he could see.

About the village, from the well and ashes of the Council around the junkpile and through the tamarisks and by the dwellings down to where the garden had been, the people of Mouse Sits were spaced at intervals to form a kind of gauntlet. They stood impassively, old women and their daughters and the children, each holding a small switch or whip. Along the route trod one of the horses. When the animal stopped, the nearest Indian would switch it onward. A rope was tied round its neck. Over its withers and along its flank the rope tautened out and down to a knot tied about the wrists of Claude Walkingstick. He lay upon his back. The pull of the rope extended his arms above his head. Stripped to the waist he was dragged like a cotton sack very slowly over the ground, disturbing pebbles, raising dust, stopping, starting, now dragged slowly again. There was no way to tell how many circuits of the gauntlet he had completed or what his pain must be or if he were unconscious.

"They used to do this till they died," said his father, Ramon, to the German. "He's my son, but how long we punish him is up to you."

Whisking her tail, huffing at her task, the swayback mare lagged along the route, past the Ford coupe beneath a tamarisk, and neared the house of Alice Walkingstick. It passed directly before the doorway. Its burden left a trail of blood. In Bitter Boy's upturned face the eyes were closed. Matthe Teege took two tottering steps and falling awkwardly, covered the dragged body with his own. He moaned. It seemed to be a plea in German. "*Nein, nein,*" he seemed to moan.

33

Hair grew again, yet did not entirely cover the livid upper left side of his skull. To hide it, he wore his billed Afrika Korps cap with its bold cockade of black and white and red. During another four days' convalescence he ate well and regained much of his strength but there was still residual paralysis. His speech was slurred. To articulate he made faces ugly to look at. And although he had some return of function on his right side, his arm and leg were wooden, their use limited.

When Alice was out, he practiced walking, limping from bed to wall and back again. He was doing this one morning when someone entered and, before he could turn, knelt behind him and clasped arms about his knees. He knew who it was.

"Stand," he said.

"My holy God, I'm sorry."

"A soldierr you have been. Like a soldierr stand."

He was released. Without turning he moved to the bed and sat down.

"I didn't know, I didn't know. I couldn't even get a job myself. Tansie gave me your Iron Cross and I sold it and got drunk, sick drunk, I didn't know what he'd do, Thode. Nobody told me about the other five of you, when they caught them. So I did it. If I was you, I'd beat me to death, it'd be no loss. I don't even know who I am or what I'm doin' any more."

The German faced away from him. "It is not yourr fault."

"And something else you better know. I never saw combat. I never killed a German or even shot at one. All those ribbons and things I bought, and the sher'ff found out. Overseas I was dog-robber to a colonel, his orderly and shoeshine boy. I really lied big around here."

180

A light rain lulled upon the roof, the first rain of winter. "In service it is not what you can—can select. Ourr friend, who was in the camp hanged, Willi Loffelbein, he was in an Unterseeboot, and the crew he served as a waiterr."

In Matthe Teege the Indian youth perceived the change the Council had observed. He did not so much speak to others as to himself.

"How can I make anything up to you?"

"Help me to walk. To the graves."

"Sure." He put Matthe's left arm over his shoulder and flinched. "It's OK. My back, half the skin scraped off behind that horse. I had it comin', I don't blame anybody. Alice wrapped it up with some roots."

Together they went outside the house, Matthe stumping along assisted, his right arm heavy beside him. Indian and German were equal in height, but the German was sturdier. It was less a light rain than a mist. The Moencopa watching under watos, through the mist and village they made slow way, passing near the well the unused water wagon and the toy Tiger, its stovepipe cannon broken out of the turret and one wheel off. The climb along the rocky path took them a long time. On the ledge they stopped at two new graves, damp raw mounds of recent earth with two crosses, one blue, one white. In glass jars at the foot of each were wilted flowers.

"That blue one, that's Lies About His Age. We don't put names on them. Yours is white."

Matthe freed his arm. "Please, will you do another thing? Paint find, it may be in the junkpile, and a brush or piece of rope."

"Sure. Be right back."

The air was sodden. The top of the black mountain was shrouded in mist. Still higher, rain clouds rumbled up from the distant ocean gulf and across the steel sky like formations of armor. Richter stood with his weight on his left leg. This was the place to which they had come that night three months ago out of the red, inhospitable desert. To twinkling luminarias and food set out upon the graves for small, departed, hungry souls. To surrounding by the *Indianer*. "Peace," had been his first word to them. "How," was Hampelmann's.

"This is it. All there is."

181

Matthe took the small open can, removed the scum with a twig, stirred, then sat down on the mound and using his left hand began to letter in Latinate script with the stiff brush. The paint was pink. On the cross he printed "Albert Anton Pomtow 1922-1945 *Gefallen für Amerika.*" and put down the can and brush. It was a wretched job, all but illegible.

"So that was his name," the Indian said. "All that work on my car and I never called him anything but you or Fritzie and never said thanks. And I got him killed. What's your name in American?"

"Matthew."

"Matthew. Mine's Claude."

"Tell me about those men, those eight."

"The ones caught you and the others?"

"Yes. In the prisoner camp we called them the Krautfange. But I have seen them before, in Phoenix, in a show riding. They were announced the Vaca Valientes."

"Valientes!" Claude Walkingstick squatted. "The same ones, you sure? I'll be damn! I know them, from before I went in service. They started ridin' in parades around here, in fancy outfits and horses like movie stars, you know. Hamp and Mister Buster and Lloyd and Tate, they're growers. Coye runs the bar in town and Doc has that drugstore, but they lease land. Joe Mack and Thode, they run the gin. They're all in cotton, one way or another, and they've got rich off it. And they're the same ones, I'll be damn. How come you want to know?"

"Now, the town. Describe to me the town."

"It's nothin', just a cotton town."

"Census?"

"People you mean? Couple thousand, why?"

Matthe handed him a twig. "Here. A map draw."

Bitter Boy scratched a line on the mound. "This is the main street. Along here's the stores, the bar, movie house, jail, bank, gas stations, so on. There's some side streets, not many, not even a train station." He made an X. "Cotton gin's out here. Why? What's up?"

Moisture darkened their shirts and glistened upon their faces. The German seemed oblivious to it.

"Forget I asked. It's your business."

"*Ja.*"

Claude Walkingstick shivered. He did not like to be in this place, sitting on a grave with someone as strange as this. He assumed the German was OK in the head.

"You don't have to tell me."

"I will tell."

"If you want."

"I am going to get them."

"The Valientes? Eight men?"

"All."

"You crazy?"

The German looked at him, blue eyes into black. The Indian shivered again.

"OK, you're goin' to get them. How?"

"I do not know. But for them to come again for me I will not wait. I will now attack."

"Attack. Sure." Bitter Boy wondered if the German army gave Section Eight discharges in cases of the head. It had never occurred to him before, but he supposed it did, like any army. "Sure."

"You have heard of our commanderr, Rommel? If a Panzer stopped, he would drive up to it and on its turret with a barr of iron hit and shout the crew to move on, always to attack. I will want a gun. One of those old rifles."

"Can do. But there's no ammo, no cartridges."

"It does not matterr. And transport I will need. To be driven into the town."

"That's me, my car. But listen, you're in no shape."

"I will be in two days ready."

Richter put his left hand atop the cross and hoisted himself, swaying for a moment, then standing erect and grim. Claude Walkingstick stood with him.

"Matthew, I'm goin' with you."

"*Nein.*"

"You damn well can't do it alone. You can try, but you'll never make it."

"No."

"Back in the house you said I've been a GI, so stand up like one. I am. I'm goin' with you."

"You do not owe this."

"Hell I don't. To you and this one down there and the People. And to me myself."

The German shrugged. "Very well, do as you like."

Claude Walkingstick grinned and put out his hand. "Now you're talkin', buddy! Shake on it?"

Richter looked at the hand. "We go as soldiers, not friends, now or everr," he said curtly. He turned away.

Together they started down the path from the cemetery through the mist, Indian assisting German. Behind the mountain, behind the massive armor of the clouds deploying, there was thunder.

34

Albert's he folded neatly in a tuba case. His own Afrika Korps uniform he rolled into a compact bundle and tied. His Iron Cross had been stolen and sold, his shaving things lost among the stones of the Sonoita. The case and the uniform were all he had to take.

To steal away secretly they met by the car at dusk. The Moencopa were up on the mountainside watching the sun go down over their beloved desert, and the two boys could hear above the treetops children's voices singing in German the song that Hampelmann had taught them:

> "The penny went to water,
> The dollar went to wine.
> *Hei di, hei do, hei da,*
> *Hei di, hei do, hei da.*"

They stowed the tuba case and Matthe's bundle and the two relic Springfields in the back seat. Then the Ford would not start. The Indian pounded on the dashboard in frustration. He had not driven it for days, the goddam battery was dead, it would not even turn the motor over. They got out. In the gathering gloom, skirts hitched up and her face tattooed with anxiety, Alice Walkingstick came running. She knew, she knew, she sat up there on her butt and knew those boys were sneaking off! Where? Why? She spied the case and bundle and the guns, she flung her thin arms around Matthe and clung to him desperately. Dear, dear German boy, his head wasn't healed yet, he was too poorly, he couldn't talk right, he didn't even have a pair of clean socks, damn if she'd cry but he was going away and never coming back and breaking her heart! He was gentle with her. There was a thing he had to do, he said into her gray hair. Only a small while he would be gone. He would never forget what she had done for him. But now please, would she please help them? The runs-by-itself would not start. A little push would she and Claude give? The way was downhill, one push and it would roll toward the dry wash and he could start it. The project diverted her. Matthe got in the car, turned the key, put the gearshift in second, depressed the clutch with his left foot, and stationing the old lady and the Indian at the rear, said *"Vorwärts!"*

They pushed. Down the slope bumped the car, Matthe steering it around the junkpile and the well and the ashes of the Council toward the riverbed. It began to rattle and shake and as it gained momentum he let out the clutch. The Ford convulsed and bucked, convulsed and bucked as though it would strip its gears, then roared into a crescendo and belched blue oil smoke and red carbon sparks and struck the bottom of the wash with such force that the remaining rear fender, suspect for some time, dropped and hung by one bolt and clanked inauspiciously along. Matthe pumped the accelerator and raced the motor, then braked to a stop in the middle of the wash and looked back and up at Mouse Sits. Peering through the twilight he could trace the small figure of Alice Walkingstick waving and the squat shapes of the adobe dwellings and still higher, in proud, hygienic isolation, the government outhouse. Through the trees one bare light bulb glowed good-bye.

Bitter Boy jogged up, planted a foot on the bumper, and with a grunt ripped off the vestigial fender, climbed in, took the wheel, cried "Geronimo!" and they were on their way.

If the war party which had set out on rickety horses in pursuit of Otto Skubovius had been comic, this one, mechanized in such a contraption, was pathetic. Then there had been three to take a single man; now the odds were two against eight, an Indian youth who had been an officer's orderly and whose lacerated back was bandaged with greasewood roots and a German whose skull was not yet sound and whose limbs on the right side had not yet recovered full function. Matthe Teege huddled in his AK cap and patched khaki trousers and a denim jacket. It was dark now, the December dark was cold, and the coupe had no top. It had but one headlight, too, as Claude Walkingstick discovered when he switched them on. He wore his paratrooper boots and suntan shirt and trousers with only those adornments to which he was entitled: blue-piped infantry cap, Thirteenth Division patch on his shoulder, and the European Theater ribbon with three small campaign stars. His companion requested that he drive slowly, he wanted time to think. Glancing at his speedometer, which was still out of order, Bitter Boy did not know whether to be excited or aghast at what they were doing. If only the car were faster, and the rifles loaded, and this German not so sour, so hostile, so withdrawn. There was something wrecked about him, too. His timing was off, his instruments did not work properly, and he had a lot of screws loose. If the Ford was a used car, Teege was a misused kraut, by too many owners over too many miles.

"Matthew?"

"What?"

"*Wie geht's,* buddy?"

"OK."

"You got any idea how in hell we're goin' to operate?"

"As yet not."

"What'd you do in the Africa Corps?"

"A tank drove."

"Swell." Claude Walkingstick hummed a few bars of "Lili Marlene." "How'd you get that Iron Cross? Buy it?"

"*Nein.*"

At the reservation line the road into Vaca became tarvia. "Listen, buddy, shouldn't we some way get some ammo for these cannons? They play dirty, you know, they might call our bluff."

"*Nein.*"

A kilometer out of Vaca, Matthe checked his wristwatch. 19.10 hours. He was on military time again, and planning in kilometers. "How is it farr from this town to Taft?"

"Nine, ten miles."

"Where will those men be, at this hourr?"

"Out at their ranches prob'ly, Lloyd and Tate and Hamp and Mister Buster. The rest I don't know. In town somewhere."

"*Jawohl.* Now, as I say, do. Up the principal street, drive, and patrol until you have the location of the others. I will take coverr. Do not stop. At all times be moving."

The order surprised Claude Walkingstick. His companion seemed, if not a friend, at least a German again, with a German's efficiency. As he took a deep breath, Matthe lowered himself out of sight on the floor between dashboard and seat.

"Yessir, Lootenant, I hear you loud and clear."

The road became the main street. He cruised it, the V-8 motor churning on about six cylinders and loud because the muffler was also shot. The streetlights were on, the stores open, Vaca had finished supper and much of it was out buying Christmas presents and window-shopping and looking at itself. There were many Moencopa and Mexican field hands spending cotton tickets and doubtless many more inside the outdoor movie, on the fence before which a sign advertised "Along Came Jones," a Western starring Gary Cooper and Loretta Young. On the sidewalk in front of the hardware store new postwar stoves and refrigerators were displayed and a phonograph blared "Hark, the Herald Angels Sing!" The air was dusty. Along the curbing, under the wheels of automobiles, eddied rags of cotton blown from trailers passing that day. Bitter Boy drove as slowly as he dared, hoping to God that if he saw the sheriff the sheriff would not see him because he was supposed to be in California. But the jail was dark. He had to stop for a woman trying to park a car too big for her. What if someone he knew, like from Goat Drink, crossed the street by his car and looked beside him? What would he say? "Hi, like you to meet a buddy of mine, *Herr* Teege from Duisburg, Germany, he's just over here seeing the country?" The woman parked and he moved on, his hands sticky. Through a window he spotted Coye behind his bar. Doc's drugstore was doing a rush business, so he must be there. That left Thode and Joe Mack unaccounted for.

In two blocks he was out of the business stretch, in two more beyond the last house and at the edge of town where the cotton gin occupied several acres of desert. Near the street was the one-room frame office of the Vaca Ginning Company. It was lighted inside. Through the window he identified the two men talking. Driving on, he turned the corner, continued, turned right again, cut the motor and headlight, tapped the German, who came up beside him, and reported. Coye and Doc were in town. Out in the gin office he'd seen Joe Mack and the sheriff, who were partners in the gin. Such darkness was this, where were they now? In the bale yard. Then the rifles bring, they would make a reconnaissance.

Claude Walkingstick had parked between two stacks of bales so high that they overhung the car. Leaving it over the doors, Springfields in hand, they climbed a cliff of processed cotton, each bale wrapped in jute bagging and banded with steel and tagged with owner's name and grade and number and weighing five hundred pounds. Indian helping German, they reached the top. Kings of the cotton mountain, from this height they could survey the entire gin area. On either side of them in the yard was another stack equally high, built of another hundred or more bales. Before them was the gin itself, a building of corrugated tin perhaps 150 feet long and 60 wide and 60 high, sliding doors at each end, and on this side at roof level an iron bunker into which cottonseed was conveyed by auger from within the gin, stored, and unloaded by gravity into trucks. Beyond the gin, in another graveled area open to the street, some loaded, some empty, four-wheeled balloon-tired cotton and motes trailers of mesh were parked in rows, and near them, the car of the Taft County Sheriff's Department, painted badges on its doors. Light from the office window made a yellow square over the scales on which the loads were weighed.

Matthe Teege sat down and muttered a series of questions. Was there a telephone in the office? Sure. Why was the gin in production not? Down to a day shift now because the crop around Vaca was almost in and ginned and they were sitting on it. Why were some trailers meshed on top, some open? Motes, or trash, trailers were covered to keep the trash from blowing out during hauling. What were the dimensions of a trailer? Maybe 30 feet long, 8 high and 8 wide maybe. How many kilometers, miles, from here did the four growers live, those not in the town? Two, three. Would anyone be apt in the next half hour to the gin to come? Not likely, but you never knew. What was the engineer, the motive force of the gin? Electric motors, big ones, sucking the cotton up through pipes out of trailers at one end of the plant, blowing it through the machines and out into the bale press at the other. Somewhere a board, a panel of controls, of switches, there was? Yes, other end, by the door, he'd been through the gin once and remembered. Why?

Richter sat for perhaps another minute. Under him the bolt of the harmless, senile 30.06 poked into his thigh like a thumb. He wondered what American had carried it in that earlier war, his father's war, and if the American had ever had his father in its sights. Old guns and young men, how much in common they had. Issued, aimed, fired. Cast away as surplus or given to dust or, when time enough was past, exhibited as souvenirs. The air was laden with sweetish cotton smell. The December stars were brittle. He nudged the Indian down beside him.

"Attend. I have been *Taktik* studying, and I have decided. That these guns are unloaded they will neverr believe. Therefore it is possible we can capture them."

"How?"

"We will be a *Jäger-Kommando,* a rifle commando. We must *blitz* very fast, to confusion them. As they did to the village that night of the fiesta, on horses."

"Brief me."

"No. In such actions it is advisable one to lead, one to follow. Betterr that you do not know, that you obey merely. Now, the first orderr. We will toward the office move, where they are. At the gin, you must open the doorr and wait. I will in the office assault them. When you see that I enterr, do you enterr the gin and quickly every switch throw. So that the machines commence. All the controls start excepting lights and then run to me. Comprehend?"

"Why start the gin?"

"To make much sound, to deaf ourr sounds."

"My achin' goddam back."

"Now we go, and recall—silence and *blitz* and obey exactly. Comprehend?"

"Oh, sure, hell yes." Bitter Boy stood his rifle on its butt in disgust. What a squad. Follow the leader who had no use for you, who wouldn't even shake your hand, a cripple who couldn't even give orders without crippling his face. It was going to be one hell of a fouled-up operation. No wonder the krauts lost the war.

"OK, buddy," he snapped. "Here goes nothin'!"

189

35

Down the blocks of cotton they descended. Crouching, German in the lead, they prowled like shadows from the bale yard to the end of the gin, to a sliding door hung on rollers. Pausing to be certain that the Indian opened it a foot or two, Richter limped across the corner of the trailer yard to the Vaca Ginning Company office, avoiding light from the window. Before the door he entrusted the old Springfield to his right hand, took the knob in his left.

He turned it. He burst in blinking.

"Hände hoch! Hands up!"

Three things immobilized them, made them unable to raise their hands—his shout, the sight of him, and the whines and howls as a battery of electric motors was switched on at the gin.

He waved the muzzle in their faces. "Up, up!"

They raised hands. They were seated. A telephone stood on the desk, a ledger lay open.The deputy was uniformed.

Claude Walkingstick came full speed. "She's runnin'!"

"Coverr them!" He aimed at Thode. "The *Telefon!* On the telephone call them, those six! To come here *schnell,* quick!"

Thode stood as though to reach for the telephone, then spinning, boot heels against the desk, hurled himself full-length through the office window. Glass shattered everywhere.

"Get him!" Richter yelled at Bitter Boy, who gestured helplessly with his rifle as he dashed out.

It had already gone wrong. Richter could not leave Joe Mack. "On the floorr lie, lie!"

White-faced, the gin owner half slid from his chair and lay on his stomach, limp. The German's eyes looted the office. Cardboard bale tags with long attaching wires were stacked on top of the safe. On the rolltop desk was a decorative mass of pure white processed cotton. A shot in the trailer yard. That pearl-handled revolver!

Richter tore at the cotton, stuffed Joe Mack's mouth full, trussed his wrists and ankles by winding the tag wires round and round, and leaving him prone amid the glass, headed outside.

The boys bumped into each other. "He's in there, in the gin! I cut him off from his car but Jesus, he's shootin'!"

"You to the otherr end—that he does not escape! Stay out! I will go in afterr him!"

"I'm goin' in too, buddy!"

"Do as I command!"

Bitter Boy sprinted toward the far end of the building as Matthe limped rapidly to the door on rollers which, for some *verdammt* reason, was closed again. He slid it open, edged inside, and a bullet smashed against the corrugated tin inches from him.

The darkness, the din, were infernal. He had not even heard the report of the revolver. He had to whet his eyes and ears. Huge blowers and burr machines and gin stands and lint-cleaners and comber-cleaners and dryers rumbled all about him. Overhead, a complex web of tin ducts racketed, the pipes or ductwork through which cotton was blown by forced air from one process to another. On its foundations the entire building shook as though in a cyclone.

He could not cut the machinery and risk silence and shooting.

He could not turn on the lights and make himself a target.

He could not seek out the deputy in the dark. But he had to have him, he was the key.

If only Albert were there—the *Pionier* would invent something! Despairing, he hesitated.

A gun flash, up high. But there was no impact near him. Why was Thode firing at the other end of the building?

Claude! He had entered against orders!

Till he adjusted his senses, the Indian would be vulnerable. Would he, Richter, act again too late and still another kill? *Nein*, he must draw fire in his own direction! Jumping to a comber-cleaner, swinging the Springfield by its barrel, he hammered on the duct which fed the machine until the tin resounded above the roar.

At the flash he dropped and dropped the rifle. This time, two slugs clanged like cymbals against the tin and screamed off. Thode was up high, near the roof. He had fired five rounds. Five out of six.

Along the vibrating wall Matthe groped. His hand found the rungs of an iron ladder. He climbed, not as he had once climbed a beech tree in the Duisburger Wald and later a tamarisk, but clumsily, relying on his left arm and leg, higher and higher into the maze of ductwork throbbing with the thrust of air under pressure. Prone, he clambered onto a catwalk.

The sixth flash, the sixth slug. He felt it near his face. Opening his eyes, he could see. Skylights above him. He squinted.

Down the catwalk. Boots and black belt. Kneeling, working frantically to reload.

Matthe pulled himself upright by the handrail and lunged. Striking with the pearl handle, Thode met him.

Crashing backward against the handrail, Matthe went down, the deputy upon him, taller and forty pounds heavier, the Smith & Wesson flying and clattering below.

Lights.

They wrestled high in the tumult on the narrow catwalk. Beside them, great iron snake in its iron lair, the auger rotated, the auger which conveyed cottonseed to the bunker outside.

Thode's big hat fell into the auger and was sliced into strips.

"Nazi—Nazi—Nazi—Nazi," Thode panted, straining the German in an embrace ardent and deadly, bending his flaccid right arm and hand toward the bite of the auger.

"You—the Nazi—are!"

Jack Thode bit his tongue at the sharp tap on the back of his head. Claude Walkingstick stood over him, rifle lowered.

He prodded the deputy on his feet, gave Matthe the weapon, went down the ladder, located the other rifle, waved Thode down. Matthe followed.

On the lighted floor of the gin the German pointed toward the office, made telephoning motions. Thode shook his head.

It was Bitter Boy's idea.

He forced the tall man down, jabbed him with the rifle till he crawled into the bale press. He pushed a red button. As the oily steel jaws closed slowly and hydraulically, exerting fifteen hundred pounds of pressure to the square inch, he squatted grinning at Matthe while the deputy cowered on all fours in the vise, making himself smaller and smaller, a vein pulsing in his forehead, eyes retreating, opaque in their sockets, sweat falling in drops from his chin.

Bitter Boy nodded the question at him.

Thode nodded yes.

The Indian scrambled up, pushed the red button, and hissing, the jaws opened.

They turned out the lights and hurried the deputy back to the office. Stepping over Joe Mack, who lay as he had been bound, Richter sat Thode down at the desk, stuck the muzzle of the Springfield in his ear and ordered him to begin phoning or he would blast his head off, the four growers first, then the other two in town, one after another, telling them only to come to the office at once. Thode did as directed.

While he telephoned, Richter whispered to Claude Walkingstick to get the man on the floor outdoors and into one of the motes trailers, those meshed over, but not one near the office where he might be seen. Then go to the gin and find rope or chain. Then return *blitz, blitz,* they had only minutes and things were now swiftly to occur.

Over the broken glass, out the door the Indian lugged Joe Mack. Thode completed his calls. Richter had him lie flat, crammed his mouth with cotton, and tied him with tag wire.

Bitter Boy returned with an armload of steel bale bands. They were all he could find.

Together they dragged the deputy out to the row of trailers and through the side door of one dumped him in with Joe Mack, his partner.

The headlights of a car coming.

They dashed into the office again. Richter posted Claude Walkingstick behind the open door, drew the shade to conceal the shattered window, and seated himself at the desk.

The car pulled in over the scales.

The German removed his Afrika Korps cap.

36

"*Guten Abend.*"

It was Coye.

At the "good evening" and the apparition and the skull with its horrible cicatrix Coye blanched. At the punch of a rifle barrel in his back, he started.

Before he could speak he was on the floor, his mouth full of cotton, he was trussed with wire and being hauled out the door and dumped into the trailer. They drove his car off the scales and took up stations again as another car turned in.

"*Guten Abend.*"

Doc fainted.

"*Guten Abend.*"

Hamp and Mister Buster arrived together. But now the *Jäger-Kommando* operated with split-second precision. Greeted and bound and gagged with their own cotton and loaded, they were processed as efficiently as the others.

"*Guten Abend.*"

Tate's reflexes were faster. He moved, might even have put up a fight had the Indian not dissuaded him with a recoil of the rifle into the kidney.

"*Guten Abend.*"

Lloyd, the one who had used a rock in retribution for his son, was last.

"I wish that always you will know his name," Richter added. "It was Albert Pomtow."

As they wired his wrists and ankles, Lloyd groaned. "No don't, don't, I'll go peaceable. I haven't slept much since that day." To their disgust and embarrassment, he began to cry. "Boys, I'm sorry as hell—and I'm not the only one of us. Beatin' on a German didn't

194

help my boy's walking again, I know it now. I never thought so small of myself before. I'll take my medicine. Boys, believe me, I am so damn sorry!" Cotton choked off his conscience.

It was not until German and Indian added him to their load and latched the side of the trailer, not until they stood back, trembling and breathing hard, staring at the Vaca Valientes, all eight of them gagged and tied and tagged and cooped like animals in a cage, that Bitter Boy understood what they had accomplished.

"Ayee-ayee-ayee!" he whooped, hopping about the trailer in triumph. "Hey Sher'ff, I'm dancin'! Hey you crazy one-legged, one-armed Heinie, we did it, we did it! Why, this is neater than you krauts taking off in your own tank! Why, we got our own Apaches in a basket—I'll be a ruptured duck!"

It was Claude Walkingstick's moment of revenge, of prankish exultation. "The Valientes ride again!" he shouted over the rumble of the gin still running. "On their fat Nazi asses!" He seized both Springfields and scraped the muzzles up and down the mesh. "Look at these, you Sears and Sawbuck cowboys! Here's what we took you with!" He stepped back, leveled a rifle under each arm, and pulled the triggers. "Look you bastards—no bullets!"

The prisoners' eyes rolled. Plump with cotton, their baby cheeks worked grotesquely.

"Matthew, we did it." The Indian put out his hand in congratulation. To his disbelief, his insult, the German ignored it. On his stern face there was no trace of fulfillment, even of satisfaction. He was staring through the trailer side at the men of the West, contrasting perhaps his memory of them in their theatrical splendor with the figure they cut now, imprinting their bloated, foolish faces on some inner negative.

Then Richter settled his AK cap at an angle which would cover the side of his head. "The car bring," he ordered.

"What for?"

"The action is not complete. Do you as you are told. The car bring and reverse to the trailer."

"*Jawohl!*" Claude Walkingstick snapped off a defiant salute and trotted away as Matthe wheeled and started for the office.

When he returned with several bale bands the Ford careened around the gin, braked with a screech, and slewing gravel, backed to the trailer. Working together, they raised the trailer tongue and with the steel bands hitched it to the bumper, tested it by jumping on it, and climbed into the car. The driver asked where to. Taft, was the short answer. Taft? To the headquarters of the police, and was it required that they travel by the main street of Vaca? No, they could take the next street over and connect with the highway. We go, then.

But when car and trailer rounded the gin and were passing through the cavern created by two towering stacks of bales, Richter called a halt. "These bales, how many are here?"

"*Quién sabe?* Five, six hundred."

"What is the value? Of each?"

"Two hundred pesos, dollars."

"Who is the ownerr?"

"Mostly these guys, our POWs. It's about the whole damn crop around here."

"Cotton. Is it not used in munitions?"

"Sure is. Powder, shells—I heard they can get a hundred thousand rounds of machine gun ammo out of one bale."

"Will it enflame, burn?"

"Will a player piano?"

"You have matches?"

"My GI God! Hell yes, here."

From his shirt pocket he handed over several wooden kitchen matches. The German took them, stumped past the trailer barking "*Achtung! Achtung!*" At the end of the stack he struck a match and applied it to the jute bagging of a corner bale. The jute smoldered. When he had struck two more, one at each corner of the other stacks, he returned to the car and paused to watch. Claude Walkingstick had risen from his place behind the wheel. Clutching themselves upright against the mesh, the prisoners stared in speechless anguish. No one could have been ready for the result. As the jute burned through, the cotton, dried and mechanically compressed by tremendous force, ignited like powder. It burned white-hot. Glazes of flame swept up the stacks. In seconds the bales incandesced from within and began to explode their steel bands in fireworks of sparks. Coupe and trailer were almost trapped between seething, roaring, smokeless pyres. Matthe hung on the running board as Bitter Boy jerked the vehicles ahead and out of the bale yard. Three blocks from the Vaca Ginning Company they could still hear the inhalations of the holocaust, could still see by the super-flare of the fire which turned the sky over the town into a Götterdämmerung.

37

Bitter Boy drove as though the Ford itself were on fire, flooring it to fifty. It shook and shimmied and the motes trailer fishtailed on and off the highway. About the metal bed the eight captives tumbled. Wind flapped their Stetsons off their heads and around the mesh like birds. The German ticked him off, sitting there stolid and stupid as a damn Indian, more Moencopa than he was himself. It took the fun out of the escapade; it reflected on his own daring and discipline. He'd played his soldier's part in the *Jäger-Kommando* as well as anyone could have, white or Indian, German or American. They were all alike, the krauts, and this one beside him was typical, a little Hitler. The master race, bull. No wonder the world hated them and always would.

When they neared Taft, the county seat, Richter asked the location of the police headquarters. Center of town, he replied, in the basement of the courthouse, and the jail was there, too. The kraut looked at his wristwatch. What time? 20.25 hours. Thanks.

In town, on a dusty, ill-lit sidestreet adjacent to the business district, the German directed him to stop. "Here are the last orders. *Eins,* to the police drive them. *Zwei,* tell them what they have done to prisoners of warr escaping. These are the names written." He passed a slip of paper. "Ehlert, Boehm, Mohrdieck, Fuge, Buchting, Pomtow. The Army will know of them, and the government, and it may be the Red Cross International. Also in that tuba case is his uniform. Show them and it will prove, they will accept. *Drei,* say that I have the fire set tonight, not you."

Bitter Boy listened, nodded. "Sure. Roger. And where'll you be?"

There was no response. Instead, the German got out of the car.

197

Only then did the Indian grasp the implication, did he supply his own answer. His jaw dropped.

"No."

"*Ja.*"

"No. You wouldn't. Nobody ever did."

But the German was reaching for his bundle.

"My God, you're not! No!" Bitter Boy leaped over the opposite side of the coupe as he had retreated in confusion to the far side of the junkpile the day they had first encountered each other. He still could not believe his own inference. "But why, why? You can stay now—we've caught these guys! You can stay at the Mouse till the camp's closed and then move out on your own—you can be an American now! Don't you get it? She's all over—you're in the clear!"

He stared across the car. He swept a comb through his hair, put the comb away, finally convinced himself. "You're really goin' to. You really are."

All at once he ran around the coupe. "Hell no! You can't do it, you're in no shape! Christ on a crutch, Matthew!" He turned away, in his anger slapped the car door, whirled. "Now you hear me for once! You know what I sold that ring for? A tank of gas! You know what I got for that Iron Cross? A bottle of wine!" He took the German by the shoulders. "You stubborn crazy kraut, all I got in the world is this car—but all you got in the world is me! So you have to take it! Here's what we do. I ride on the tongue, you drive and gun up in front of the courthouse, I unhitch and you take off, okay?"

"*Nein.*"

"Yes! Matthew, I know where you're goin' and you can't make it without this pile of junk—I'm beggin' you, goddammit! You do this for me!"

He waited for the yes. He saw the affirmative twist of the mouth, then the set of the jaw muscles. His own face contorted in sympathy. For a moment the German resembled Jack Thode in the bale press, vised between pride and raw physical need. Then Matthe Teege nodded, a slight submission of the head, and the word itself was unnecessary.

"Thanks, thanks, buddy! I still don't believe it but I hope you make it. And we see each other again sometime."

"So Gott will."

"Listen, don't blame Tans. That kid, she doesn't know which end is up—all she wanted was to get the hell out and find something better'n what she had. Same thing I wanted. And even you guys. OK?"

"OK."

"So now. You've made up your mind. But will you please shake hands with me one time?"

It was a poignant instant, not long in resolution. For something in both German and Indian stirred, a consanguinity of loss and exploit. They had fought a common foe, valiantly. By him, in the long run, both might be defeated, but this battle they had won. And from him now, in a sense, both boys were free. And while the Americans bore witness from their cage, the two shook hands.

"Wait a minute, I forgot. A present, here." Bitter Boy thrust into a pocket and placed something in the other's hand. "You thought you were goin' to the Apaches and you got gypped. So there's one to take with you. I hope to hell it brings you more power'n it did me. Merry Christmas, Matthew."

"Auf Wiedersehen, Claude."

They embarrassed each other. As hastily as he could, Matthew got behind the wheel. Bitter Boy collected the rifles and instrument case and slung them up on the trailer, then sprang onto the tongue, shouted at the prisoners to lie flat, butts or bellies down, and motioned the driver forward and around the corner into the main street of Taft. The stores were still open and there was considerable traffic, but cotton trailers were an ordinary sight and they were not stopped. The Indian pointed at the courthouse and the lights behind barred windows in the basement and the curb entrance. As they pulled in Claude Walkingstick hopped down, cursed at the bale bands as he unwound them hastily from the bumper, and standing in a snort of exhaust smoke, waved the car onward with the nonsense arm signal used in movies by the US Cavalry.

38

Betrayed am I, and I betray.

Tod und Flamme I lead, Death and Flame are my commanders.

"War's over!" shouted the boy on the bicycle. And near here, among these vineyards, they rejoiced.

In the turret of a runs-by-itself. Shorn of fenders, rear tires shrieked upon the pavement. The single headlight wavered.

Seekers three were we. Of freedom one, fortune one, truth one. The only one am I who found what he was after.

The night of Animals Thin grew colder. A knife of air around the windshield slashed his cheek. He maintained a speed close, he estimated, to fifty kilometers per hour, shifting now with his right arm and operating the accelerator with his right leg although both ached and cold did not dull the ache. What had taken them four nights to hike, he could cover in two hours.

How many wastes of sand he had crossed by Panzer, seeking oasis! How many reaches of the Rhine he had breasted in a *Faltboot,* homeward bound!

He swam among the schools of aircraft, starlight gilding their aluminum scales. They had spawned. They were innumerable now, on each side of the highway, netted in depth and dark. In the belly of a whale we slept.

The motor coughed, caught, coughed, died. The tank of *Benzin,* bartered for a gold ring, had run out.

He let the coupe roll to foundering on the shoulder, and taking his small bundle, began to limp along the highway. Infrequent traffic bustled him. He was spent, as though he had been in battle. 21.42 hours.

Tod und Flamme I lead, Death and Flame are my commanders.

Sailor, dog, Indian chief, horse, Oberfeldwebel of the Wehrmacht, clown, Ford—these are my *Soldaten.*

A side road intersected. A few meters beyond, he looked back as a heavy sedan spilled out of the side road onto the highway, passed him, braked on impulse, pulled off, stopped, and waited, lighting his approach with two red lamps. The door opened. He got in.

"Hi. Where to?"

"Phoenix."

"Lucky boy, so am I."

She wheeled the black sedan onto the highway, shifting easily. He sat at attention in a seat soft as a divan. Perfume and liquor seduced his nostrils.

"I'm staying at the Posada, up that road. For the season. But it's a bore evenings, so sometimes I run away into Phoenix."

"The Posada?" he asked politely.

"Resort, hotel, you know. We've been out here every winter the last three. Chicago winters are unspeakable. My husband's back there now, but he'll be out for Christmas."

"The hotel, a dome it has and gardens and a pool to swim?"

"Yes, you know it?"

"I have stayed there, with a friend."

"Really? You speak with an accent." And with a defect, she did not say.

"I am a German soldierr."

"Really?"

"From the prisoner of warr camp I have escaped."

"Really? How exciting." Negligently she lit a cigarette and did not offer one. She smoked with short, sharp gasps as the black sedan, long as a *Leichenwagen,* a hearse, dominated the road. She stubbed the cigarette into an ashtray and immediately lit another.

"The camp," he said. "It is closed?"

"What camp?"

"Of prisoners. That nearr Phoenix."

"I'm sorry, I didn't even know it existed."

Her voice was indolent and pampered. She was a woman in her forties with long, blonde, chemical hair. She wore black. On her fingers were diamonds, around her shoulders a cape of voluptuous fur. "How exciting. I recognized your cap."

201

"It is of the Afrika Korps."

"Oh, yes. What is your name?"

"Richterr I am called."

"Richter?"

"Judge."

"Really? Mine is—but I won't tell either. How old are you?"

"Twenty-one."

"You look older. Believe it or not, I have a son twenty. He's in the Navy, in college."

She drove swiftly. By the time she had smoked a third cigarette they entered the environs of the city. Lights and pedestrians and stores and bars and gasoline stations seemed to reassure her.

"Well, I'm sure we're both glad the war's over, aren't we? You more than I, of course, but it's been very hard on us civilians, too." They were downtown. Strings of tinsel arched the streets. Business establishments were closed, but throngs still gathered before their illuminated windows to enjoy the display of merchandise. In one city square was a giant Christmas tree constructed entirely of tumbleweed and frosted with artificial snow. "You have no idea of the inconveniences. Gas rationing, for example, and meat coupons and standing in line for cigarettes and how unpatriotic they made you feel about traveling. Thank God for my husband's sinus trouble. That's how we could winter out here, doctor's orders." He counted only a few young soldiers and sailors in uniform but many girls assessing them, white and colored and Indian girls. They had a rueful, flotsam air, as though peace and the tides of supply and demand had stranded them on street corners. "Now that you're here, and free, why not stay in the United States? Life, liberty, pursuit of happiness, you know. And someone as young and handsome as you—it would be an adventure." The luxurious car gained speed as they left the downtown area along an avenue well-lighted and lined with palm trees which was familiar to him. He had seen it once before, through the driver's slit of a Mark IV Special Cruiser. "Besides, Germany's a shambles now, from what I read. Have you a family there? A fiancée?"

"*Nein*, no."

"Well then, no reason you shouldn't stay. Your being German, I don't think anyone would hold it against you. It's the Russians we worry about now—there's the next war, take my word."

He was craning , trying to get his bearings.

"Must you leave?"

"I would like to continue, this way a little. It would be—be—much convenient."

"Why not? It isn't that we judge all Germans harshly, just some, that awful Hitler, for example. Now if you'll only stop mistreating the Jews and be nice."

Thoughtfully she drove a kilometer or two, then leaned toward him, scented and confidential. "I'll tell you a teeny secret, we have our own Jewish problem. The Posada, where we stay, is the best resort in Arizona, with guest restrictions naturally, but they're trying like mad to get in. I don't know how much longer the management can hold out. They have the money. And once they're in, as you very well know, you Germans, they simply take over. There used to be a marvelous dude ranch near Scottsdale, for example, the Bar Butte. Now we call it the Bar Mitzvah. So about the Jews we understand, we understand."

They were out of the residential sections now and headed, he believed, in the right direction.

"No need to sit there like a wooden Indian," she chided. "You might smile once in a while."

"Excuse me, I have also a secret," he said. "There is a thing I wish an American to tell, a civilian."

"Really? I adore secrets." She slowed the black sedan, glanced about her, and turned off the street onto a two-track road into the desert, stopping after a hundred meters and switching off the lights and motor. "There. Let's be comfy. Now tell me. This is fun."

"I hold the Iron Cross."

"Iron Cross? Oh yes. How exciting, and only twenty-one! What did you do, dear boy?"

He began to describe that day of the fifteenth of February, 1943, in Tunisia, near the village of Sidi bou Zid southwest of the Faid Pass, that afternoon of rain and mud and butchery and low, indifferent clouds, and what the 501st Tigers of the Tenth Panzer had done to Battle Group A of the First Armored Division, to the undergunned and -armored Grants and Shermans. He tried to make her see through telescopic horror the tracer patterns, to sicken on the taste of cordite, to shrink at the screams of crews, American crews, cremated as tanks burst into flames. With misshapen mouth and halting tongue he told how he had steered the tank unbuttoned down into a wadi on orders to seek more prey.

"From behind we were struck, by a shell, where a tank is, is—how do you say—indefended. Cans of *Öl* were tied there for the *Dieselmotor*. The officer of the tank was burning to black. I was thrown from my seat, among bodies and blood, and not conscious, and when I was recovered all were dead, gunnerr, loaderr, radio man as well, all dead." Poor boy, poor dear boy, murmured the woman in black, moving closer to him, introducing a maternal arm about his shoulders, consoling him with sable.

"I must save myself. I could see, out the slit before the driverr, and down the wadi coming were many American soldiers in helmets of leatherr with in their hands pistols. In the wadi, crews from destroyed tanks walking to find coverr and be safe themselves, comprehend? To capture me, and we had orders that a Tiger being new must not be taken by the enemy to inspect. I push the bodies of my *Kameraden*, through the machine gun sights look, and the firing start. Do you see, do you see I had to fire overr their heads only and they would surrenderr?" Of course she saw, she understood, he was so sweet and young and strange. She put a covetous cheek to his, cosmetic skin sucked his. She turned his head, forcibly, and kissed him, her mouth a maw, yet she was not appeased. Of his lips her teeth took small cannibal samples.

But I did not overr their heads shoot! But at them! *Ach Gott,* such a killing! Of Americans! As in a house of slaughterr!" Rather than revolting, the story excited her. She breathed in short, sharp gasps upon his face. She opened the front of his trousers and exposed him with almost gourmet pleasure, as though his flesh were a feast of rare fowl, imported wines, exquisite meats, and his Germanity itself a delicacy she had not yet tasted. She fastened upon him, her hand clammy and the diamonds cold, and in remembrance and sensation Matthe Teege writhed.

"Up the sides of the wadi they were crawling and downsliding in mud and could not escape and the machine gun I did not stop! Fourteen I wounded and killed for the Reich, fourteen! Young men like myself I did not know or hate except in that minute! To an American have I wished this crime to confess! To the *lieberr Gott* have I prayed this shame to forgive me, to pardon my soul!" Oh my darling, how terrible, how awful it must have been, let me comfort you, she panted, with her other hand caressing the cap from his head, fondling his wound with her fingers, toying with the matted, scabby tufts of hair.

"*Nein, nein,* woman!" he begged. "Do you not do this to me—please, please, I cannot any more in *Amerika* bearr!" He fought her hands with his arms, with an elbow hit the door handle, and depressing it let his weight and hers expel him sprawling. On his knees he reached over the seat for his bundle as she scratched at him, and rising on his left leg stumbled from her. No, no, she snarled, no you dirty foreigner don't you dare leave me now, don't you dare. But he had disappeared.

"Hun!" the creature screeched after him, her face hideous, "Hun! Hun! Hun!"

39

Where was his AK cap? In the black sedan. Now the woman would have another souvenir of war besides a son. It was bone-cold, no more than a few degrees *über null,* above freezing. Shivering, he checked his wrist. 22.50 hours, getting on toward midnight. He limped up a low rise. The good soldier must always determine where he was.

There! Matthe Teege warmed, thankful for the homing instinct which had served him well both in Tunisia and Arizona. That great electric Star of Bethlehem, set high in the east by municipal miracle so that the entire city might reverence the season, was hung upon the Sleeping Indian. He had only to put it behind him and one foot before the other and march, his leg allowing, another two or three kilometers.

Eins, eins, eins, he trudged out of the desert and into a paved, lighted street which curved through a neighborhood of modest frame homes, indistinguishable one from another except by decoration. Most could afford only a holly wreath upon the door or, in a window, a tree with multicolored lights. Across one rooftop, however, reindeer dashed a sleigh filled with toys and a jolly *amerikanisch* Santa Claus instead of the German Nikolaus in priestly garb, while on one green lawn was a complete *Krippe,* or Nativity scene, with life-size papier-maché Virgin and Joseph and Christ Child and the Three Wise Men and a lettered placard in the foreground: "Peace on Earth, Good Will Toward Men."

As he passed beneath a final streetlight and the city was subdued once more by desert, three figures approached him out of darkness. He met three young men, boys really, none older than sixteen, and he recognized their garish attire as zoot suits. They were the latest mode among youths of lower class who, too young as yet to be inducted into military service, dressed themselves in costumes which would attract even more attention than uniforms. Every line of the zoot suits was false—the coats wide and padded at the shoulders, nipped in girlishly at the waist, and draped halfway to the knees, the trousers rib-high with narrow legs. The correct accessories were suede shoes and thick watch chains without watches which looped below the coats.

The zoot-suiters stopped. They looked up and down the street and then at him, at his average height and build and then at his horrifying head. Coarse, ignorant faces wreathed in smiles, they freed ends of their watch chains and began to spin the chains in hissing circles. They spoke to each other in an idiom he could not follow. He attempted to go round them, but two barred his path and one darted behind him. He was exhausted, he could not have run in any case, but he did not want them to become aware of his affliction. He stepped this way and that as they circled him nimbly, shifting, stalking him away from the light and into dark, breathing plumes in the frosty air, their movements almost like the formal, stylized sequence of a dance. Then a sudden, expert climax. The zoot-suiter at his rear dropped to his knees, those at his flanks sprang and pushed. He was toppled.

It was as though they did not deign to attack him with their hands. They kicked him—in the chest and stomach and groin and back and genitals and head.

He did not lose consciousness. He lay still as they went through his pockets. One found something—the doll of human hair, feath-

ered and dressed in deerskin—and with an oath tore it in shreds.
Each kicked him once more in farewell.

Betrayed am I, and I betray.

Tod und Flamme I lead, Death and Flame are my commanders.

Sailor, dog, Indian chief, horse, Oberfeldwebel of the Wehrmacht, clown, Ford—of these my *Kompanie* consists.

So Gott will.

The bleeding brought Matthe Teege to his hands and knees, a viscid flow down the left side of his head where greasewood roots had not entirely healed the wound. The brutal shoes of the three boys had reopened the scalp. Dizzy, he sat up, somehow removed his denim jacket and with it stanched the bleeding. He groped for the bundle which had rolled into darkness as he toppled. He crawled about and could not find it. He wept. His tears were those of a foiled, befuddled child in pain. Then he remembered: we don't cry. Sniffling, continuing to search, he found the bundle at last, helped himself erect, and almost fell. The means of balance, that delicate leveling mechanism which bubbles in the inner ear, had been kicked into anarchy. As he put the electric star on the mountain behind him, his walk was both a stagger and a reel.

Erratic, through a garden of night and suffering he marched, and because it was familiar and dear, through the library of his boyhood. Tom Sawyer and Becky exploring the cave, lost, hunted by Injun Joe.

He slid down into a wadi, and crawling up the far side, slipped down again as had the American tank crews in his gunsight near the Faid Pass. When he had groveled up and regained his feet he seemed to see a million luminarias.

But that was irrational. He looked into the light, and recognized it as the continuous façade of searchlight and fence at the rear of No. 80 Camp rather than the front, or street, side. What he had planned—what had become his obsession since the instant he peered from his coma into that tender, tattooed Indian face—what Bitter Boy had guessed only at the time of their parting tonight in Taft—was to present himself in full uniform to the Americans at their main gate. So far as he knew, no prisoner of war had ever renounced freedom. No prisoner in all the records of conflict had ever given himself up by deliberate choice to the very captors from whom he had successfully escaped. He would be the first. Such an act would speak for itself. Only such an act would constitute a final, damning, irreversible indictment. But now, gazing through agony, he understood that he was physically incapable of going round half the perimeter of the camp and reporting at the main gate. Very well, he would reach objective however he could.

Seekers three were we. Of freedom one, fortune one, truth one. The only one am I who found what he was after.

Of all the books of Karl May, his favorite had been *Weihnacht im Wilden Westen,* or *Christmas in the Wild West.* At its conclusion, having survived many a crisis, Old Shatterhand, the frontiersman, and Winnetou, the Apache chief, attain the very crest of the Rockies and guide their party through a blizzard into a secret vale of eternal spring. It is a prehistoric crater, its grass and trees kept ever-green by zephyrs passing o'er the surface of a warm volcanic lake. There, in a cavern lined with buffalo robes and under a Christmas tree bright with tallow candles they dine on elk, thanking *Himmel* for their deliverance from the storm. And there on that Christmas Eve, in the arms of Old Shatterhand, his friend of student days in Germany, dies Capio, a poem on his lips. Over his grave the intrepid man of the West permits himself the frailty of a single tear.

Grass underfoot. Black shapes of beasts surrounded him, nuzzling him, befriending him with their warm breath. He touched the gentle, curious things with his hands. He was in a field with horses.

Matthe Teege crossed their pasture and crawled beneath the lower rail of a white fence. Nearer the wall of light, it was possible for him to see clearly. Supporting himself against the fence he took off his shirt and trousers, untied the bundle, and as he had planned, put on his Afrika Korps uniform. He regretted the loss of his billed cap, but the khaki tunic, with its palm tree and swastika, seemed to transfigure him. He wished he had a girl to see him, to kiss goodbye, an Erika or a Laughing Corn.

The distance to the wall of light, to the end of the odyssey which had routed him from Duisburg to Tunis to Sidi bou Zid to New York to Phoenix to Mouse Sits, he could measure now not in shores or months or seas or zones or states or kilometers but in meters. He marched. As though many were with him, he spoke aloud.

Owl, Bear, and Coyote he thanked for counsel, and Alice Walkingstick for mercy.

208

He told his small brothers, Klaus and Wolfgang, that the consolation of an infant death was this: they would never know war.

To Lies About His Age he expressed abiding sorrow.

Claude Walkingstick and Tansie Scout he wished Godspeed, wherever they might go.

He assured Willi Loffelbein that his sacrifice would never be forgotten.

Albert, my clown, my Silver Six-Shooter. To the sea we came together, and there was no salt.

Ach, mein Huckleberry Hampelmann. We shall one day steal away again. And on a raft again down a river ride. A better raft than books are. A river, *Kamerad*, that to a land of truth will take us. Where men and women fair and free and noble are. Where dreams will institutions be. And where we may by love belong. To the *Heimatland* of the heart.

Matthe Teege stopped. For he heard the organ. Over the desert to him, high into the nave of night above him, voices in their hundreds joined. The instrument was open-throated, as sonorous as that in the cathedral at Cologne. He knew the music and the language and the theme. They welcomed him. *Sieg Heil!*

Stumbling over stones in last extremity, tilting through cactus, he marched toward the haven of music, toward the rampart of light. Radiance blinded him. He crashed into the chain link fence. He climbed, clawing himself upward with his left arm and leg. At the top he became entangled for a moment in the three strands of barbed wire which angled inward. Two of these he separated, and dropped or fell through them twelve feet to the ground. Wire thorns tore his uniform, the palms of his hands.

Inviolable now, immersed in light, he staggered to the second fence and began to climb as the organ pealed:

> *"Stille nacht, heilige nacht,*
> *Alles schläft, einsam wacht*
> *Nur das traute hochheilige Paar. . . ."*

40

Like children forbidden to be out of bed on Christmas Eve they stood along the fences of First, Fourth and Fifth Stockades. They were an unkempt lot, their hair tousled, their sleepy faces pallid in the light, their mouths open and steaming as they sang. A few were dressed in the usual green fatigues with white POW stencils, but most of the six hundred had brought Army blankets from their cots to pull around them over GI long johns. It had been some weeks since insomnia had swept the barracks, since the men of the Luftwaffe, the Kriegsmarine, the Wehrmacht, and the Afrika Korps had straggled out of the barracks to muster at the fences. To their version of "Silent Night, Holy Night" they gave a reverence, a longing, and a patriotism almost inexpressible. It was, after all, a German song. But in their chorus was a new note, a thanksgiving almost like that of a *Te Deum*, perhaps because of the day's announcement. No. 80 POW Camp would be closed in early February, immediately following transfer of its inmates by train to ports of embarkation. They could be no happier, however, than the American guards in the wooden towers, listening and watching their charges solemn along the fences and wishing them good riddance. The sooner they shipped out, the sooner their own release from the Army must ensue. Leave it to the crazy krauts to celebrate by giving a concert of Christmas carols on a midnight colder than a witch's teat. They could put plenty of schmaltz into this one, though, the guards conceded. They sounded damn near human.

In his tower above the wall of light, above the fused beams of the searchlights, Billy Cahoon looked down upon the prisoners in what was formerly the Fourth Reich. It had been a year almost to the day since, persuaded by his sweats and in his soul that he would die a hero's death in combat, through his martyrdom deliver-

210

ing his buddies and winning awards and ten thousand dollars for his parents, he had joined in France the Thirty-Sixth Infantry Division, which was then busy with a fine slaughter, the reduction of the Colmar Pocket of last-ditch German resistance. He was a rifleman replacement. Assigned to a company, a platoon, a squad, however, he was less than forty-eight hours in the lines. As an infantryman, an engine of war, he was totally and irreparably useless to the United States Army. Berated as a gutless wonder, kicked, chastised by superiors of every rank, he sat in a stone house, the company CP, his face to the wall, immovable; he would neither load his weapon nor venture into the open where military immortality, he was sure, awaited him. From battalion to regimental medics he was passed, and eventually, as a mental case, to the psychiatrists at Corps. He was seventeen then, still an adolescent, and to them his condition, while interesting, was not unprecedented. They had several times encountered it, a freakish paranoia characterized by delusions of martial grandeur—but grandeur beyond the grave rather than this side, the ironic converse of the normal foxhole affliction, simple yellowbelly cowardice. That was terror at the prospect of death or mutilation; this was fear of fearlessness. The alternatives with such a psychotic were three: to return him to the lines and unhinge him permanently perhaps, to grant him a Section Eight discharge as mentally incompetent, or to ZI him to noncombatant duty in which he would be quite harmless and for which he was adequately equipped. Billy Cahoon and his obsession were forthwith dispatched to the Zone of the Interior, to the States, and eventually to the Military Police at No. 80 POW Camp in Arizona. Yet even here, at this menial and untrumpeted task, he had signalized himself.

One night while on tower the previous August he had fired, in childish, delighted ejaculation, an entire machine-gun belt at a prisoner named Skubovius, the only man to escape the camp through the wire, and failed to hit his mark once in two hundred tries. It was a feat he was not permitted to forget. Instead of occupying a pedestal in the pantheon of American valor as he had once shuddered, he sat in the dunce corner of an MP barracks. He became a laughingstock, the oddball butt of every crude, conceivable joke.

He was eighteen now. Snug in overcoat and gloves he leaned on the barrel of his .30 caliber machine gun. He listened to the singing.

It made him think of home, of how he had not long ago hung his stocking by the chimney, and of how, on weekends in the winter, he had gone out with his father, his friend and mentor, into the Michigan countryside to fish. Together they had chopped holes in the ice of a lake and let their lines and baits down into the black cold water. Once he had hooked a large pike, and his father had warned him not to lug it in quickly or sharp ice would sever the line, but to play it, to let it exhaust itself. He remembered sitting ecstatic and fearful on the ice while the wind applauded, line taut in his mittens, and as the heavy fish lay stubborn in the deep, twitching the line so that the pike, stung by the barb of the hook, threshed and swirled out of sight. The power, the mastery over the living thing far below him, had thrilled the young fisherman.

In the corner of his eye, a living thing. In the wall of light, a prisoner. Deranged evidently, the man was dressed in an Afrika Korps uniform ripped at knees and elbows. He hung halfway down the inner chain link fence.

A veteran now with a chance to redeem himself, Billy Cahoon had learned his lesson. He removed his right glove. He did not even alert his fellow guard in the tower. Calmly he traversed the Browning on its tripod, calmly sighted below him. He took a deep breath, exhaled, and fired a short, staccato burst.

Sacrilege of gunfire cut the carol. In battlefield silence the man cringed, stung. Then, apparently in shock, he dragged himself not down but up, to the top of the fence, and hooked himself between the angled strands of barbed wire.

Billy Cahoon the fisherman twitched the trigger, let go another burst. The man threshed. He seemed to be trying stubbornly to spread the strands. In the lake of light every detail of his person was vivid. His hands dripped red. He was capless. Lacerated probably by a bullet, one side of his blond head was ghastly.

A thrilled, omnipotent Billy Cahoon fired a finishing burst and another, riddling his target. The man dropped through the wire. A sleeve snagged on a barb. Hanging upright by one stiff, upraised arm, he seemed in death to pantomime the Nazi salute.

He was later identified from fingerprints as Matthe Karl Teege. Until then, the body was believed to be that of a prisoner attempting to escape.

ABOUT THE AUTHOR

Glendon Swarthout was born in Michigan and received his A.B. and M.A. from the University of Michigan and his Ph.D. from Michigan State University. He has been an advertising copywriter, a foreign correspondent in South America, a rifleman in the third Infantry Division in Italy and France, and a professor at the universities of Michigan, Maryland, Michigan State, and Arizona State. Mr. Swarthout is married and has a son who is attending college in California. In addition to his six novels, the author has collaborated with his wife on two juvenile books, and his short stories have appeared in *Esquire, Cosmopolitan,* and *New World Writing.* Mr. Swarthout is the recipient of the Hopwood Award in Fiction (1946), the Theatre Guild Award in Playwriting (1947), and the O. Henry Prize for Short Stories (1960).